PROPHET OF LOVE

FARRUKH DHONDY WAS BORN IN 1944 in Pune. After graduating in physics from Wadia College, he won a scholarship to Cambridge to train as a quantum physicist, but ended up reading for a BA in English. He is the author of a number of books including *East End at Your Feet* (1977), *Poona Company* (1980), *Bombay Duck* (1990) and *The Bikini Murders* (2008) which is soon to be a major motion picture. He has also written screenplays for film and television, including *Split Wide Open* (1999) and *The Rising: Ballad of Mangal Pandey* (2005). Farrukh's opera based on Rudyard Kipling's *Just So Stories* was given its world premier performance at the Riverside Studios in London in 2012.

PROPHET *of* LOVE

Farrukh Dhondy

HarperCollins *Publishers* India

First published in India in 2013 by
HarperCollins *Publishers* India

Building 10, Tower A, 4th Floor, DLF Cyber City, Phase II,
Gurugram Haryana – 122002, India
www.harpercollins.co.in

ISBN: 978-93-5029-667-7

2 4 6 8 10 9 7 5 3 1

Typeset in 11/14 Weiss
By Saanvi Graphics Noida

Printed and bound at
MicroPrints India, New Delhi

'It's only words,
And words are all I have
To steal your heart away...'

The Bee Gees

'FUCK IS THE MOST VERSATILE word in the English language. It can be used to show attraction: "I'd love to fuck you"; longing: "I'd love to fuck her"; aggression: "fuck you"; surprise: "fuck me!"; disgust: "fuck off"; realization: "I'm fucked"; personality distortion: "He's fucked up"; exhilaration: "fucking great!"; largeness: "fucking huge"; smallness "fuck all"; destruction: "I'll fuck them"; warning "don't fuck with me"...'

The voice was shriller than the sombre long white beard and flowing wavy black-and-white hair promised. The voice of the prophet had something of the shrew in it. The crowd was delighted. It was delivered with complete confidence and the pretence of spontaneity but, like everything else he said, to me it seemed recherché, something he'd looked up in a book of amusing semantics, someone else's idea presented now as the flow of wisdom and guidance which would shape new attitudes, dispel old inhibitions, form the new world.

At the end of this little oration, a sea of crimson rises around me. White men, women and children, in the throes of applause, giving their Guru a standing ovation which he acknowledges sitting on what looks like a kitsch throne on the wooden platform.

He wears white. He has designated that all the others, except his chauffeur, will wear crimson. The chauffeur, an American girl in her twenties, wears a white uniform, smart but marking her position in the hierarchy of functions which makes up the ashram of Bhagwan Shree Saket.

I remain sitting, squatting cross-legged on a canvas sheet spread with rugs under a canopy, open on three sides to the weather. The canopy is skilfully erected—not the sort of job you see around the rest of the town giving temporary sanctuary to a god or goddess for a festive celebration or sheltering the guests at a wedding. It seems to be of firmer canvas and has been erected on metal with bolted brackets rather than the native, frail, bamboo poles tied with rough jute string bundles. It is built to last and looks as though some German or Scandinavian devotee, a crimson man who has given his life, for a few years perhaps, to the service of the Guru and the ashram, has designed it with the benefit perhaps of a computer and some stress-load analysis.

I have been placed in the front line of the audience which built up behind me after I was ushered in with other journalists to take my place in the outdoor auditorium. It filled up and there was a spontaneous hush as the Guru was driven thirty yards from his bungalow in a Rolls Royce to the theatrical wings of the auditorium and climbed the few steps to take his place on the waiting throne to a ripple of applause.

The 'fuck' speech done, the Guru's eyes darted around the congregation taking in the reaction.

Perhaps it was my own paranoia, bred of being the lone dissenter in this sea of devotion, but I fancied that in a flicker he noticed that I was the only one not standing for the ovation. His face and smile were fixed, satisfied that his speech had done its work, but his eyes, always written up in the press as 'hypnotic and piercing', the large black eyeballs darting about above the faintly smallpox-pitted cheeks and cheekbones, searched for details. Did he register my insolence in refusing to stand for a second-hand speech? Would he be in the least attentive to or disconcerted by such a petty act of defiance? I thought not.

POONA COMPANY, WHICH ONE COULD call an autobiography, though the narrator is virtually missing from the action—*Hamlet* with brief appearances by the Prince—covering my early years of school and college and my sojourn with the more colourful characters of my neighbourhood, a concatenation of short stories, or a coming of age novel had been published in London. My fourth published book. I earned a meagre living at the time by writing for the Brit newspapers and periodicals when I managed to sell them an idea.

The editor of a weekly called *New Society*, for which I had written a piece or two called me in one day.

'Read *Poona Company*, very amusing', he said.

'You're too kind,' I said, having picked up this English way of accepting a compliment.

'Any plans to return to Poona? Sounds a fascinating place.'

'No plans right now, but it's much in the news with the Bhagwan's ashram and the crimson people flooding the town. Now if some editor thought of buying me the airfare, I'd go like a shot.'

Tony smiled.

'I wonder who might buy you that airfare and give you a commission,' he said.

'Such an editor may not be a million miles away,' I said.

'Yes, but we're broke,' he said. 'Or at least we're not economically endowed. Can't you write up the facts from here? But I should ask what your attitude to all that is first, shouldn't I?'

'I think he's onto a good thing. I don't think his thoughts quite match up to Spinoza or Schopenhauer, it's all second-hand stuff with bits of Buddhism and the *Bhagwad Gita*,' I said.

'But the sex thing?'

'I don't quite know what he says about sex, but I can interview him in depth if the great spirit of Ahura Mazda will get me to win the lottery and of course stump up for the ticket first; I shall report on the great social phenomenon of our times. Tell you what Tony, my aunts still live in the house which you read about in my book and they will feed and shelter me, so the per diem I can forego.'

'Generous of you. Pick up your cattle-class ticket from my secretary's desk. Get as much as you can. Should be worth three weeks of a serial run, or one or two really long feature pieces? See how you go.'

'Ask your travel-wallah to leave the return date open,' I said.

MY AUNTS WERE SURPRISED TO see me. I used to write to them occasionally and send them money now and then—whatever I earned in rupees from articles I wrote for Indian newspapers. I had sent them the whole advance on the book when an Indian publisher picked it up. It wouldn't have made much difference to me if I'd received it in sterling, but it made a great deal of a difference to them.

Both my aunts were unmarried working women and still lived in the house in which they had brought me up through my school and college days. The book I had written began in their house and was about their neighbourhood. It was about the neighbours, about my friends and some of the unsavoury types round and about and, I dare say, it contained a lot which as a teenager I could not share with my poor shockable spinster aunts.

Returning after eight years I found the house the same from without but with new shrines within. There was a television with a doily and a vase placed on top of it. The old chandeliers had been replaced by designer-styled lighting, the crude, cane looped-and-windowed sofas replaced with plush, cushioned ones.

Their kitchen, which used to be in my time an outhouse with a cook installed to service the needs of a grandfather, my working aunts, myself, my sister and an old grand aunt—their mother's sister who had been imported from Bombay because she was on her own and too old to fend for herself in any clean fashion—now had a gas cooking range they proudly said they used mostly to cook for themselves now that granddad and their aunt were gone, but they had a part-time cook to do the heavy stuff. The old 'meatsafe', a wooden larder cupboard with doors made of thin wire netting in wooden frames had been replaced by a large refrigerator and the corner table boasted a toaster above which a food processor took pride of place on a crockery shelf.

'Your room is still as you left it,' said Shera, my older aunt, prompting me to find it just as I had left it. It wasn't really a room. It was a converted side-veranda with a narrow alley separating it from the sheer wall of the next house. The conversion was no more than a dark green bamboo blind three yards square which rolled upwards on a rope-and-pulley system, making up one wall of my room, the others being a thick cloth curtain and a cupboard placed athwart the veranda to shut my space off from the rest of it. Beyond my curtained entrance were the household washing line and a dirty clothes chest with a cubic wooden frame and woven cane sides—just as it was before I left for England and university.

My books were where I had left them though someone had taken care to dust them. The bed was not made up. In the monsoon, on very stormy nights the rain would come through the curtains and the blind and soak me till I moved the thin mattress to my sister's room indoors and slept on the floor.

'Why have you kept that space as it is?'

'We knew, or we were hoping you'd come back and need it someday,' Shera, said.

'It reminded her of you, so she didn't want to get rid of your very nice books,' said Amy, the younger one.

Of course they'd read my book.

'Everyone who's read it is very amused by it,' said Shera, intending it as the highest compliment. 'They all agree that you have a very good command of the English language,' she added.

'Of course he does,' says Amy. 'He is a writer.' This with appropriate pride.

And what am I doing visiting them like this without notice? How long am I going to stay?

I tell them.

'Those people. Horrible people,' says Shera. 'Since they've invaded the town, the price of tomatoes has gone up so much we can't buy them anymore.'

'And eggs,' says Amy, 'You can't imagine, they are a rupee for one egg!'

'The shopkeepers are having a great time, but no one can get a room to rent. Even these stupid neighbours of ours have converted their house into a hotel and are renting rooms out to these filthy people.'

'Don't they bathe?' I ask.

'I don't know, but they are filthy in different ways.'

'How?'

'They kiss in the street. On their mouths.'

'I'd kiss in the street on the mouth given half a chance,' I said.

'Chhhut! Don't say stupid things, Farrukh! You learn all this rubbish in England. It may be all right there, but this is India.'

'Be honest, Amy masi, wouldn't you like a nice gallant handsome man to kiss you on the street?'

Amy smiles.

'If he was really handsome and I loved him,' she says, 'but not on the street. You have to have some decency.'

My aunts had thrown away their years and their chances. I had heard my mother and father say that they were offered marriages and matches in their times but out of flighty romantic notions and an idea that modern women had to fall in love and be loved and chosen, not be bartered away, had turned them down.

I had arrived on the evening train from Bombay. My aunts told me where the ashram was located and whatever facts they knew and rumours they had heard about this great occupying army of the crimson folk who had invaded their town and were to be seen everywhere on the streets, in the marketplaces, the parks, hospitals, posh stores and even, they said, in their own little enclave of a seed-retailing firm in which the two of them worked.

The firm was called Pocha Seeds and was the enterprise of an old Parsee family of Poona who owned farms and nurseries where the seeds were grown and cross-bred, a small factory where they were dried and packed and a showroom in an old Parsee bungalow which exhibited them and their produce and accepted orders.

My aunt Shera sat in a cashier's cage in the front room of the bungalow and Amy performed secretarial duties for the boss, a reverend personage and doyen of the town universally known to his near and even not-so-dear as 'Popsu'. The slogan of the firm was 'Pocha Seeds Satisfy'.

The Pocha dynasty is a study in itself with a fascinating and twisted history which I always told my aunts I would one day turn into fiction. They didn't want me to as long as they were alive. They feared for their jobs and for any association with scandal that I might bring through my exposure of the constant gossip and stories they brought home from work.

Their indignation now was directed at the cheek of some crimson people who had gone into their showroom and asked, not for a packet of seeds, but whether the firm would sell them their whole bungalow and farm. 'These Saketis thought they had the money to buy our Pocha Seeds' premises and start some sort of subsidiary colony there.'

It was a preposterous suggestion, they said, and the employees were up in arms.

'How dare they come there? We told Popsu to launch a court case against them.'

'For what?'

'For being rude like that. The insult to Popsu was they said they weren't interested in the seeds, just in the land and the "run-down bungalow". You can't come into someone's showroom and call it a run-down bungalow. Just imagine the cheek!'

I pointed out that calling a run-down bungalow a run-down bungalow was possibly not against the law and said that I would ask Saket himself if he intended to buy Pocha Seeds. Did they have any idea how I could make an appointment to see him?

'They have everything. They have a press office and we have a phone now,' Amy said proudly.

'You can use the phone,' Shera said.

I left the use of it to the next day.

I cycled around Poona on my old bicycle which, with pumping up and oiling was in rusty but workable shape.

Yes, they were everywhere. I didn't speak to any of them. I would get their measure as the days passed, I told myself. I was fighting the prejudice I felt against them. The price of eggs and tomatoes inflated? Was this a blow against Western materialism?

They walked about this town, my town, with an air of possessiveness. Poona had never been a great tourist spot. The only Europeans (or 'Caucasians' as my history teacher haughtily called them) I saw in my short and happy childhood were either Christian missionaries of the American variety who had established a chapter of Christian Science in a leafy suburb called Salisbury Park, or the occasional engineer with a family, who moved to the town as a consultant to one or other of the factories that were beginning to locate themselves in this hinterland town far from the commercial bustle of Bombay. It was, though I didn't know it then, the very beginning of India's industrially expansive boom—something that was still far in the future.

The certainty of why I'd left this town was now upon me. I could see myself getting old there in ways I didn't want. I had to go away, far away and I did.

The streets had changed. They were crowded with rickshaws and cars and still the bicycles, which used to be the hallmark of the city, every street in the rush hour resembling the start of a Tour de France, seemed now, though just as many or more in number, pushed to the sides of the newly expanded and proud thoroughfares.

The shops of Main Street, inevitably named Mahatma Gandhi Road, were plusher, full of rich clientele and overflowing with the Saket people. Austerity was not one of their credos.

I phoned the ashram that afternoon and said I was a journalist working for a British publication. An American voice on the switchboard put me through to an English accent in the press office, a man. No, the Bhagwan didn't give personal interviews ever. But I had read some, I said. That was then, he said, and the circumstances would have to be very special. I said I was good at engineering special circumstances but his English ironic humour had deserted him.

'We can offer you a tour of the ashram,' he said.

'You got yourself a deal,' I said. I put on a cod American accent and it made him uncertain. 'Gimme the lowdown, what's the schedule?'

'Er...if tomorrow morning suits you, you can start with the Bhagwan's lecture at seven. Please arrive by six at the gates and give me your name again.'

'Hiram P. Ingleburger Jr.,' I said. I hadn't given him a name to start with so he'd have to accept this one. It was a subconscious prompting that had invented the necessity and the name. I had heard from my aunts that they didn't allow Indians into the ashram. At the time I had taken it as a ban against Indians being initiated into the cult and becoming crimson folk, not against Indians entering the premises. It would be preposterous if the latter were the case in our own country.

The name silenced him for a suspended moment.

'Well, Mr Ingleburger. Can you turn up at six a.m. and kindly refrain from using any unguents for twenty-four hours before.'

'Hey, we don't have twenty-four hours till take off. We have eighteen.'

'Well don't use any soap, aftershave, perfume or deodorant from now on.'

'I appreciate you bending the rules,' I said.

'And do you have a cold or any stomach problems?'

'I don't think so,' I said, not quite seeing what he was after.

'We have to be certain. The Master has severe bodily reactions to people sneezing or releasing intestinal odours.'

I was sure that among the Saket disciples there'd be expert nutritionists and bio-gaseous scientists who could invent the odourless fart, but I kept the thought to myself.

I turned up at six, chained my bicycle to a lamp post and entered the ashram. It was like gaining admittance to the pearly gates. They took me through a wooden shed and two white women in their robes, the duty noses for that morning, sniffed me from head to toe. It beats being frisked for guns and bombs by airport staff. You can feel their sensitive proximity and the up and down scrutiny is very suggestive of kinky foreplay, but I put such thoughts out of my head. It could have become embarrassing.

Another young Saketi, who told me her name was Ma Agnivarsha, accompanied me to the open lecture hall. She read my name from a clipboard and betrayed no surprise that my Indian features didn't match the name Ingleburger by which she addressed me. She said she'd been assigned to show me the great work of the ashram after the lecture. I said I'd like to see it in stages, there was so much to absorb. There might have been a tinge of sarcasm, but she was so absorbed in her role that she thought my caution mirrored her fascination with the change she had brought about in her own life by opting for what I suspected was licentious piety.

After the 'fuck' lecture, the Bhagwan went into some homily about sticks and stones being harmful objects only when wielded with nasty intent—a discovery which he laboured to death. After the lecture was overMa Agnivarsha, the 'year of fire', took me around and showed me the vegetarian canteen and the machines that washed the plates in its kitchen. There was a posh modern version of the Gandhian ethos about the place. The crimson people worked the kitchen wearing token aprons to denote they were on duty and tying their hair in stark bandanas, like so many prisoners in a concentration camp, to maintain head hygiene.

I told Ma Agnivarsha that she could call me 'Junior' and not go through the whole rigmarole of Ingleburger. She was Dutch I found out, but she didn't reciprocate by asking me to call her Kris or Beth or whatever her name was before it turned into the 'year of fire', a name she was proud to have and would try to live up to.

The ashram, situated in several acres of compound is fenced and hedged to keep out the unwanted. The bungalow, whose site was converted into this complex of rapidly built, beautiful structures, always had its own gardens, trees and wild patches and these had now been cultivated by the landscape gardeners among the devotees and they had made a great job of it. It was in itself a tribute to the busy, logical, resourceful minds of the disciples drawn from the Western professional classes, their diligence and their faith in the unseen realities of modern science which fitted in seamlessly with this new skein of knowledge. No one has seen atoms or viruses, but science has taught us to reckon with and by them and the manifestations we know, which follow from their presence and properties, give us our world. Surface is all.

Then why were all these professionals, which most of them were, unless they were the idle rich, the lost children of the slightly past-the-post-hippy generation, turning to a lecturer who laboured, not very incisively the semantics of the 'f' word? What did they see which I was missing?

Agnivarsha gave me several free publications and cassettes of tape recordings when I said I would come back another day. She wanted me to listen and read.

'You will surely understand after,' she said.

I strolled out of the gates and got on my bicycle. The ashram is in what used to be a quiet suburb of Poona in my boyhood, a redoubt outside the town where some of my rich friends whose families owned motor cars—a luxury no one in my neighbourhood shared—had bungalows with servants' quarters and, in some of the larger houses, a swimming pool.

Now the lure of the ashram had caused the side streets to sprout shacks and shanties, the fronts of which had been converted into permanent structures and shops, some of them cafes, tea shops, curio shops and Indian traders on the make who had set out to fulfil the demand for ready-made crimson robes, beads and photographs of Saket. There were small name-engraving stalls which would put the new name of the devotee on a watch, on a bracelet, or on anything metallic or leathery. There were Saket mugs for sale, and crimson robes in different sizes for mummy crimson, daddy crimson and baby crimson. With an unerring eye for the mote in the aesthetic vision of the Westerner, the artefactors were selling idols, counterfeit erotic carvings passed off as genuine excavated pieces and aids to meditation, including Tibetan prayer wheels of whose use the vendor would have no clue.

And then there were the postcard and Coca Cola stalls and, for the nostalgic, fast foods stalls selling lamb-burgers and Southern-fried chicken.

At the edge of this market, addressing herself to the flow of crimson people in the heat of the afternoon, was a young woman in her twenties, dressed in a man's T-shirt and jeans, in bare feet, handing out leaflets. She appeared to be crying and hysterical.

'Please read it. You have to know the truth. Denial is wrong, rape is wrong. Take charge of your selves, your minds, you fucking idiots…' and so on.

Her tone was enough to stop me. Very few people were taking her leaflets and those who did seemed to peruse them and instantly throw them away. Others avoided her as they would a dripping leper. Like a madwoman, she would rush to the discarded leaflets and pick them up. She would shout abuses at the people who had discarded them.

'Fuck-heads, cock-suckers, blind…'

I stopped and watched her. She put the leaflets she had picked up at the bottom of the pile she held, or tucked them into a faded crimson shoulder bag she carried. She was either trying to preserve copies of her leaflet or eradicating the effect that a litter of discarded leaflets would have on fresh passers-by. No one stopped to talk to her. No one asked her who she was or what the matter was. Perhaps she was the village idiot to whom they were used, curious only to see what the latest of her leaflets contained.

She was pretty, but grubby. She had blonde hair which was tied back but looked like it needed a wash, sharp angular features and eyes that looked out with a gaze of contemptuous pity for the fools who passed by. She had a large mouth, her lips turned down at the ends in intriguing little darts.

From her language she wouldn't have been the perpetrator of an alternative religion to that of the Bhagwan. She was aggrieved. Everything about her said she'd been hurt. I went up to her and stretched my hand out for a leaflet. It took her by surprise—a man at the other side of a bicycle deliberately asking for the leaflets she was finding it so hard to give away? Not a crimsone.

She stared into my eyes and I averted them and, wheeling my bicycle, pretending to be absorbed in the leaflet while I was actually wondering how she would follow up my interest, I went some distance. I could feel her watching me to see whether I would throw the leaflet away. I read the headline. It said:

'YOU ARE EVIL. YOU ARE THE DEVIL. YOU FUCKED EVERY HOLE IN MY VULNERABLE BODY.'

I folded the leaflet and put it in my shirt pocket. I would read it at my leisure. As I turned round to look at her, she was screaming at a couple of girls in crimson, the first ones to pause and perhaps listen to her.

'Has he fucked your arse yet?' she asked loudly.

The women moved on and just as they did, a dark blue police van drew up and an inspector and constable got out. They grabbed the woman, who didn't resist. They pushed her into the back of the van. The van drove off and I could see that the bystanders and stall-holder had watched the little episode and seemed quite unperturbed.

'Where are they taking her?' I asked the holy artefacts man.

'She is always come here and say foul thing, Saar. Spoiling trades. They will let it go after six miles outside Poona over lonely roads. Then this person will walking back in towns or asking truck lift.'

At home, sitting on my back veranda, having reclaimed my old room, I read the leaflet. It was badly printed. The ink was smudged, perhaps because the printer or the customer had been impatient to pick the leaflets up before they dried.

It wasn't terribly informative.

It said:

> Your Holiness the Damned Beelzebub,
>
> Those who pose as gods are really the devil. No living being can arrogate to himself the position of a god and you have blatantly called yourself 'Bhagwan'. But of course poseurs have no shame. But what am I talking about? You are the devil and you invented shame so that others would wear it. You shall wear white and The Others, the damned, shall blush in crimson.
>
> And how deep red is my own shame that I fell for you. That in my lost and confused way I gave you what was most precious inside and outside myself. I gave you it all, spiritually and physically, I gave myself to the shape of the

body of the man I thought I loved, the man who betrayed me and the little child whose innocence I would beg you to respect and return. But I know that that begging will get me nowhere with you, the devil.

Devils only exult in making people beg. Gods answer prayers, devils think they have triumphed in not answering them.

You have used me, you have used every single being you came across. You make me feel filthy even talking about you, thinking about you. They say the devil leaves a foul smell in his wake and you have left it on my body, in my body—in my cunt, in my arsehole, in my mouth, in my ear, in my nostrils, in the crevice of my cleavage, in my palms, in between my toes, in my armpit, anywhere where you have penetrated.

And the fools won't listen. They worship the fatted calf, the evil that you are and have made them worship in themselves and they think they are being liberated when all you are doing is, like the Pied Piper with your sweet evil music, leading them to drown like rats.

May God destroy every atom of you. I curse you.

Jai Shambho, Jai Sree Krishna, Jai Vishnu.

I would pray for the circle of your life to be broken and for you to be free from rebirth even—because your rebirth means more people deceived and betrayed.

Let my daughter go.

There was some thread to the thoughts and the curse with random overflowing anger.

I put the leaflet aside.

Freak rain in the night, a light drizzle and I pull the curtain back and hold out my hand to catch the rain. Despite the narrowness of our alley, the smell of the earth fed with a little moisture comes steaming up. From beyond the alley I can hear someone repeating 'Hail Mary, mother of God, blessed art thou...' and I lose the distinctness of the words in the mumble.

I return to the ashram and am informed that I have been elevated to being the guest of the press department. I get to see the Englishman in charge of the press. He calls himself Swami Raktavijaya. He looks like he could be called Billy Bunter. He wears round spectacles and has dark hair which he throws about with a flick of his head. He takes himself seriously. He doesn't for a moment believe that I am actually called Hiram P. Ingleburger Jr. But then, if he can hide his true identity behind a preposterous name, so can I. There is an unspoken truce between us, a truce about who we really are. I won't ask him his name and he won't ask me mine, though names, I suppose he'd say, are only the tags we convicts of eternal sin have to wear. He addresses me, like Ma Agnivarsha used to, as Mr Ingleburger. I don't invite him to call me 'Junior'.

I petition him repeatedly for an interview with the great man himself. That will be my coup. Somehow tooling around the ashram and hearing about hydroponics from the gardening freaks and about the generation of sustainable energy from garbage and sewage and of plants to harness the flow of the river and the winds on a large scale so as to make the ashram self-sufficient in energy, seems removed from the real purpose of this constructed little oasis. There is about the ashram, a base odour of manic conviction and I want to know what this conviction is. These people, who behave as though they are in a seminar about saving the planet or about more efficient marketing and growth of some enterprise, are actually here driven by some irrational force or by the fear of some irrational force and the dread of falling prey to it.

I'd make a fool of myself writing about the good governance of the ashram, which is all that Billy wants me to write about. Mention this, mention that, he says.

'Shall I mention that the Bhagwan has fifty cars parked in a field? Cars for which he has no use?'

'Ninety-nine,' says Billy, 'And you can say what you like. We can censor it, but they are all gifts. He can't help it if they give him cars.'

'Why doesn't he give them to charity or sell them and give the money to a project to help hungry kids? There must be those around.'

'Charity is false consciousness. People suffer and are hungry because of the karma of their past lives,' says Billy.

'You don't want to go around saying that blind people asked for it and cancer is godsent. Or is that the official line?'

'I've told you Mr Ingleburger, you can report the words of the Master exactly as they are or you can say who told you what. You can't put my words into his mouth. We'll take your newspaper to the cleaners. And our lawyers don't simply remove the stains, they corrode the cloth. Remember we have some of the world's best, fed up of the rat race in wigs and gowns, the travesty of justice in the known world, jurists and young Turks of the law who have come over to us.'

'Over to "us"? Since when was it "us" and "them"? At war with the world? And you will use the corrupt world's libel laws?'

'Of course. We stop at nothing on the road of rectitude,' says Billy. Oh he's tough. He won't grant me an interview.

'Talking about your bloody good deeds is like going to a Soviet Gulag and writing about the efficiency of the kitchens. Something else is going on over here,' I protest.

'You know that something's happening here, but you don't know what it is, do you Mr Jones?' he says. I recognize the quote from a Bob Dylan song. He smiles. The first time he has indicated that he is a creature driven by something other than solemnity.

'Okay, so what happens in the closed sex sessions? Can I attend?'

'You know the meaning of "closed" Mr Ingleburger? Opposite of observable. You would disturb their routines. These are sensitive medical procedures.'

'Ah, sex as medicine again. I thought the whole teaching was that sex is not medical, it's spiritual and fun.'

'Maybe, but that's not what I expect the press to understand or to go along with. Sex as medicine is the best they will get from me.'

'Have you ever heard of Dr Goebbels, Swamiji?'

He smiles again.

I see her again at the gate when I emerge from a mind-numbing session on meditation techniques which Billy has fixed for me in compensation for not allowing me into the sex sessions.

As I leave the ashram she is outside, attempting to get in. As she argues with the crimsones at the gate, men and women, she hands out leaflets to the emerging devotees who refuse them or promptly demonstrate their allegiance by throwing them away.

So, just as the ashram can boast professional architects, engineers, designers, dieticians, dentists and doctors, they probably have a heavy squad too, people who've been military policemen, perhaps. One of the women dealing with her certainly has that cold, efficient appearance. The crimson is only a loose burkha over her officiousness.

She wants to go in. The crimson man is being kinder to her than the women have been.

'No, Diamond, banned means banned. Whoever you are looking for will come out when they feel like. You know you can't go in.'

'My name is Ma Vidhyadhari, you know that. I received a necklace from Bhagwan himself.'

'And he has banned you himself. You can't distribute leaflets in a one mile radius...the police...'

'I'll just go in and find my daughter...'

'No you won't, Diamond. You'll go away and if you take my advice you'll seek help. You need it,' he says this and then firmly grabs the limp, muslin bag she has over her shoulder. He pulls at it and it falls to the ground, spilling the bunch of leaflets.

This is too much for Diamond, or Ma Vidhyadhari as she calls herself, to take. She punches the man in the face and he reels. The two women fall upon Diamond and drag her away from the gate. Another woman comes running up and joins them. The man she struck pulls his hand away from his cheek and spits blood. Her blow has caused his cheek to split.

'Are you okay?' I ask and he nods. Other sanyasis and sanyasins, as I have discovered the devotees refer to each other, have come out of the ashram and are looking after him. Diamond's faded crimson muslin bag with all her leaflets are on the ground a little distance away and I pick them up. I pick up the ones that the wind has scattered as well. This is a new leaflet but it contains, by and large, the same diatribe.

I cycle towards the road bridge that crosses the railway lines. The three sanyasins are returning without Diamond, talking to each other animatedly. They walk towards the ashram.

I cycle on and come to the bridge. There are unpaved gravel paths on either side of the bridge which lead to the fence along the railway track. From under the bridge I can hear a faint sobbing.

I wheel my bicycle to under the bridge. She is there crouched in a foetal position, crying.

'I brought your bag,' I venture, feebly.

She doesn't look up but the sobs shake her body and her back undulates.

'Can I help in any way?' I ask.

The sobs are not hysterical and neither are they pitched in the registers of self-pity. There is a genuine pain there.

She won't look up at me. She doesn't know who is talking to her.

'I'll leave your bag here.'

As I am about to go she looks up. Her eyes are watery, huge pools.

'Just fuck off, leave me. You can't help,' she says.

I shrug and move to cycle away, leaving her crouched and crying. She shouts now.

'Bicycle man! You took my leaflet.'

I turn back.

'Yes. Are you really all right?'

'Of course I'm not all right. They won't give her back. I'll die without her.' She begins to howl, neglecting my presence. All I can do is wait.

Then she rises from the stone she is sitting on and picks up her bag. She walks away, casting one glance in my direction. It is not a glance which says she doesn't want to know, but one which says that I wouldn't want to know her and she will remove the embarrassment of herself from my sight.

'Diamond, wait,' I call out.

She turns round.

'You heard my name.'

'Yes, but you wanted to be called something else.'

'I was trying to get into their damned concentration camp. They've got my daughter, sir.' The American 'sir'—'I won't give up, you know. They are abusing her. He is abusing her. He can't do that. I'll fucking kill him.'

She grabs the handle of my bicycle out of passion.

'Yes, okay,' I say.

She turns her face away.

'Where were you going?' I ask her.

She shrugs.

'Are you going home?'

'No.'

'Are you hungry?'

'Yes.'

'Can I offer you some food?'

'I have no money,' she says.

'Not a problem. Come with me.'

'I don't want to go to their cafes,' she says.

'Then we'll go towards the town, towards my house. Come on.'

She follows me and we cross the bridge. As we descend she says, 'I can't go with you. I don't know who you are.'

'No, you don't, but I am safe. And I am interested in your story. All of it. I am a journalist from London.'

This seems to interest her and she has evidently made up her mind to come with me because she starts walking again.

'Can I ride your bike?' she asks.

She swings her leg over the seat like a man and rides off. She turns deftly fifty yards on and cycles back.

She is transformed and smiling.

'Get on,' she commands.

'Get on where?'

'Sit on the crossbar like everyone else in town does.'

'If we are going to do that, shouldn't I pedal and you sit on the crossbar?'

'No, dude. You do as you're told.'

I GOT ON THE CROSSBAR and we cycled into town drawing the mildest attention from passers-by. She asked me my name.

'Why are you interested in my story?'

'I'm here to research the ashram. The fellow won't give me an interview and you seem like… '

I didn't want her thinking that I was treating what may be her tragedy as a news story.

'… it was some sort of deeper truth.'

'I'm hungry,' she said slamming on the brakes and nearly projecting me over the handle bar.

I stopped at a cafe where no crimson people would venture. I guessed that the separation between the crimsones and the townies would have taken place by now, most townspeople avoiding the cafes that the crimsones used and vice versa. It's the pattern of all invasions and colonial enterprises. The invaders stick to their own, especially if they have arrived with a specific purpose and an even more specific disdain for the uninitiated. And having grown up with the townspeople I knew that certain types would shun the newcomers and others would pay to follow the foreigners into hell if permitted.

This was a cafe my crowd used to use when I was in college. The menu was the same as it had been, only it was printed on a proper card and not scribbled on a blackboard.

'You're the rascal who wrote that book about all of us, aren't you?' the proprietor asked, pretending he'd forgotten my name till he gauged the attitude of the others who recognized me, either as the perpetrator of libels against the neighbourhood, or the literary lion who had immortalized it.

Two fellows whom I recognized came over. Their attention was at first drawn by the fact of a white woman venturing where most would fear to tread. And then they recognized me as the chronicler of their neighbourhood. I had in fact written about this very cafe and of the gangs of ne'er-do-wells that congregated there.

'Worldwide, you've made us famous worldwide,' one of them said to me.

'My niece's sister-in-law's sister read your book in Canada, Farrukh. Did you know they have a copy of your book in Canada?'

'I had no idea, but since it was published there, I'm glad to have it confirmed.'

'Worldwide,' said the other fellow.

'This is the fellow who wrote that story about the cat cutlets. Selling in my cafe. Lies. Don't worry, I forgive you. Give these people a free tea,' said the proprietor.

Years before, in my boyhood, the rumour had spread that in the early mornings in the alley behind the kitchen of this same cafe, the wails and dying screams of cats could be heard. The rumour soon spread that the cooks were murdering cats for their meat and the famous burgers, a specialty of the house, were made of it. The story spread and instead of putting people off the cafe, enriched its reputation. As college boys we used to walk in and order 'cat cutlets' in defiance of the truth of the rumours. Soon the serving staff of the cafe were referring to this delicacy of the house as 'cat cutlets' and offering it as the jewel in the menu.

In the episode I fictionalized in my book, I may have exaggerated and said that the menu itself boasted 'cat cutlets' and ended the episode with the municipality and police closing the cafe down. It had been closed down and I suppose the family that owned it must have been relieved that I didn't write about the real reason for its closure which was to do with dead rats in the kitchen. Rats and rat poison in the food were routine in our town's cafes. Cat cutlets made a unique story.

I offered Diamond the menu.

She pointed at the only word she understood. It said 'Rice plate'.

'That's poor people's food. Are you a vegetarian? '

'I could and would eat a horse,' she replied.

'With rice? Eat the dhan sakh,' I offered and ordered it when she smiled and nodded her longing approval.

'So you've taken cat burgers off the menu?' I asked the proprietor in Gujarati.

'So, Farrukh, you've come back to make fun of us poor people?' he asked.

We were drawing attention now. Her food came and she was so busy hungrily eating it that she didn't seem to mind assuming the traditional role of women in that cafe, to be seen and not heard. Undoubtedly in the old days she would be obscene and not heard, but Diamond sat through the quiz the clientele were anxious to put me through.

'I have been told that in London you don't have to work, that the government just gives you money. True?'

'Up to a point. If you are unemployed they don't let you starve. They give you a subsistence wage.'

'I am happy with daal and a chapatti each meal. I wouldn't ask for more. How does one get to London?'

'Why does anyone do any work then?'

'They want more than daal and rice and a TV set.'

There was a murmur of approval. London sounded like a good place.

'But these fools to whom the government gives money to live, waste it betting on horses,' I said.

This sounded even better to my audience. London was the place.

'Even in Canada they give free money,' the man with the niece's sister-in-law's sister said.

Diamond had eaten the rice and I asked her if she wanted an over-sweet ice cream.

Her eyes were wide and glowing now.

'Yes please.'

One of the company, most of whom had drawn up chairs, leaned forward.

'Now tell me, Farrukh. In England they tell me that people want themselves whipped and pay you money to kick them in the face with heavy boots and all this. This can't be true can it?'

Diamond smiled.

'Well,' I said. 'Yeah, true. Not everyone, just specialists, you know, guys who shoot foxes and dress up in red coats and go to prostitutes and are really perverts beneath a sort of veil of decency.'

'Fantastic,' said my questioner. 'I will go there and give them the thrashing of their lives and become bloody rich.'

'It doesn't work like that,' I said. 'They don't employ just anyone to thrash them. These are slightly sick people who hire women, prostitute women, to dress up in cruel costumes and whip them.'

'And the victims pay the women?'

I decided that the S&M concept must be culture specific and turned the subject back to cat burgers.

'I was acquitted in the magistrate's court. There was no evidence,' the proprietor protested. 'So fuck off, Farrukh the great poet.'

'The bastard bribed the police to hide the evidence,' one fellow said.

All this in English so that Diamond nearly choked on her ice cream.

When we stepped out of the cafe and I fetched the bike, she stood on the pavement and thanked me profusely.

'Where will you go?' I asked.

'They let me sleep in the church compound,' she said.

'It's where I go. Look, let me tell you,' she said, 'A white woman in India can share a bed whenever she wants. I've done it when I get fed up of sleeping on graves. Okay, it's prostitution but you make friends through it too.'

'If I take you home, you won't have to sleep with me,' I said.

'That's what they all say. But thanks for the food,' she said. 'You're a beauty.'

'Back to the churchyard?'

'No, no, no. I just said that to see if you'd make a play. I've got a friend,' she said. 'Thanks again.'

She went and I watched her go.

I cycled to the Bund Gardens, a spot by the river that flows through our town where the river is dammed and where, at low tide, you can walk across the dam to the other side.

It was where, as a child, my sister and I would be brought by our ayah Chandrabai, to play amongst the flower beds and the swings, and where one day we saw a crowd gathered to watch a man tying newborn puppies into a sack to drown them by descending the stone stairs to the river and weighing the sack down with stones. Even at the age of three or four, I understood the terror that accompanied the realization of what he was doing. Chandrabai hurriedly hustled us away from there but my sister and I persisted in asking why the man was doing it and what would happen to the puppies. We knew.

I got back home late. My aunt Shera said that an old friend Praful had dropped in, having heard from the cafe owners that I was in town.

'He said you should go to his place, same place, whatever time of night you came back.'

'I thought he'd gone to Bombay or somewhere. Isn't he a journalist?'

'He's back in town. His father died and he lives with his mother in that haunted house. Go and see him. But don't bring him here.'

'Why not?'

'We don't have to see him. You see him if you want. He has some cheek coming back into our house,' Amy said.

I didn't ask why. In our neighbourhood there were always petty grudges and quarrels which could last for decades. People crossed the street to avoid each other.

I went to see my old friend who used to hang around our house every day when we were teenagers. He was older than I was and was in the same college year as my sister Zareen who, very disdainful of his attention, would get him to do errands for her—running to the corner to buy stuff from the chemists, getting her bicycle punctures repaired, delivering records or parcels to the houses of her friends. My other friends would make fun of him but my aunts and I always put it down to his natural kindness and resented the fact that Zareen referred to the poor boy, with his slightly hunched back, as 'my Mycenaean slave'. In all these years neither I nor he ever discovered what Mycenae had to do with his willingness to run errands.

Praful's house was a little bungalow in severe need of repair. There was no doorbell, and the house didn't need one because the door was half off its hinges. I shouted his name to draw the household's attention.

Praful came to the door. The same dark features, his eyes set deep under his forehead. Balding now though, I calculated, barely into his thirties. We grin and embrace.

'I thought you were working for the *Times of India* in Bombay.'

'I'm finished with them,' he says and leads me in.

The house is as I remember it—flag-stoned floors and the same moth-eaten sofas, only a little more derelict. The ceiling consists of sagging canvas, whitewashed but now brown and full of holes through which, I remember, the scampering rats that lived between the tiled roof and the canvas in the walls and rafters, would occasionally fall into the living room and bedrooms.

As we sit down he shouts to someone in the next room to get some tea.

His mother comes to the door and I stand up to greet her. She is very thin, very dark and was in her youth a real beauty. Her features are still an icon to that vanished past.

'So good to see you,' she says in Gujarati. 'Why don't you take this fellow to London with you. Get him some work.'

'Sure, we'll talk about it,' I say and she approaches Praful and whispers to him, 'There's no sugar for the tea. I didn't have any money.'

'Hey, forget the tea,' Praful says, 'Let's have a drink, yaar! Sweetheart, come and meet FD,' he shouts.

His mother retreats to her own room and, from what I know to be the door of the bedroom adjoining the street, his father's bedroom as was, emerges none other than Diamond.

'I know FD. The kind man on the bicycle who fed me.'

PRAFUL LOOKED FROM ME TO her.

'He took one of your leaflets,' she said.

'Your leaflets?' I looked at Praful.

' Praff helped me write it. I'm not a writer, I'm a dancer, Diamond said.

'It's part of the exposé,' Praful said. 'You don't know what's going on in this town, yaar.'

Diamond went into the bedroom and came back with a bottle of Indian rum and three tea cups. She poured the drink.

'They are very powerful. This story—I was breaking this story and doing an investigation, like Shera aunty said you were, and I met Diamond and sent the story in to the *Times of India*. They rejected it. The editor said it can't be proved, any of it; and they have these gora American and European lawyers in their ashram—devotees who wrote thirty letters to the *Times* saying they will sue him in every court in the US and every country in Europe and then in India and bankrupt the paper. Boy, they are bastards. I know you are writing for Britain but they'll get there too, they'll stop you writing anything.'

'British newspapers don't scare that easy and my editor said he'd take any verifiable copy.'

'Don't be naïve, man, they have money. They'll buy the owner of the newspaper off. Or they'll buy your bloody newspaper. They have ex-advertising people from Madison Avenue in their fucking sex-pit of an ashram and those guys threatened American publications and TV channels with withdrawal of expensive advertising accounts if they wrote anything nasty about Saket.'

'Good to know,' I said. 'Is the stuff you wrote verifiable?'

'Go and find my daughter in the ashram. And my so-called husband whose arse the Guru is presently fucking,' Diamond said. 'Ask them the truth. Verify and preach.'

I sipped the acidic rum.

'Why do you think they sacked me from the *Times*? The day after I filed my story and kicked up a fuss about it not being published, the general manager called me in and asked me to clear my desk and go. No explanation. They wouldn't be giving me references, the pimp said. It was clearly a punishment and they wanted me to know it.'

'Why would they sack you—for a story they didn't want to print? Surely they should keep you on payroll to stop you taking it to other papers?'

'I called five editors after that. Including the ones in Poona here where you and I used to work—the *Messenger*—saying I'd accept the job of a stringer even. They wouldn't even take my calls. A friend in the editor's office told me that I had been hung out to dry.'

'They can't have that much influence.'

'They have a pocketful of powerful politicians they've put on their Swiss bank payroll. How do you think they make these land deals? The politicos take money in dollars only, you know, and the dollars stay in the US or Europe. The devotees pay by standing order from their international banks. The ashram spends in rupees and converts them into hard international currency.'

'Must debrief you about the details,' I said.

'Why do you think I called as soon as I heard you were in town? And your aunts told me what you were here for? But listen, baba, I'm fucking broke—not even cash for food man. I know the stuff. If your papers want articles about… you know…'

'Yeah, yeah, yeah. I am sure we can collaborate on the deals as I pull them and…' I could see that he would be too proud to ask. 'Of course I am sure you are the best source so I can give you an advance now just to see you don't run away and sell the info to London and cut me out.'

He bit his lip. He knew it was charity of a sort, that for him to try and get a story into international newspapers would be a long shot. I pulled out my wallet and held out two thousand rupees.

'No time to waste,' I said.

He didn't take the notes. He looked solemn and then he looked away. Diamond stepped towards me and took the money.

'Thanks, bicycle man,' she said.

I said we'd talk the next day.

I didn't talk to Praful. He was investigating some other story, Diamond said. It was only later that I discovered he had gone out and bought three bottles of the same rum with my money from a bootlegger in the early hours of the morning and was still dead drunk and sleeping it off.

Diamond met me at the cafe in the early evening and then I brought her home.

My aunts were shocked to see me bring a white woman with unkempt hair into the house. Did they take any comfort from the fact that she was not in crimson?

'This is Diamond,' I said, introducing her. 'My aunts, Shera and Amy.'

'Call me Di,' she said.

The aunts asked her to sit and looked at each other. At least the woman had brought no suitcases or possessions with her, so she was probably just dropping in, not someone I had picked up. But still I had to reassure them.

Di asked to go to the bathroom and Shera discreetly enquired whether she was staying to dinner.

'She is staying at Praful's place. She has rented a room,' I said.

'In Praful's house? But there's nothing like that, is there?'

'No, nothing like that,' I said.

Diamond came back into the room and we stopped whispering.

Shera was staring at Diamond's head.

'Under the tap. I didn't use your towels,' Di said. 'Or the shampoo, just the soap. I left the basin clean.'

Her hair had been washed and rinsed and she'd smoothed it out and bundled it together. It was still wet. 'Where I am staying, there's no proper water.'

'You should use the shampoo and the hot water, darling. Have a shower. We have a geyser, you know. Electric. Instant hot water. I can show you how to use it,' Amy said. 'If you are staying at Praful's just come and have a bath whenever you want.'

'I can show her if she wants a shower,' I said.

Shera stood up. 'No, no, not you. She's a lady. Come, darling. I can show you now. For other days, next time you want to come.'

'Are you sure?' Diamond seemed a bit overwhelmed.

As they went into the bathroom, we heard Shera asking her what she'd like to eat that night, even though dinner had already been prepared.

'Now who is she? Why have you brought her here?' Amy asked.

'I want to hear her story. Praful tried to write it but it got complicated. I think scandal is the only interesting thing about the Saket project. Until, of course I get some handle on why it's a disease of the twentieth century and how a great confidence trick has become trans-cultural.'

Amy didn't get what I was saying.

'They are not good people. They may be religious but what kind of religion is this?'

'The religion of the lost. I must first answer the question—why are these people here? And why they give him everything as the price for what I can see is nothing but self-delusion?' I said.

'What is she doing in Praful's house? Is he safe with her? A single woman living in the house?'

'My darling, you've been two single women living in this house for thirty years?'

'Don't be silly, you know what I mean,' says Amy.

WE SIT IN THE SAME cafe that we have now made our haunt. I see Di most days and we spend time at Praful's. He drinks.

He drinks incessantly. I pay. He exudes bitterness. Diamond calms him down. He promises her that he will get her daughter back and fight a duel with the husband. Obviously my aunts know that he drinks and his reputation as an alcoholic has spread through the neighbourhood.

So Di visits the house as my aunts have invited her to do and spends time in the room in which I am sleeping, the room my aunts have preserved as it was when I was still in college in Poona. There was no reason to change it. The shelf still holds the dusted volumes. Diamond goes through them.

There is a paperback copy of *Thus Spake Zarathustra*, good teenage reading, which I tackled with the peculiar conceit that I was the only person in my town who realized that it wasn't an interpretation of Parsee Zoroastrian texts but Nietzsche's attack on the ethics that flow from monotheism. Then there were the Hardy novels with my scribbles in the margins, pretentious musings on the metaphorical significance of landscape. There was the D.H. Lawrence collection, every book I could get hold of from second-hand bookshops, all of them except *Two on a Tower*; paperbacks; and Bertrand Russell's *History of Western Philosophy* which had served as an armoury to bluff one's way through arguments about the Western Intellectual Tradition.

Very few of my companions, the teenagers and wasters I moved with, understood any of this. They had all, in the time I spent at Poona University and later in England, joined their family firms to run petrol pumps or they now drove trucks and ran welding yards for a living. D.H. Lawrence didn't enter their frames of reference. He had nothing to say to them. And even less so Giuseppe Di Lampedusa, Nikos Kazantzakis or Lawrence Durrell or difficult treatises on aesthetics and ethics by George Santayana or Spinoza. Diamond spent hours on my veranda and went through that collection. Reading.

'I'm learning about you,' she would say in the rare moments in which she could forget or cast off or take a rest from her preoccupation with her mission, her daughter, her revenge.

'You want to tell me the story?' I asked her one day, soon after she started frequenting the house for her showers. It was late evening, dusk, and we sat on the veranda having rolled up the bamboo blind so we could see the wall of the next house a few feet away. We could hear the flocks of birds coming to rest in the trees beyond the house, making the awful screeching din with which they greeted dusk. I switched on the table lamp which was, and had always been, the only source of illumination in that cut-off veranda.

'I'll let it play—here in my subconscious.' She touched the middle of her head. 'Maybe I've been a bit impatient. But there are days when I feel there is no time to lose.'

I promised her that I would go back to the ashram and try and identify a young child, a girl of four called Sapphire, Saffy. But of course they would have changed her name. She would be called some complex, if beautiful, Sanskrit name and be forever lost to the world as Saffy. As far as Di knew the child's initiation had not been complete when she was forced to leave and so Saffy might still be Saffy. It was a hope.

The next day at the ashram I asked to see what they did with children and a very willing Ma 'year of fire' took me to their nursery shacks, the prefabs dedicated to happy children in crimson.

I was allowed to peer through the windows but not allowed to address the children who were dashing about as in any rich well-equipped nursery the world over, knocking over towers of bricks and pouring water from ladles into heaps of sand before busying themselves with some other task of make-believe grandeur.

'Is one of them called Sapphire?' I asked.

It must have rung some bells in Ma Agnivarsha's head, because she said we had better go. Or was I over-interpreting? Did she really have an appointment with the next client of the press office? If she hadn't, it was not a good sign.

I didn't tell Di any of this.

She didn't ask and was waiting for me to volunteer some reassuring detail when I had it. She suggested that she take me to the dissidents' cafe in the city.

These conversations and proposals mostly took place at Praful's house and in his presence. Over the days I gauged what had happened to the sprightly investigative, tenacious reporter I had known when we were both starting on our writing careers with the *Poona Messenger*. Had he started drinking before the *Times* kicked him out, purportedly for his attempt at an ashram exposé? The three of us would sit in his room. He would preach and ramble and curse, sitting on his bed always with a glass in his hand. He wouldn't come out with us but when Diamond spoke to me I felt an impotent jealousy welling up in him.

'We must help her,' he said to me. 'I gave up my career and my life for her. She is my common-law wife.'

Why was he saying this to me? I had no desire for her or intention to steal her from him.

'What is your status?' he asked me out of earshot from Di.

'What status?'

'Are you married, do you have a family, are you in love. Come on, yaar, we were the best of friends!'

'No, I am not married. I've been through some things. I lived with a woman but things haven't worked out. I thought an assignment for a few months in India would help me see things more clearly.'

'You left your girlfriend in London? She's waiting for you?'

'No. She ran away with some Frenchman who hugs trees for a living. A fraud with some idiotic French philosophy,' I said. It was true. He didn't want to hear that. It meant I was not committed to any woman and that my mind could stray to Diamond. I could see the thought crossing his face but it would have been ridiculous, if merciful, to tell him I wouldn't want Diamond if she were the last woman on the planet. Instead I said, 'You should help her and if I can I will and if you get Saffy back then maybe you can adopt her.'

He looked into my eyes to get an index of my sincerity.

'But you should stop drinking,' I said.

'I just drink socially,' he said.

Di came in and said she was ready. I asked Praful to come with us, but he said he had work.

Di took me to a tea shop in the city, a few miles from my house, a newish part of town being developed with broad cement roads and glass and steel buildings, a place that had been empty land when I grew up, with a large native clientele but with a few hippy types at several tables in a corner or section that seemed reserved for them. Some of them wore faded crimson kurtas but they weren't crimsones, or at least didn't from the way they talked, like young people in any European bar, appear to be.

Di seemed to know them all. She introduced me to Vincent. He was a Dutch psychoanalyst and psychotherapist who had abandoned his technical titles and now called himself a 'socio-sexual healer'—which is how he introduced himself.

Vincent, like Di and the rest of the 'dissidents', had also been expelled from the ashram. He said he was the pioneer of the sex therapy unit that had now proliferated into the ashram's chief money-spinner and had been corrupted beyond all recognition.

Diamond and I went again two days later, making appointments with Vincent to meet in the cafe. And then again. I took down his story as he told it sitting in the cafe over several days, sometimes with Di and sometimes without her. I preferred the technique of writing notes to using a tape recorder, because that way I would ask Vincent to repeat himself and then I could go over the sentences and reform them to make written sense out of their spoken flow. He said:

'I studied medicine in Holland in The Hague and came to Britain when I was twenty-five. I wanted to continue studies in the mind and its relationship to the body. I read everything I could on the neurological structures and everything more on the psychoanalytical theories of Freud, Jung, and Adler. It is difficult to explain, but today we can see that Freud had a model that superseded the model of mind as clockwork when something goes wrong with the wheels and the cogs. He thought of the mind as a computer, though he didn't know about computers which hadn't been invented in the form we know today. It had memories, and dreams were evidence of activity that went on behind the current opened screen. And then he moved on to say this computer is connected to all the other family computers that programmed it.'

Computers, when we talked, were just instruments of word processing and e-mailing to me, but apparently Vincent knew about them and constantly through his ramblings alluded to them hanging themselves as does the human mind and having to switch them off and on again to get them to function properly and so on analogously and boringly.

Jung, Vincent said, had a wider vision, seeing a sort of connection between a universe of minds (he called it an internet of minds), and when the mind goes wrong we call it madness, but we mustn't. That's what he said he grasped fundamentally and completely in England—but do we know something is displaced and how to bring it back?

'To cure madness?' I asked, using the word he shied away from provocatively.

He took it in his stride. He stared at me across the tea cups on the table.

'Okay, my friend. What is madness? Why are there two spirits bottled in one? What is schizophrenia? Practitioners like R.D. Laing, who came into consciousness with this great blossoming of the alternative world, the resistance to the Vietnam War, the Civil Rights Movement in the States, the consciousness of burning bras to unstrap the female libido, it all came together in the accusation against the family. The family became Ronald Laing's scapegoat. He owed everything to Freud but wasn't willing to pay his debts and so he tore up the IOUs and distorted the other notes of debit.

'Then there was David Cooper who broke from R.D. Laing and his therapy sessions at the Tavistock. Man. I tell you, I was there in situ myself at the Tavvy. Cooper was pulled into dialectics. Bullshit Hegel, bullshit Marx. And he could roll it. He said everybody, society, social laws were responsible for crippling minds. Everything was fucking everybody. Nothing was innocent and he could prove it guilty.

'I learned so much from that man. And still he was old-fashioned. He told me to get out and find out for myself. Somewhere there, though Saket never met them, originated the guru who bluffs his combination of Tantric arts and sex and the needs and uncertainties of the lost children. Here is Peter Pan, as you call him, the fount of eternal youth and there are the lost children and you put them together and a mission is born.

'I met Saket by accident. I was thrown out of Holland for my own practices of psycho-sexual therapy. I was accused of abuse, exploitation, perversion, God knows, man. I did what I believed in. I don't believe that the psychoanalyst can sit, like you are sitting there with a book in hand scribbling and listening.

'I think he has to take his underwear off and show the patient his erection. Yes, yes, yes, it's tasteless, dirty. But what else can one do when one is curing the mind. The disease is people and the therapist is the protagonist, the person. Okay, extreme case, you fuck your patient—let the bodily contact speak. That's not what I was after. I was not Saket.'

I asked if I could take all this down and he grinned.

'Then why are you still here?' I asked.

'I've got nothing, so I've got nothing to lose,' he said.

THE TAPTAVAN MONASTERY WAS A lonely place. It had this romantic name but was really a rock temple in a rocky terrain by a fast-moving pebbly stream in the Himalayas. It hadn't been built in a spot of beauty or a spot of convenience, a place with a view or with pastures next to it. It had been built on the craggy part of a bare mountain. A quarter mile's trek in any direction, up the mountain, down its shoulder into a deep valley, sideways across the bare mountain to the next ridge and one would come across the most breathtaking sights of forests, valleys and, on a clear day, even snow-capped peaks. They would have been perfect sites for this rough stone monastery, part carved out of rock and then mostly built of crude brown brick, but it was as though the asceticism of the founding monks of our order was such that they chose the ugliest spot.

The children of the monastery were sent out to wash the robes of the monks and their own little saffron and brown wraps in the bubbling brook. It was one of their tasks. They washed the clothes and spread them out to dry on the rocks and the mountainside would become a patchwork of saffron and brown and white while the sun shone. When it was cold the frost would bite into the fabric and stiffen it and then the boys would be sent out to collect dry wood from the jungles higher up the mountain and would return with sackfuls on their backs.

Each Jayanti, the birth celebrations of our Lord, there would be new recruits, new apprentices, some of them mere infants, brought into the monastery from the cities of the plains. Three or four monks would be delegated to go to the temples in Varanasi or Bombay and spend a few weeks there examining the candidates who were nominated to join the order. It was a hard journey from Taptavan—fifty miles down the mountains on foot to Nyoma and then a twenty-day trek into the Kulu valley by donkey train and thence to the towns and to Ludhiana from where the train would take us to Dilli and Varanasi and over three days to Bombay.

We carried blankets and a change of clothes and were fed by the generosity of villagers in the mountains and of fellow passengers on the trains. I was born in a city so the streets and the crowds were no shock to me. I had voluntarily gone to Taptavan having been orphaned at the age of eleven, gone on the streets and been picked up by roving monks and brought to the monastery. I rapidly decided that the broader world was not for me and being taught to turn within I concluded, even at that age, that I had found a universe that was vaster than the realm of all the stars and I resolved to devote the time of this illusory consciousness and selfhood that we possess, to explore it or any corner of it that I could illuminate through concentration and the simple life. It was an assumption of monkhood and took me away from the terror of my parent's deaths and the terrifying life on the streets, alone where I was thrown in with seasoned children, cynical eight-year-olds who begged and stole and smoked cigarettes and talked in the rough terms and tones of the streets. Many years later I read Dickens' books—I shall tell how and why—and I can only now see myself as a sort of Oliver Twist.

I was twenty-two when I was delegated to go on the mission to fetch our young acolytes. I went to Bombay with three others. Our head monk, he who was called The Enlightened, had addresses scribbled in a book and a Jain guide came each morning when we reached the city and took up residence in the forecourt of a dark temple, to take us to the houses from where we would fetch our future acolytes.

I remember the home from which we took the young Saket, though he was not called that then. It was a flat in a building off a main road with a 'nursing home' on the ground, first and second floors. There were residences on the third, fourth and fifth floors. We went up in the rickety lift with its trellised metal door.

The entire floor had been converted into this rich, vast Jain household. The family came to the door and touched The Enlightened's feet in turn as we waited to be admitted, queuing in order of seniority behind him.

This ceremonial obeisance took place before the huge dark door anointed with marks of piety. The large room we entered was tiled in marble, vast, empty and even cold in Bombay's heat. Yes, there was an air conditioner rumbling away with an occasional small explosion but I thought then that the cold came from the marble floors.

The room had chairs along one wall but otherwise was devoid of furniture. We were motioned to be seated in a row on the chairs which were sculpted like mini-thrones with gold-plated arm-rests and stiff gold-braided green cushions on their upright backs.

We waited in that room. There were other priests who came and went and I could hear chanting from the inner chamber.

The infant, perhaps a few weeks old, was brought without ceremony by a servant and handed to The Enlightened who gave him to me to take charge of. The mother had declined to be part of the handover. The father, his grandfather and uncles and an older woman came in with the child. The grandmother handed me a wicker basket full of feeding bottles and milk-powder and began to instruct me on how to make one up with boiled water that had been cooled. There had been other bottle-fed infants in our monastery and though I hadn't tended to them myself I was aware of the procedures and familiar with cloth nappies and their care.

The infant had wide eyes and I felt that they were studying me. No cry escaped him. He was a contented child, sucking his thumb and fingers. Did he smile or is that my memory playing tricks?

I knew I had been designated as the carer and that this was my mission in the big city. There were others in our group who were assigned the care of older boys.

My boy, this child, was called Rahul and I was told that he was dedicated to us from the day he was born, but I wasn't told why and never thought to question it. Being in the holy order, I thought, was a blessing that karma bestows.

I was constantly made aware that as an orphan from the streets I had been taken in at a more advanced age than the other monks of my batch in an act of extreme charity. Rahul came to us in an act of reverse charity—the family was giving us a substantial sum of money to take him from them.

My own first days at the monastery and the memory of my parents, the memory of loss remain with me. My mother's face and ways, my father's drunkenness. And then the instruction of The Enlightened, younger and insistent, teaching me to repeat the mantras, the chants and how to empty my mind of memory.

Faces—bald, polished heads replacing faces—the washed and anointed heads of elephants, glistening brass urns, mountain peaks. And women, my mother a form in my dreams, become an abstraction. Aliens.

As boys, myself and other 'companion monks', as we acolytes were called, found a chilli tree in the wild and plucked the red pods and brought them in. The older monks reacted with horror. Chillies were forbidden fruit. The three of us had to undergo three days of purification. What I didn't tell the monks was that I had already tasted one and it burnt my mouth. The chilli itself taught me that punishment, karma is here and now and not in some hereafter where the soul is accommodated to a new body and sent down to earth to suffer again. The wages of sin are regularly paid.

A YOUNG MAN, MYSELF, CHANDRIKA, still in his teens, is given charge of the infant on the donkey trek up the mountains. The tiny boy, his little pink fingers twisting constantly, evidence that the body is not a supernatural creation but a nest of nerves made from ropes of chemicals, cried all the way and his feeble cries turned into tiny spumes of steamy breath along the mountain paths. Now and then I would pick him up as I must have observed the hill-tribe women do. They strapped their babies into slings under their chests or on their backs, but our procession of monks had no such slings and though our uniforms had shrouds of cloth in which we wrapped ourselves, no one thought of devising such a portable, body-warmed cradle. Besides, the infant had been handed to us with woollen caps and coats and baby blankets galore.

The mother in parting must have insisted, though we never saw her or spoke to her. The grandmother handed over the child and the clothes with instant relief on her face. She was the one, it seemed who had managed this whole transfer and she looked determined. The father immediately took to telling his beads, chanting under his breath, his eyes filled with doubt, as though asking the heavens, in which we were not supposed to believe, for forgiveness.

The taking or the transfer of the child became a ceremony and the vast and echoing empty reception rooms of the family household were filled with incense and the sonorous chants of prayer from squatting monks. Was there a ceremony associated with the handing over of children to the care of monasteries? Was it Hindu, Buddhist, Jain? Was there not a confusion of prayer, of belief and of ritual?

Yes, we begged for our food and were given it, but our troupe also had a marketing delegate who kept the money and bought the fruit we ate and the curd and milk we drank. He was probably in charge of the transaction that accompanied the transfer though no one mentioned it.

When the tins of dried milk were exhausted, the child drank diluted goat's milk from a bottle. Unclogging the rubber teats and washing out the stale, sour milk became routine as we journeyed upwards to the monastery in the clouds.

It was when we camped on the trek up to Taptavan, in the huts that the villagers vacated for us, that I gathered the courage to ask The Enlightened why this child had been entrusted to us.

'They are a very rich diamond-trading family and own the huge endowments which pay for the order,' he said, solemnly. 'The boy, who is given to you to bring up as though you were his mother, will die on his seventh birthday. His life on earth will be without the sin of man. He is born under a special star which shortens the present trial of his existence as substance in the cosmos. No temptation, no thoughts, no bad deeds, a clean sheet of karma at the age of seven and one trial of life put behind him. He is truly privileged.'

'How do you...how do we...know this?' I asked and even as the words were pronounced I knew I had brought disfavour on myself. Of course he would answer. It was the mission and duty of the master to answer every question of the acolytes.

'It was seen at his birth,' he said. There was an eclipse of the sun as his mother laboured in pain and the house was in darkness. It was a difficult birth and through the deserted streets the dervishes walked crying 'dey daan chhootey gheraan!'—offer charity and release the eclipse—and the snake worshippers who carried their cobras coiled around their arms, giving them a lick of milk from a terra cotta salver when the devout emerged from their doorways and gave them alms to feed the slithering deity. The city wasn't silent. The bells of the temples clamoured in the darkness and the muezzins called the faithful from their turret loudspeakers.

This unborn child's mother cried out in her torment that she would offer the child emerging from her womb to the gods, to the cosmos, if only a chink, a spark, a flash of light could be brought into the eternal darkness she saw in the pain of birth. She cursed her womanhood, she cursed the marriage that made her a vassal of sex. Her grandmother was by her side with aunts as midwives through the long agony of this birth.

'And the prediction? Seven years?'

'The prediction, my son, there is no escaping the prediction,' he said and it was all he would say.

Through subsequent questioning of the 'treasurer' and of the other senior monks on our expedition I got to know the truth.

The child, my child, Rahul, was born after a hard labour and his father waited with his astrologers for the exact moment outside the birthing chamber and the pundits, taking their cue from the cries of agony beyond the forbidden doorways, made their divination. They read their scrolls over and over and made their calculations. The life the newborn had inherited would be pure because it would be short. The child should in the seven years he was destined to live, be out of harm's way, out of the ways of the world even.

Then the grandmother determined that we should be called. The family would part with him. They didn't want to be there, to stand by while the prophecy was fulfilled.

How would it happen? How would the infinite summon the seven-year-old soul? Could a mother bear to see fate at work, the hunger of the eternal maw? No, how could she? And would that mother and father be tempted to do all they could to resist the act of The Inevitable? Would the terror of regret not grip the stomach and paralyze the blood as the days went by and The Day approached? Suppose the child grew to be the most alluring, the most amusing, the most precious. How much would they invest in the child as he grew? Would the mother hold back from speaking to him so he was deprived of speech? Would he be confined to a childhood of meditative silence in order to prepare himself for the predicted fate? Would it not be tempting to circumvent that fate and cut short the time of its coming?

No, there was no other way. They couldn't live in the light of a candle that they knew would be snuffed, leaving desolate darkness. That would be our privilege. Better this way.

How could I argue, though it was my very thought that every mother, presumably, was conscious that her children would die? Not before her perhaps and not before they had fulfilled the futile promise of life. A mother was surely conscious of that truth even at the ecstatic moment in which her child was conceived—even in the throes of fornication—and then the forgetfulness that life breeds.

But we, The Detached, are conscious of the figure at our shoulder, the presence that holds our elbow and is on our back, the shadow which resembles us and yet grins at our vanities. We live with death and expect its release. The Detached learn to value non-life, not-being. And yet.

We took the child to the monastery. There was no reason to give him a name other than the one his parents had, reluctantly, given him. The moment before the prophecy was pronounced, the horoscope had predicted that his name would begin with 'R' and that this child would be near God and that the child would be God—as all things are God. And his father was asked to pronounce his name so that Eternity could register it in the book of happening and could then pronounce his fate. The father didn't know what was coming. They hadn't then told him what the stars foretold.

The father said his name should be Rahul.

Then the astrologers, after some meditation, said he would die at the age of seven and could not live a second longer and the clouds filled the window of the house and the mist of darkness floated through it and there was a distant discordant music made of a mixture of the crashing of cymbals and a creaking sound like timbers in pain or the braying of donkeys. The father and mother saw it, heard it and were reassured that they were in the grip of greater powers. They looked in each other's faces. Was their sight obscured by the dark mist? Did they hear the distant donkey music or would this portent have only been sensible to The Detached. Our elders could see eclipses years before they happened and I was told as I lived, meditated, recited the mantras and detached myself from the mud that was my flesh, that the gift would descend on me, on all who passed through the dimension of being that the key of Detachment unlocked.

The boy grew up under my care. In time I was assigned other older boys to manage, one of them the boy Harkishan. Each of us acolytes was assigned up to four boys to mentor apart from fulfilling our other duties. It was very much like being an elder brother and much more. These boys had to be taught not just the disciplines of the monastery but the perspectives on life, the gift or burden of the granted, temporary flame.

The story of the Buddha goes that his father, fearful of the flow of life and its consequences, instructed the young Siddharth's tutors to keep him from ever catching sight of old age, sickness and death. That was the blindness that unenlightenment, misguided love and concern bring.

My task was the opposite. I had to demonstrate to my charges that old age, sickness and death were the threads of the woven and patterned fabric of life which continued into the next life and was beyond time and space. These were easy lessons to preach. The discourses had come down to us through the ages, but the entirety of their meaning was impossible to absorb, even for me who had passed the stage and ceremony of apprenticeship.

And that was not all. The young acolytes were becoming aware of their bodies, the burdens and lures of being made of material. One had to address oneself to those knowing that the infants were not yet struggling with the greatest temptation, the distraction of all flesh, the illusion of the garden, the whisper of the blood and the beacon to all the senses. Subvert and subdue was what we had been taught. Control the urge, negate it and pass the energy into peace. Sex is violence, it leaves the body exhausted, the spirit depleted. Let the blood circulate to the rhythms of meditation, not the pulse of arousal and detumescence.

The boy grows. I teach him the ceremony of hands in which we touch each other and transmit the energy of being. Do I believe in the ceremony of hands? I have had infusions of the power of elders throughout my life but am I at all capable of transmitting it to this boy? I grow to love him.

He is a happy boy and shows no dismay when he doesn't get the answers to the questions he constantly asks. He is curious about everything, anything. Why we need to cook our food when wild animals don't? What's metal made of and why are some things softer than others? There are those in the monastery who could teach him physics and chemistry and answer some of what he asks and I refer him sometimes to them, but these questions are outside the realm of his discipline and routine.

What are the stars? How far are they? Where did we come from? Why did his parents give him away?

I answer the last by saying that we monks have a calling and there was a prediction that he would be one of those who were called to the higher service of the Universe. How does the Universe make its will known? How does it anoint those who are called? I try my best. Curiosity is the mother of faithlessness. Enquiry casts doubt on received wisdom and destroys it. This much I began to learn even through his questioning and my struggle to answer him. And I told myself that doubt is a strong test of detachment, because if you doubt you don't know and that is a lack of something; and surely, detachment is learning to live with the lack of things—even knowledge—the discipline of doing without knowing.

Today I know, and Rahul who later became Saket—and this is the story of that transformation—taught me—and this is also partly the story of how he did—that Descartes said 'I think therefore I am'. The subject of meditation comes to unthinking through thinking, to abandonment of the chain of consciousness through concentration, and that is the most desirable state of being—I have ceased to think, therefore I am not and in not being, I am. Or so we were taught to think.

The elders of the monastery never spontaneously alluded to the prediction or to how and why the child had arrived at the monastery. I found myself wishing, in what I felt was a guilty sacrilegious state, that they had forgotten the prophecy, that Rahul would pass through his seventh birthday and grow to be a man.

But they had not forgotten. They keep dates, these astro-loving monks, but they didn't mention it to me till the day before his seventh birthday. The future must not influence the present. Thoughts of the future can mean you take precautions and that disturbs the harmony of the Universe in which every decay of a petal is deliberate, decreed, decided and destined.

'Clothe him in dark blue, give him three blankets and take him to meditate tonight on the bare mountain above the stream.'

I had my instructions. I couldn't tell the seven-year-old child the truth of why he was required to stay awake and meditate through the night in the cold. He asked. Not once but four or five times and I elaborated my lying answer each time. I said all of us had to undergo the trial of a night on the bare mountain and then I said the night would reveal something to him, something important and eternal, and he was excited.

We walked up, wading waist deep in the very fast-running rocky brook. We knew every twist and turn of this mountain water which would descend to the plains and become a mighty river. At this height and speed it was a dangerous stream and would sweep you away if you didn't avoid the rapids and didn't know where the treacherous strong currents prevented even the strongest from gaining a hand or foothold. There were routes across the stream which we knew we could take, using embedded rocks to hang on to or ones which would shelter us from the forces of the current.

I carried the blankets on my head. The sun was huge and pink and sinking beyond the arc of mountain peaks. Rock snakes dived into the water. The dusk air was chilly.

There was a spot under a cliff where I told him he should settle.

'Will you come for me in the morning?' he asked.

I didn't answer.

'Are you afraid, little one?' I asked a moment later.

'No,' he said. 'This will be good. If the moon comes out I can look on the black and silvery water and pretend it's the snake that holds the world on its back. That's what I shall use to focus on. And if the moon's not bright enough or there are clouds, then I'll just listen for the mountain wolves.'

He seemed ready for this adventure and the panic made my gut knot itself. I arranged the blankets round him, crouching by him as he assumed the squat-legged meditative pose and he looked into my eyes. There was no mistrust there, but possibly the panic showed and he saw it. What was I doing?

'I'll be all right,' he said. He wanted to reassure me.

No, you won't, I thought. Why was the world ordered so? I had seen people die before, old, wise, reconciled monks who knew the great peace was upon them. But this child? My child! I was this strange parent on the precipice of loss. I was the father stabbing his son to prove his allegiance to God. Not that we believed in God, but here was the Universe claiming its youngest. I wanted to die in his stead.

'You better cross back before it gets dark,' he said.

I kissed him on the forehead and then again and, without a

word, turned away. I didn't want him to see me crying. Why would I be crying? How would I explain?

Where had all the years of practising detachment gone? A waste. I felt the pangs of parting more acutely than I would a blunt knife sawing through my throat. This was not what I was supposed to feel. Atoms and space, nirvana, form is an illusion, the infinite ocean of all that we were awaits us all, the soul is not immortal, merely the tiniest, irrelevant part of the universal soul.

'See you at dawn. You always wake up first. Promise I won't fall asleep,' he shouted behind me as I waded across the stream again.

There was no sleep. I sat in the meditation room all night and counted my beads and repeated every mantra I could. In my mind I was betraying the faith. I was praying that the mantras would redeem him and that was the worst thing a soul seeking redemption could do—to ask a mantra for a wish. No matter how many times through this darkest of nights I told myself to melt into detachment, I felt the wrench of parting with this boy. The dread of it. I was no monk. I was as far from enlightenment as the lustful goat in the alleys of the market.

The moon was very bright and then towards dawn the clouds came and eclipsed it even as it faded to white. Destiny had come for the child. The Abbot, The Enlightened, had come looking for me.

'Retrieve the body and we shall have a ceremony by the stream.'

It was dawn. The night of his birth had passed, his seventh birthday, the passage of seven years to the second. What would I find? How would I face this? The Abbot knew what he was putting me through.

'Go. Earn merit,' was all he said.

I went. I walked through the paths leading to the bare mountain and came upon the stream. It was fresh but covered with mist and through it I thought I heard his voice.

'I can see you,' he said. 'The moon lit up the river and I saw the serpent that carries the earth.'

The mist cleared and I saw him at the height across the stream, standing now wrapped in two blankets and waving the third with his right arm.

I didn't cross the stream.

'Wait there, I am coming back with The Enlightened,' I shouted and turned and ran.

Had I seen a ghost? No, the timing of the birth had gone wrong. His hour of birth must be later in the long dawn, except that the dawn in the southern parts of India is instant. Light and darkness come fast and suddenly.

I ran to the monastery and encountered The Abbot. He read my face.

'What did you do with him?'

'It hasn't happened?'

'What do you mean?'

'The boy is alive, waving a blanket. Where I left him,' I whispered.

He put his hand on my shoulder and led me out of the meditation parlour.

'That is not possible.'

'But it's true.'

'You located him in the wrong place. Take him down to the stream and ask him to wait for the blessing of the waters and then cross at the broad point and you come away.'

I shook my head in disbelief. I hadn't heard what I had heard.

'Go. Gain merit,' The Abbot said.

'You mean murder him?'

'Don't say ungainly things. The prediction is of the first order, it cannot be faulted. If the prediction fails, all predictions fail and the language with which we understand the Universe becomes a silence. Go.'

I was stunned. The night's fears and panics had told me I wasn't a monk. Now I knew I wasn't. If that was the language of the Universe which I must learn to speak or interpret, I wanted my tongue cut out.

I turned away from him and ran back along the path to the high valley of the stream.

Rahul was sitting in his meditative pose now and I crossed the stream as quickly as I could.

'Come on, we are going,' I said.

'Can I sleep now? I stayed awake.'

'Just follow me,' I said.

He stood up and smiled.

'Come on then,' he said. He treated me with no reverence as my other charges, his constant companions, did. He didn't seem to notice that they talked to me in hushed and respectful ways and that only he talked to me in the manner they used with each other.

I embraced him and a flicker of puzzlement crossed his handsome features. Then we set off and just as I led him along the left bank of the stream down the goat path, I heard a small cascade of rocks on the other side of the river. Against the cliff stood one of my other charges, older than Rahul, Harkishan.

'Don't go. Chandrika, Rahul!'

I shouted back. 'Go back. Don't say anything to anyone. Just go back.'

'But where are you going?'

'We can't stay. You won't see us again. Forget us. Just go back and say nothing, not even if The Enlightened questions you, say nothing. You will get a new tutor.'

I hurried Rahul along the track and looked back as we turned round a curve of the hill and saw that Harkishan was still standing there.

'He is my best friend,' Rahul said. 'We play coonjis.'

'How do you play that?'

'It's a secret. We get very close and then we rub the tips of our soosoos together. He doesn't want us to go.'

'He has to forget about us,' I said.

I knew the way. The road down the mountain from the monastery followed the contours of the mountains. It was an ancient road and had been built away from this river valley because the stream, when the snows higher up in the mountain knots melted, became a torrent and would wash out any road. The goat track led to a village maybe fifteen miles down.

We walked down the track and passed the village hanging in the little side valley. We were following the river.

'Where are we going? Aren't we going back?' Rahul asked.

'We are never going back,' I said.

He must have pondered this long and deep, because he didn't ask why. After a while he said, 'How long is never?'

'That which doesn't end,' I said.

'I saw that in my dream,' he said, 'a snake whose head was in my lap but whose tail went into the sky and kept going.'

I knew the goat track passed the village and we had often trekked this way down to the Kulu valley and then to the villages, farms and crowded towns. We walked till early evening and climbing away from the stream which had, being fed by smaller streams along the way, become quite a river, joined a proper road down used by trucks and cars. We didn't walk on the road but on the dusty, dry track below it.

We hadn't come across a soul all day and then I saw a car parked on the road and a man and woman standing next to it. From their clothes, one could tell they were city people and they both had wavy lines of white ash and yellow paste, anointments on their foreheads, which indicated that they had been to a Hindu temple and bore the mark of the ceremonies. They were both looking towards the river. I looked too and just as I did I heard a shout from the water. A young woman in a white sari was bathing in the river and the undercurrent had dragged at her feet and legs and was pulling her away. She screamed and went under. The woman by the car saw this and shouted what must have been the girl's name.

I ran along the bank and when I saw her body thrown up by the fast moving current I dived in. I wasn't familiar with this river, but I was the strongest swimmer in the monastery. I grabbed the girl. There was no point in fighting the current. I let it carry us and tried to steer ourselves, moving sideways through the strong current, knowing we would attain the bank. I anticipated hitting a rock and we did. It was just under water and I reached out for it, grabbing the girl by the hair and lifting her head above the deceptively unmoving surface. The rock was slimy but I managed to hold on to it and to the girl and held her head above the raging water.

The man had come down from the car and was very soon on the bank nearest us. He was carrying a rope and he slung it to me. It took him a few tries to fling it far enough and then it got to me and I grabbed it. Rahul grabbed the end of the rope to help the man haul us in.

As we got to the shore, the girl went limp in the water and when we dragged her onto the bank I saw why she was in the water. Her hands had no fingers and the flesh of her ear lobes and the tip of her nose seemed to have dissolved. Leprosy. I turned her over on her stomach and she vomited a lot of water and coughed. Then she rolled onto her back and closed her eyes, exhausted. She said she was okay and she gripped my wrist.

'God saved her,' the woman said.

I propped the girl up. She was breathing hard.

'This monk saved her,' the man said.

Then he turned to me, 'We came here to purify her flesh. Thank you, Baba. Thank you. She would have drowned.'

'God sent him,' the woman said.

'Please, let him decide who sent him. Only he knows,' the man said kneeling over the young girl who had now opened her eyes.

'I drowned,' she said.

'God saved you from drowning,' the woman said, kneeling by her now.

The man stood up shaking his head and looking at me.

'We can't repay you,' he said to me.

'We don't deal in repayments. It's the trade of the world,' I replied.

'We can drive you where you want to go,' he said.

I looked at Rahul.

'I am tired, Chandrika,' he said with a twinkle in his eye, catching on to the game. 'God sent these people to take us where we want to go.'

The couple and the girl drove us all the way to Dehradun. I told them it was where we would get off. I had no idea where we were going. Rahul was in his blue robes and sandals with his blanket and I was in my ochre robe with two more blankets. Apart from that we were carrying nothing. The man must have observed this.

'Are you going to a monastery here?'

I should have lied but I said, 'No, I don't want to be a monk any more. I am going to look for some other clothes.'

'What sort of clothes?'

'Anything. Indian, western, anything,' I said.

We had stopped on one of the main streets of the town. He went to the back of the car, opened its boot and unstrapped a leather suitcase. He pulled a pair of cotton trousers and an ironed and folded shirt from it and held them out to me.

'Here. I think we are about the same height, but I can give you my belt to pull the trousers in.'

I took the clothes.

'And Sarika has jeans and a top which could maybe fit master here.'

He went to the suitcase again and dug around and came back with jeans and a T-shirt which advertised some designer brand.

'God sent her to us,' the woman, Sarika's mother, said standing with her arm over Sarika's shoulder. The girl was much darker than these city folk and I presumed that they had adopted her and cured her of her leprosy. They had sought out their form of ultimate attachment—a child to whom to be devoted. The false continuity of the blood.

Rahul was, quite impolitely, looking over his jeans and holding them to himself. They looked long in the leg and I asked him whether they could be folded over, I had seen tourists doing just that. Rahul had never worn jeans, trousers or T-shirts. This was new to him. He hadn't once asked why we were here or why I was saying I didn't want to be a monk any more.

Sarika's father gave me three thousand rupees.

'Let us pretend you are still a monk, young man and I am completely entitled to give you alms—in fact the gift will count towards my own karma won't it?'

'I need to feed him. Dressed in a shirt and trousers, I can't beg,' I said.

Rahul put his new clothes on. Sarika helped him with rolling the trousers to length and then took his robe off him and helped him on with the T-shirt, pulling it down and over his little hips with her stubby fingers.

I said I wouldn't change in the street and that we had delayed them enough. The man embraced me. Sarika and her mother touched my feet, though I stepped smartly backwards to avoid their stooping figures.

'God bless you, holy man,' Sarika's mother said.

They got into their car and drove away. They had come two hundred miles out of their way.

We went to the railway station and boarded a train for Delhi. I got Rahul to change back into his robes and we bundled the blankets and clothes into a pack. We were ticketless travellers but when the ticket inspectors came around in their grubby white coats, we could, as monks, get away with it. They would let us sit on the floor of the carriage. They would think they were gaining merit.

We emerged from Old Delhi railway station no longer monks. We were wearing these improbable western clothes and had discarded the monks' robes. On the train I had explained to Rahul that we were following the path of destiny and that all this had been foretold by the stars and we were no longer religious people. We would be householders. We'd find a room, I would find work and he would go to school. He asked if The Enlightened would come looking for us, because from his point of view it must have seemed as though we had run away. I said he wouldn't, because The Abbot himself had told me that he didn't want Rahul there any more.

We found a room in an old brick building in the crowded lanes of Old Delhi. It had dark staircases leading to the second floor. From our one barred window we could see the Jumna river. I looked for work the next day. I could read and write and went to the pavement outside the high court and offered myself to a gang-master who hired people like myself as a reader and translator of official documents and a writer of personal and official letters. He said he'd give me twenty per cent of what I earned for him. I found, a few alleys down from where we lived, a school to which Rahul could go.

Four weeks later, having set up a regime of school and work, we were visited by Rahul's schoolmaster. He addressed me as Rahul's father. I corrected him. I said he must think of me as his half-brother, much older, from our father's first marriage. He seemed to understand.

He had come to say that Rahul was a very bright boy and he would recommend that he be sent to an English medium school now that he was seven years old.

'Those schools cost money,' I said, 'which we don't have. My earnings will barely get us food, clothes and this roof.'

'Then convert to Islam and come with me to the mosque twice a week. Once the mullah notices you, he and I can recommend the boy for an extraordinary Muslim foundation scholarship. His fees will be paid. I have done it before. For a real Muslim boy.'

I asked for a few days to think it over and put it to Rahul. We discussed the advantages and drawbacks of this plan and of the future it promised. I said converting to Islam was the main problem.

'In the monastery you said the idea of god exists but God doesn't exist,' he objected. 'So if there is no God he won't mind if we pretend there is and if there is one then we are saying the right thing and he'll be happy.'

We converted and Rahul got the scholarship.

THE CHILD, NO EXPERT IN comparative theology, nevertheless interrupts the ceremony of conversion by telling the mullah that we don't believe in God and we don't believe in prophets, that neither exist, only the void and kindness as a weapon against it.

I shut him up and sternly tell him to start again and follow what the mullah is saying and to do as he says. We are now people of the world, I tell him. We have converted to Islam to get a scholarship to a Jesuit school which accepts pupils the mullah recommends for reserved scholarships. This is India.

Rahul, enlisted as Abdul Miah, goes to Saint Ignatius Loyolla School and is taught by the Jesuit priests. He comes home singing Christian hymns and on Fridays we go to the mosque together. Does he have to believe all this, he asks. I tell him he must believe whatever convinces him.

'Do you believe anything?' he asks.

'I have been reading a book called *Astronomy for Idiots*,' I tell him, 'and I now believe that the stars are billions of miles away from us and are nothing but burning gas with nuclear explosions and they don't even make up the pictures and patterns we see in the sky because some of them may not even exist by the time we see them. So they can't predict anything.' He absorbs the idea and, so many years later, uses it.

'So what?' he asks.

'So the people who wanted to kill you when you were seven years old are fools and criminals, because that's what idiotic belief does. It rots the brain.'

'Who wanted to kill me? If you are reading a book for idiots, are you an idiot?'

'No one will be allowed to harm you and yes, I am an idiot. I have wasted twenty-six years of a precious life on nonsense.'

'Are you going to get married?' he asks.

'No. That's one thing I don't know how to do,' I reply.

THE YEARS PASS AND HE does well in each exam. He takes it for granted that his role is to study and to read and mine to earn our daily bread.

He is now a graduate and dutifully resolves to look for a job. He finds one at a college affiliated to Bombay University in that city. It is to teach philosophy. It's the city of his birth, but we have never discussed his birth or how we have come to form this odd partnership, this family of two.

They require him to present himself for an interview and we scrape together what money we have, abandon our room in Delhi, leaving early in the morning with all our belongings in order to avoid paying the rent we owe and make our way by third-class carriage on a train to Bombay.

We find a room and he goes for the interview dressed

in a tie and jacket we buy in a second-hand shop. If the interviewers cared, they would have noticed that he was wearing slippers with his jacket and tie. Neither of us had a pair of shoes. He passes the interview and modestly assumes the job.

I go to the high court and try and sell my services as a translator and writer of letters. Bombay is bustling and its energy infectious, its stink of dried fish, sewers and the crush of humans—if indeed a crush can exude a smell—is pervasive.

ONE DAY HE COMES HOME despondent. He has not yet cultivated the art of hiding his emotions. He flops on his bed. We share a single room with two beds and a range with a sink and two oil stoves for cooking. There is no gas and electricity is expensive.

I've installed a shelf above the head of his bed which he has weighed down with so many books that it threatens to come down over his head. While he is away at college I have tried to secure it by driving longer screws into the wall, but the plaster and brick crumble with my every effort and make it worse.

He leafs through a book on Spinoza. I don't even know what that is.

'I have striven not to laugh at human actions, not to weep at them, not to hate them, but to understand them,' he quotes.

I am stewing up the tea in the saucepan.

'And what have you understood?'

'That humans are fools and you can't make idiots of those who are already idiots—if you want to fool people, choose those whose intelligence you respect.'

He wouldn't come to the point. I couldn't join in his banter, but played along.

The thinking boy had become a thinking man.

With his steady salary we had become more comfortable than we had ever been on my meagre earnings. Living off what I earned outside the courts meant we sometimes starved till the next few rupees came my way.

In the lean weeks I would subsidise our income by working at night as a labourer at a small printing press whose owner had become a friend and would let me run errands for him.

Rahul took it all in his stride. He moved from being the ashram boy, the detained ascetic, to the city scholar without any sign of discomfort. He had absorbed, in his first seven years the subconscious lesson that life was what presented itself every day and could not be otherwise.

In college he had taken to reading the communist pamphlets that one could buy on the pavements for a few rupees: *The Communist Manifesto*, *The State and Capitalism*, *The Speeches of Lenin* and *Quotations from Stalin*. He also picked up some American novel called *Peyton Place* and would read it in bed. I looked through it once out of curiosity and easily turned to the well-thumbed pages of sexual description that he must have repeatedly read. There were other books which he had bought and kept for the same purpose, something called *Tamerlane* which was, while being a history of battles and conquest, full of descriptions of the conqueror's encounters with women he had enslaved and kept as concubines.

One of them, the tyrant's favourite, was a white woman, a 'Frank' called Ali-Soun-Agha, a corruption, the author noted, of her original name Allison.

I read these pages from his books but the descriptions of

the encounters between master and slave left me cold. Not him. He would wait till I slept, read the same pages in bed and I could hear his breathing getting more pronounced and careless as he was aroused. At that stage, seventeen years old, he never broached the subject of sex with me. We lived like the monks we were destined to be.

HE GRADUATED AND GOT THE job in Bombay. It was the same routine. He would go to work and in the evenings he would read and scribble notes.

On day he brought home a paperback called *The House of Dolls* written by someone with a strange name: Ka Tzetnik 135633 or some such long number. It was a strange authorial signature. Rahul told me that it was not the real name of the author, who may have been a man, but the name with which the character was branded as a Jewish prisoner in a German concentration camp where she and other Jewish girls were used as sex slaves.

He seemed to be reading the book over and over again. He read lying in his bed propped against the wall. When he was writing his essays and assignments he used the trestle table I had improvised out of discarded planks I had found on the pavement, an old bicycle frame and the legs of a tall bedstead. He marked passages in the book with his pencil.

I never asked him what he was reading. I had no truck with the dialogues of Plato or the unpronounceable name of the man who wrote *Thus Spake Zarathustra*. I was curious about Ka Tzetnik because of the name but didn't venture to ask Rahul any questions about the book. In the day, when he left for college, I delved through it. It described the degradation of the female prisoners sent to The House of Dolls, the brothel annexe of the concentration camp for pleasuring the Nazi soldiers.

Of course I was taught to read English but these were not the kind of books I had been allowed to read. But they opened a world. I was now working for entire days at the print shop delivering orders. I went early in the mornings and came back late at night. There were very few times when I could get at the books to discover why he was fascinated by them.

But this Ka Tzetnik he seemed to dwell and frown over. He read it every day, page by slow page as I cooked our early morning breakfast and late at night when I turned over and tried to sleep despite the light from the naked bulb above his bed.

'Sex is the root, love is the illusion we invent to make it palatable. I think love was invented by women,' he said.

'Is that in the book you are reading? It's a funny name for a writer.'

He mulled that over.

'It's the name that she was branded with, they were given numbers. Like cattle. The number was burnt into their arms. Then, if they were young and presentable, they were carried off to the brothel and groomed and the soldiers were allowed... they were allowed...' he broke off.

'I read a small bit,' I said.

'It's not the kind of thing you should be reading,' he said. He grinned.

'The Jewish women are compelled, coerced, slaves...and then they realize that giving themselves is part of their fate, inseparable from the suffering, call it the function, of their gender.'

'But they can choose to whom they give themselves,' I said.

'Really? In India? With child marriages and arranged sell-offs for minimal dowries. It's a trade. What's the difference between that and the Nazi soldiers being allocated a slave girl from the concentration camps? She eats better, she is treated better, she is allowed to have a shower without the water turning into lethal gas.'

He stopped.

'Some of them develop the illusion that they are in love with the men who use them,' he said. Then he folded the book, turned the single light out and rolled over under his sheet to sleep.

In the morning he told me that he had lost his job. The book had triggered some thoughts in his head which he had tried to share with his first year philosophy class.

'What thoughts?'

'The Freudian idea that reproduction is more fundamental than survival. We survive in order to reproduce.'

'This is what you teach in philosophy?'

'I didn't put it like that,' he says. 'I wanted to see what would happen and what honesty there was in my hundred and fifty students, so I asked them to consider the answer to my first question which was "would you rather fuck or eat?" Some of the bolder boys in the class began to shout "fuck, fuck", so I raised my arm to shut them up and said we should ask the girls. Now these twelve girls sit in the front row, four benches, three on each bench and they were very eager as we went through the Socratic method and Plato and we have had real conversations going. So I turned to one of them and said "Hemlata, what do you think, which would you rather do, fuck or eat?" I didn't know she'd take it as a non-academic question. She blushed and took her book and walked out of the class. Three other girls followed her before I could clarify what my question was about. "I put Freud on your reading lists," I said. Some boys started whistling and one of them shouted "You want Hemlata, Rahul sir? You asked something difficult, sir. She might be wanting to eat you up! Like cannibals!" Now the rest of the girls walked out of the class in a rush for the door. I let them go.'

'You've gone completely mad,' I said.

'The boys were still there, a hundred and twenty of them and they were rattling the desks now. I had them excited.

'"The answer to the question is of course you want to do whatever you need to in order to survive but the purpose of surviving is so that the species goes on. And for that to happen you need men and women." The class was hushed now. "Evolution doesn't make one gender shy—they have equal energies towards reproduction—but our minds, civilized minds, are layered and plastered with inhibitions—do this, don't do that, hear this, don't hear that. You see how the girls walked out?"

'One of the students asked if I thought the girls were just pretending to save their reputations, that they really loved talking about sex and using dirty words. "There are no dirty words," I said. "You can say anything you like in front of me. I am a college lecturer, not your priest or your daddy. I have given up being shocked."

'The boys started shouting words that came into their heads, English, Hindi, Konkani, Marathi, Punjabi, whatever and the class was in uproar when Professor Damle, logician and Principal of the college came to the door of the class.

'"Mr Rahul can you come to my office straight away," he

said and then stepping in front of the silenced students told them that the class was dismissed.

'"I have had a delegation of your female students saying you have been making filthy suggestions to them in class."

'"What? In front of a hundred and fifty students? You believe them?"

'"I heard them. I heard the boys shouting dirty things. Is this what you teach in the class?"

'I was standing at his desk in his office and the phone rang. He answered, looking serious.

'"Yes, I am dealing with that right now. Yes, of course. No, no, please, just be reasonable, no newspapers. Please, sir, I am begging you. I am dealing personally…" His caller must have put the phone down.

'"That was a father. You have killed this college. Now get out and never come back. I have your address and the police will see you for your obscene behaviour."'

'AND THAT'S THE END OF it?' I asked. 'You idiot! What will we eat?'

'I'll apply to some other colleges. I have heard of lots of positions going.'

'It's not just the positions that are going, we are going too. You think Professor Damle didn't mean what he said? The fathers of the girls in that college are bound to have connections. The police will be round here. Definitely.'

He didn't seem very perturbed but in the night, while he slept, I packed what belongings we had into our two small steel trunks. I woke him up.

'If we bugger off we won't have to pay the last three weeks' rent even.'

We took the local train to Khandivili, as far away as we could go to the extreme suburbs of the city and went into the all-night tea shop and asked if the cafe owner knew of any rooms to let. If we paid a deposit he could rent us a room on the first floor, he said.

There was no money coming in. I pawned Rahul's watch and mine and paid the first and second week's rent. If we wanted to know the time, which we now rarely did, we would have to drift past the cafes or the shops and get the hour off their wall clocks.

Then disaster struck me too. The printing press, which was being used at night for printing pirated western novels, was raided by the police. I had seen the covers of the duplicated, pirated copies piled and awaiting their contents pages: American bestsellers in the main. The police didn't raid the place for copyright violations. They raided it because the proprietor and his partners were selling the covers with empty paddings of paper between them sealed in plastic wrappers so that the prospective buyer couldn't leaf through the book and see that it consisted of recycled waste or low-quality empty sheets. There had been some public disorder on the streets from customers and some poor vendors of this contraband had been stabbed in a fight.

The press was closed and now we were both without a job and wages.

I said I'd go back to being a scribe.

But my forays to the law courts didn't yield any employment. I suppose I looked increasingly bedraggled and the clients who wanted papers read to them and interpreted or if they wanted letters written on their behalf, chose one of the younger, better-dressed scribes.

I took to going to the street market and picking up onions and potatoes that had fallen by the wayside off the vendors' handcarts. I would make a spicy soup with the chillies, turmeric and other masala we had brought from the other flat and subsist on it for days.

Rahul didn't seem to be bothered. He kept returning to the Ka Tzetnik book and I knew that he was using it now to activate some chain of thought in his head and not, as he had originally done, for dark and dirty masturbatory purposes.

In the evenings we wandered to the beach. Bombay's beaches get very crowded after about six o'clock each evening. People come out to breathe the sea air which is tinged with the stink of washed-up sewage, drying fish and the faint scent of sweat and smoke.

Every week or perhaps every fortnight, I didn't keep track, at the far extremity of the beach where it gave way to the forbidding walls of rich bungalows and new apartment buildings, there would come a group of devotees, mostly female and clad in white, of an old man, a guru of some sort, who would squat on mats on the sand before him. The guru would sit on a chair brought for him from the coach and, rain or shine, he would have a large black umbrella held over his head by a male disciple.

The devotees would sit at the guru's feet and he would lecture them.

I noticed this gathering which came in coaches and then left in an orderly silent troupe when their ceremonies were over and the sun was dipping in pink or crimson splendour in the west across the blue horizon of the Arabian Sea. We spotted them each time but neither I nor Rahul made any mention of them till one day he walked me towards the end of the beach. He had spotted the gathering and was idly curious.

'I want to hear what the old hunchback has to say,' he said.

I know whom he meant. The guru always wore a white cloth cap, a black coat over a white shirt and walked with a doubled stoop, being helped along by disciples who held on to his arms to and from the coach and his chair.

So we went and joined his open-air congregation, standing at the back.

The guru was saying 'Voices come to me, they say simplify, purify, simplify, purify… '

His voice was feeble and strained, almost a whisper. As he spoke and repeated the phrase, I noticed three young men, louts in their late teens or early twenties, college boys who had wandered, bored, onto the beach and had joined this audience in search of some diversion.

'Oi, speak up. Or we want our money back,' one of them said.

The audience looked round. Some of them said, 'hush', old and young women in white putting their fingers to their lips enjoining respect. The guru hadn't been interrupted or addressed with this sort of rudeness before.

One woman, the only one in a dark sari, who sat on the ground by his chair facing the audience, stood up.

'He can't speak louder, he is old. You can come to this side if you want to hear properly.'

She turned to the guru and whispered something in his ear. The old man looked bewildered and looked up questioningly into her face. He didn't know what the consternation was about.

'Get an amplification system if your old crocodile has lost his croak,' one of the louts shouted in Hindi.

They clearly wanted to have their fun.

'Please go away,' the lady in the dark sari said.

The women in the audience, facing these louts, were shocked. Some gasped. They had never experienced this before and some looked frightened.

'Fuck off yourself, this is a public beach,' the lout replied.

One of the men whom I had noticed escorting the guru to his chair, a fat middle-aged fellow, one of the organizers of the meeting, stood up from where he was sitting at the master's feet.

'I will call the police if you don't go,' he shouted.

'Police? I thought you fellows only talked to God,' the lout replied. Each time one of them spoke the others laughed in a ribald way.

'You are fooling these widows and taking money from them with promises of moksha and heaven, aren't you? We know the crocodile with the long teeth is a fraud,' one of them shouted.

I had no fear of intervening. Those stray days on the street when I was eleven and still derelict, unadopted by the Taptavan monastery, had at least made this sort of behaviour familiar and I wasn't afraid of it.

'I think you should go,' I said and turned to the lout nearest me.

'Who the fuck are you to tell me what to do?' he said and grabbed me by the shirt.

Rahul instantly, coolly, grabbed the boy by the hair and jerked his head back. The other louts came to help him and Rahul kicked him deftly in the crotch making him hold his belly and keel over with pain.

One of the women in white saris near us was standing up and striking the man, whose hair Rahul was still holding, with her umbrella. She got him square in the face and he released my collar. She hit him again and again, hard. The fat man, the manager, had come through the crowd and the louts, who had been taken by surprise at the non-non-violent reaction to their offensive raillery, turned and began to run.

I ran after them. I saw a fragment of brick in the sand as I ran, lifted it and hurled it at the one closest to me. It hit him in the back and the congregation behind me clapped as he stumbled for a foot or two, recovered and then continued running.

I turned back. I was surprised to hear that the guru, probably encouraged by the lady in the dark sari and not quite understanding the extent and intent of the consternation around him, had resumed his lecture. His audience was as intent as ever.

'The simplified thought is the best. The path that has been cleared through the forest is the easiest to take...'

After a while Rahul said he'd had enough of this and we began to wander off toward the waves. The manager, the fat man who had reclaimed his place at the front, ran after us.

'Thank you for helping. Thank you very much for helping Guru Vishwadeep. I will tell him and he will bless you. I wish you would stay and meet him. These rascal boys should be handed to the police and you are very brave.'

Rahul said we'd come back in a while or another day. The manager asked us to be sure to come back and have a meal with them at their ashram, please.

This was an attractive proposition. We hadn't eaten, not even the broth I used to make with the scavenged vegetables, for two days. I looked at Rahul and he nodded.

'We have time today,' Rahul said.

We didn't want to miss out and so we accompanied the

manager who introduced himself as 'Mr Bhavnani' and stood as we had before, listening to the end of the lecture.

It wasn't a very impressive lecture. Guru Vishwadeep was saying that simplicity was made of the simple and made for the simple and probably by the simple and he must have meant something very deep by the word, but it didn't come across.

We went with the congregation in one of their two coaches to the ashram, a walled compound just off the highway to Poona, about ten miles out of the city.

The lady in the dark sari, who asked us to call her Shanti, took charge of us and assured us that we could get a convenient train back into town.

It was a very welcome meal, served on brass trays. We ate by the light of bright neon strip lights all round the walls of this ante-room. The Guru didn't eat with us, but after the meal we were taken into his presence.

He was in bed, being attended to by a woman in a blue sari who removed his urine bottle from under his blanket as we were ushered in.

Mr Bhavnani told the Guru that we were the heroes who had salvaged the meeting through our intervention when the louts interrupted it. He didn't seem to remember or have registered the nature of the interruption to his evening's activity, or have noted the fight that ensued but thanked us anyway.

He asked our names and what we did. Rahul kept silent, uncannily silent, throughout but I said he was a philosophy lecturer and I was a scribe.

Mr Bhavnani seemed very interested in this fact.

When we left, as he walked us to the gate he asked me what kind of scribe I was. I said any kind. I did court reports, wrote letters in several languages, I knew Hindi, Sanskrit and Pali as well as English and could translate documents from one to the other.

He immediately said he might have a job for me and asked if my services were available. I said they were and he asked me if I'd return the next day.

I did. Shantiji interviewed me and offered me the job. As she spoke she spat the betel nut she was chewing into a little brass spittoon. She cleared her mouth of the red juice of it before she spoke. There wasn't very much money but I was required to translate the speeches of Guru Vishwadeep into English if they were in Hindi and vice versa if they were in English and, perhaps for scholarly publication, into Sanskrit.

But where were the speeches? I had expected reams of written material, but it turned out there were none. The speeches had been spoken and had disappeared into the ether. It was too late. Guru Vishwadeep, having maintained all his preaching life that all existence was evanescent, that we were transient beings and that our thoughts were deceptions, had kept no record of his intellectual ramblings. He had taught that words and deeds would vanish and they had—literally. Shantiji, his minder, keeper and companion and Mr Bhavnani, who called himself his manager, had taken little care of it. Perhaps the old man had not allowed them to take notes or record his sermons, dialogues, or whatever one called them.

And now, in the twilight of his existence, Shanti had pressed on him the need to keep a record and he agreed to speak into a tape-recorder whose microphone I would dutifully hold for hours on end close to his mouth to catch the whispered pearls of wisdom.

I would then take them home and sentence by sentence transcribe them in English and, on my day of rest, try and translate them into Sanskrit.

Mr Bhavnani had an idea that he had found a market for these sermons. He would have them published and the Guru, the ashram or perhaps he and Shantiji would, in future, benefit.

The ride on the train and bus from where we lived to the ashram entailed three changes and took me two hours in the morning and the same or more at night when I returned. I took to spending nights at the ashram. Guru Vishwadeep kept no regular hours. He was old and ill and his body had lost the ability to distinguish between night and day.

He would wake up in the night and, sitting propped up on his pillows, begin to dictate a sermon, a thought that had occurred to him, or to repeat some lesson he had delivered before. Shantiji insisted that I be on hand when I could, to wake up with him, switch on the tape recorder and gather the impromptu wisdom. She would issue the imperious but indistinct order as she chewed and then spat out the betel leaf into her little brass spittoon. 'Understood?' she would demand.

Once a week the swami would be dressed for a public audience by his nurse Maria, the woman in the blue sari, and Shantiji and Mr Bhavnani would wheel him and carry him to the gardens of the ashram or take him to the beach where his captive but dwindling congregation would await him. He would be propped up on the throne-like chair and would begin his discourses.

'This is illusion, says Krishna, all illusion. It is brought about by vanity, the vanity of the mind. The world is reflected in every falling raindrop. But when it falls into the ocean, the reflection dissolves as it dissolves in the tide from whence it came...'

I had been brought up with thoughts and discourse of this sort, even though the monastery placed more emphasis on ritual than on philosophy, so I had a feel for what he was saying, but wondered what the women in white saris, the disciples, the widows who had signed their often meagre worldly possessions over to the Swami's ashram, made of it.

Maria was on hand day and night to clean and bathe him and to empty and wash out his bed pans and chamber pots. Shantiji and Mr Bhavnani would diligently keep away when these duties were being performed because, as good Hindus, they believed that they would suffer pollution from the great man's piss and shit. Maria was a Catholic and as such had no caste to lose and as a nurse she was trained to be without squeamishness in her duties.

Besides, she had been nurse to the Guru for eight years and had, through bathing and dressing him, grown to love him like her own baby. The 'house' doctor would come on routine calls and he was summoned on occasions when one of the household detected some irregularity in his breathing, heartbeat or responses.

The swami never complained of pain or of anything else. He had taught himself resignation and behind the constantly blinking eyelids and the ready and winning, almost toothless smile, one could almost see the skein of resignation. What will be, will be, would be the pop interpretation of it—his own would mean that he had gone beyond the veil of 'maya', of 'illusion'.

The injections, the medication, the determination of

Shantiji and Mr Bhavnani to keep him alive were not an illusion. I would sleep on the floor on a thin mattress with a single sheet next to the swami's bed, alert in my sleep to his breathing and movements and ready to wake up and switch on the tape recorder if he woke up and began his mutterings.

On occasion I heard Shantiji berating the doctor for the swami's failing energy. Wasn't there something the doctor could do to give him strength? The doctor would insist that age and a list of chronic illnesses had taken their toll and there was only so much that medical science could do. Shantiji was adamant. While she must have believed that life and reality were illusions, she also seemed to believe that the illusion should have its batteries recharged by some magic of medicine.

There had been a local newspaper item about the dismissal of Rahul from the post of lecturer from KP College. Professor Damle had been quoted. 'We had to take action because Mr Rahul was found guilty after several complaints from girl students of moral turpitude.'

Now there was no way he could apply to other colleges for a job. He had no references and he would have to put an address on his application which would lead the police to us. He was sure that Professor Damle had the clout to launch a complaint against him and that the police would have at least half an eye out to arrest him.

I contributed my entire salary, save what I required for a season ticket to travel to and from the ashram, to Rahul. Now, more and more, as the swami slept during the day and woke up at night to deliver his testament, I stayed at the ashram.

Maria slept in the same room as the swami and me. Mr Bhavnani had a home elsewhere but had a room upstairs in the ashram. Shantiji had lived with the Guru since before they acquired this ashram. From being a devotee and disciple, she had become the administrator of his affairs, personal and professional, and had undertaken the task of turning his message into a mission.

It was she who had raised money from the devotees and had come to the conclusion that one of the ways of sustaining the message of renunciation would be to attract devout and rich Hindu widows to sign over some of the wealth they had inherited to the swami's Vishwadeep Foundation which would ensure that they cultivated the right karma and a righteous dharma and inherited the best account in eternity that their sacrificing souls deserved.

Pervading this white sari-clad congregation, by no means all of them widows, was a sense of guilt. It was never said by the swami in so many words, but it was implied in his teachings which said the earthly wife's place was by her husband. Somewhere in this insistence, was the echo of a message which prescribed the passage of the wife beside her husband through the ups and downs, the thick and thin of life and fortune and beyond. The congregation would need no reminding that until the early nineteenth century, when Lord William Bentinck, the British Governor General of colonial India, prohibited the custom and ceremony by law, Hindu widows would immolate themselves on the cremation pyres of their dead husbands and pass into the beyond with them. To be of service, no doubt. To deny their husbands such a service in the hereafter, even though both life and the hereafter were but illusion, carried with it that tinge of a duty not done, a purpose unfulfilled, the final act of dharma denied by the force of colonial diktat. The corruptions of modernity!

Nothing was, as I say, explicitly stated. There was the strong assertion that life was divided into four stages and during the 'householder' stage of mortal existence, there was no bond stronger than that of the wife to the husband. It could be inferred from all the airing this principle got that the bond would continue into the hereafter and though the widows had survived their husbands, the tie was not broken and the right consciousness and attention to the teachings and oriented meditation on the 'beloved' would keep the bond intact awaiting renewal, its second honeymoon in the beyond.

The loyalty of the congregation depended to some degree on this message which the swami was, I became convinced, not even aware he was transmitting. The message was reinforced when Mr Bhavnani had what he called 'guidance meetings' with members of the congregation or the newly widowed women who came with their friends, existing members of the congregation for the most part, to enter the organization. These guidance meetings guided the widows to the bank accounts operated by Shantiji and Mr Bhavnani.

Over the months I was with the swami, recording the dictations, translating them, I became aware of the fact that a few of the widows had left property belonging to their late husbands in their wills to the Vishwadeep Foundation operated by its trustees Shantiji and Mr Bhavnani.

I was only vaguely aware of such material interests, having overheard snippets of conversation between the two, until there was a crisis at the ashram.

A widow of advanced years, an old member of the congregation who had, some years before, assigned a large piece of land and an ancestral home in Poona to the foundation fell ill and was generously given refuge in the ashram as she feared that at home her children and her late husband's younger brothers and sisters would not allow her the peace and scope to meditate or enable her to keep in touch with the swami and his teachings.

Mr Bhavnani made arrangements for her to move into one of the rooms on the first floor just above the large ground floor room that the Guru, Maria and, occasionally, I occupied.

A few days after she moved in, being attended to by the doctor and by Maria who was assigned this additional duty, two men and a woman came to the ashram to try and take her home.

It turned out that one was her younger brother, one was her son and the woman was her daughter-in-law. They wanted her to go back with them. She staunchly refused and Mr Bhavnani and Shantiji invited them to leave the premises. A shouting match ensued. The relatives accused them of kidnapping a lady of feeble mind.

Mr Bhavnani weighed in with the fact that a doctor had examined the old widow and a psychiatrist would soon certify that she was of sound mind and being a free citizen could live where she wanted. He in turn accused the relatives of neglecting and ill-treating the old widow and said he would get a legally attested statement from her to say that she had been abused and assaulted by her daughter-in-law and if they persisted in their claim to possess her, the ashram would take the complaint of such repeated physical assault and mental cruelty to the police and the courts.

There may have been some truth in the allegations because the relatives talked amongst themselves and decided to leave, saying they too had lawyers whom they would consult. The son left, shouting foul abuse at Mr Bhavnani, Shantiji and the ashram.

Shantiji and Mr Bhavnani were, in public and even when they felt they were unobserved in the ashram, quite formal with each other. He would call her Shantiji and she would always say Mr Bhavnani rather than use his first name which was Ramesh. Their bedrooms on the first floor were at opposite ends of this mansion they had rented or coerced from a disciple and converted into the ashram.

They diligently preserved their modesty, but were completely careless of mine. It never seemed to occur to them that Maria should not have to sleep in the same room as me. Of course she could sleep on a charpoy in the room of an infirm patient such as the swami, but here I was sleeping on the floor in the same space at their insistence. It was probably because in their eyes Maria, a Catholic, was not quite a woman. To both of them she was a servant, a necessary entity to cater to the swami's needs but neither of them ever enquired where she went when she took the rare day off or what the circumstances of her life were.

Living in the same room, even though it was as large as a school classroom or hall, and often being awake at night at the same time, she would make a cup of tea for us and we would get to talking.

She told me that she had two sons and that her husband had run away when they were very young and she had no idea where he was. He was a drunkard and she was well rid of him, she said, and there was some hypocrisy in her tone of condemnation because I had noticed—I couldn't help noticing—that she kept a small hip flask of something in her luggage and sometimes, even during the day when she thought she wasn't being observed, took a swig from it. I had smelt her breath. It was cheap rum.

I didn't indicate that I knew. She must have, all these years, kept the fact of her habit from Shantiji and Mr Bhavnani, because they would have dismissed her if they had found her out.

She was the only one to whom I confided the truth about my past. I told her I had been apprenticed as an infant to the monastery and that my companion and room-mate was someone who had been put in my care. I didn't tell her precisely why we left, but said that when they didn't want him in the monastery any more, even though he was just a boy at the time, I decided to leave with him rather than let him wander the world alone and end up prey to the flotsam of the country who capture infants and use them for begging, prostitution or criminal purposes.

I confessed that I was very unwise when I left the monastery and came down to the city. I had even forgotten the wily innocence I may have had as a boy cast onto crowded streets. Now I only possessed the learned innocence of the novice monk.

Even so, the spirit and memory are resourceful. I was quick to learn the ways of the city because I had not only to survive myself, I had a child to protect and bring up. When we first came to Delhi from the hills I had no plans and no idea what I was doing with this child or what I would do with him. Would some other institution take him off my hands? Would the government claim him when it found that I was not related to him by blood? Would his parents or relatives find that he was with me and take him away?

Neither had I determined that I would keep him and bring him up to adulthood, as an orphaned elder brother would. It had happened because no other choices offered themselves. It did occur to me to try and find the family from whose home we had taken the child but then it also crossed my mind that they believed in prophecies and would feel that the negation of those prophecies was the work of evil. Would they identify me as the agent of that evil?

'So then, you are not Hindu?' Maria asked.

I shook my head. We would talk by the light of a reading lamp she had next to her cot on the table full of the swami's medicines. There were more medical instruments, supplies and more drugs on top of the chest of drawers near his bed.

'But still you are not drinking?' she asked.

'No,' I said, 'I've never tried.'

'Good, good,' she said 'and no smoking also?'

'Nothing,' I replied.

'We Cat'lics are drinking and smoking like anything,' she said. 'But still we work hard and earn money and spend it, men. Lot of it on drinking and smoking. We love dancing and playing lot of useless music. You like music?'

'I like it but I don't know anything about it. I hear it on the radio when others play it, but I don't even know what it is.'

She laughed, showing her even white teeth.

'So you don't know how to dance, then,' she said.

'No, no dancing.'

'So sometimes do you feel you are a useless fellow?' she asked and before I could answer she touched my shoulder.

'Only joking, men. You are doing such useful work here with the swamiji's speeches and books. I listen but I don't understand all his stuff. I only know the Cat'lic bible and prayers and all this. Hail Mary, Mother of God … and the blessings and everything. Our mother taught us. I went to an English medium school and we had to do some compulsory Hindi but we girls never paid no attention. I can read and write a little and I can speak also. In the market, to get the price down.'

She went to the chest of drawers and mixed some medicines in a beaker. She looked around and when she thought I wasn't looking, she took the hip flask from the top drawer where she had concealed it and took a quick swig.

The mixing of the medicine wasn't just a ploy. We both knew he would be fed his draught when he awoke and if he was in the mood he would start his recitations: 'Voices come to me, they say simplify, purify ...'

'You are very good chap, men. No sinning, eh?' she said.

'I was taught to have no idea of sin,' I said.

She was puzzled by that.

'What are you saying? The devil tempts everyone. Even the high priests in your religion—whatever it is... The Enlightened you were telling me about. Even the Pope, my friend. Temptation is always there.'

The conversation would have, I knew, progressed into Maria asking me in what ways I had been tempted, but it was interrupted by the old man waking up and making a low moaning noise. She went up to him, sat him up and gave him the dose of liquid from the measuring cup. He was awake and he began to speak. I went for my tape recorder. He addressed me by name.

He wasn't sermonizing.

'I had a dream about you, my son,' he said.

I didn't know what to say. He began to speak slowly in his usual hoarse whisper.

'You have never told me where you come from. I don't ask because most people have too much sadness in their lives, so why force them to say?'

'I have no sadness, Guruji. I have happiness listening to you,' I said.

'I know about Maria,' he said, 'I talk to Maria.'

'There's not too much to know about me,' I said. 'I was brought up in a sort of ashram and then have lived in Delhi and here and worked as a scribe and never went to college.'

'The self is the best teacher,' he said. 'I don't know you well, but I love you.'

'Thank you,' I replied. It was the sort of statement you were compelled to accept from this sort of man.

'And Maria. She knows I love her. She is my angel,' he said.

He didn't progress into a sermon that night. He closed his eyes and soon he was snoring. Maria took the pillows from behind his back and lowered him into the bed as I watched.

'I gave him some sleeping stuff,' she said, turning to me. 'He doesn't get enough rest.'

It wasn't for me to ask if she was permitted to dose him with what she pleased.

She put her hand to her lips to indicate that we shouldn't disturb him and we talked no more that night. I slept on my mattress and she on her cot at the other end of the room.

I knew why, when I had never told anyone else, I had told her my story. The past, the life I had been born to or suborned to, was the only aspect of me that had any charm or mystery about it and something in me wanted to charm her. She was older than I was, darker, with jewelled eyes and, unlike Shanti and the women of the congregation, had short-styled hair. She wore saris in the evenings but during the day she would wear her white nurse's dress with a blue apron and sometimes a blue uniform sari of her nursing agency.

She had grown used to my presence in the room and some nights when she thought I was writing or transcribing or asleep, she would reach for the trunk under the cot and change into her long cotton night dress, turning her back to take off her blouse and bra as she slipped it on.

I had seen the breasts of old women who came on festivals to purify themselves in the river by the monastery. They didn't wear blouses and bathed in a trance, heedless of the other pilgrims around them. I had seen the breasts of working village women who wore them without blouses under their saris when they let the ends slip. And yet in the intimacy of a room, Maria's body was, I suppose what she had referred to as the devil's work of temptation. I had never, even through reading the books Rahul brought home for sexual pleasure, thought of a woman in that way.

The awakening was something I had never felt before. A thrill running up from stomach to my chest and throat and my heart thumping. I would pretend to be asleep when the time came for her to change from her sari or her nurse's uniform into her nightdress and, in case she resorted to turning out the light, I would adjust the curtain in the room so that it appeared to cover the window but let in enough moonlight for there to be at least a silhouetted shape and I hoped she would get careless, thinking I was asleep about turning her back.

Maria had taken the day off and gone, I presumed, to see her children who were in the care of her mother. There was supposed to be a replacement nurse arriving for the day but she never came. Shanti was angry and started ordering me about, asking me to fetch this or that medicine by reading the rough writing on the bottles of pills and even demanding, quite casually, that I empty the urine bottle from the swami's bed and bring it back.

Bhavnani came in and out and they both cursed Maria for taking the day off. Bhavnani accused her of conspiring to mislead her own nursing agency which was to send the replacement nurse for fear that they would prefer, on a day's evidence, the replacement to her and make the replacement permanent. Maria was to return the next morning.

Shanti gave the old man his injection and she and Bhavnani left me with him and with instructions to do as I always did at night and additionally to give him a dose of liquid which was placed in a glass on the dresser.

I left the small reading light on and turned to sleep.

It was after midnight when Maria came in, tip-toeing, holding a pair of high-heeled shoes in her hand. She went straight to the dresser and taking the glass of medicine, dissolved two pills in it and went to the swami's bed. She woke him up. He was used to her touch and used to the fact that he'd be offered medicines and drinks at all hours. He swallowed the stuff and sank back. She turned to me, smiling and put her finger on her lips to stop me asking questions about why she was back.

She turned her bedside light off and drew back the curtains to reveal a full moon from which the light streamed into the room. Then she turned and sat on her bed and smiled at me, still with her finger darting occasionally to her lips, for silence.

In a minute or was it an hour or an eternity, my heart pounding away, the swami's breathing became regular, the breathing of deep sleep. Why had she come back late at night dressed in a tight-fitting short, shiny dress?

'Gone,' she said. 'I love swamiji, but he is out for twelve hours at least now.'

'The replacement never...'

'Tch, tch, tch,' she clicked her tongue against her teeth, 'silly fellow, why you want to talk nonsense, men?'

I shrugged. I was sitting up on my mattress with my sheet covering my legs.

She got up from her cot and came to me and squatted down beside me. She was wearing dangling earrings and in the moonlight I could see she was heavily made-up with eye-shadow, red lipstick and rouge on her dark cheeks which made them shine.

'I have been dancing, men,' she said.

And drinking, I thought because I could smell the alcohol on her breath.

'And I was thinking of you, not dancing, not smoking, not drinking, but tempted. I came back for you.'

I just gazed into her eyes. No one had ever spoken to me like that before.

'I know you want to look at me. I have seen you looking at me, men, and I am telling you, I like it. I love it.'

'I haven't seen you dressed ... all dressed up... like this.'

'Cat'lic party, sweetie. All the women dress up to kill. But I was thinking all the time about you only, because you are innocent and ignorant and that is too sweet and better than all those bastards who hang around the parties just for picking up foolish pussy. Guys with bania's balls in their brains.'

She looked gorgeous. Her legs under the tight silky dress were bent sideways and my eyes went to the neckline of her dress.

'Don't look there, sweet boy, you are going to see all that later. Look in my eyes.'

I looked. She smiled and then with eyes wide open she leaned over and kissed me on the lips.

I was paralyzed. She withdrew her face and then holding my arms gently and edging herself close to my body she positioned them to hold her by the waist and put her arms loosely, lightly over my shoulders and round my neck.

'Haven't you seen any films, men,' she whispered. 'Put your lips around mine and stay there.'

She shut her eyes, bent her head and we kissed—as she had instructed—and it worked.

It worked too well. What I had only allowed myself to experience in the shadow of dreams and under the cover of sleep now burst forth, the real thing.

She withdrew her mouth from the kiss but still held me gently by the neck. She was smiling, gentle, beautiful, my first kiss, my first woman, an angel, realization, the truth, the mergence, nirvana?

She left one arm on my shoulder, withdrew the other hand, went under the sheet and very tenderly touched me on the crotch. She felt the wet on my pyjamas, all the time looking intensely in my face and smiling, an enquiring beautiful smile.

'You like me too much?'

'Yes,' I said.

Then she stood up and went to her bed and pulled her dress over her head and stood in her knickers and her bra which she proceeded to climb out off and unbuckle as I watched astounded, entranced, enchanted.

She sat at the edge of her cot and held out her arms.

'Come on here, men. Take your silly pyjamas off.'

I did as she said and as I reached her cot she pulled me onto her. I was getting hard again. She felt me and then she took my hand as I was lying on her and very gently led my fingers to the luscious wetness of her crotch.

I was on her, in her and kissing her.

She shut her eyes, but was smiling, subtly smiling whenever I opened mine as we made love.

There should be no asceticism, no renunciation, no celibacy, no denial, no forbearance, no taint of sin, no fall from grace, no expulsion, as I now know the Bible says, from the garden, because this is the garden, love is the garden and making love is the sap and the juice and fruit of life.

Maria.

I felt, for the first time in my life with any conviction, a conviction I had often faked and deceived myself about, that I, my sense of myself, was one with the self of another. Yes, I had faked it and deceived myself into the belief of attainment as I had been taught to do, inspired and instructed to do—the meditative trance, the surrender of prayer, the distinct and undeniable high of the brain starved of blood and nourishment through fasting—they were all as nothing.

Maria.

Even in that trance of love—No! Perhaps only after, when the fever had passed and fervour subsided, when I could distinguish thought from sensation, when the all-absorbing present allowed the resurgent memory, I understood, or half felt and half understood that all the philosophy I had been schooled in as the core teaching of human endeavour, all the Vedanta I had read in the monastery's Sanskrit classes, all the descriptions of dissolution of the individual soul in some larger purpose were nothing but metaphors for this act, this revelation with…

Maria.

I am a fool. I talk like a fool. I think like a fool—a fool who has had his first fuck. And yes, maybe religion aims at higher things and spirituality has to be strived for and the great teachings of the sages through the Upanishads and the Gita and the realizations of Shankara and the Tora and the testament of the apostles about the life of The One and the poets and madmen is much much more than the feeling for and intertwining with a woman named Maria. Dissolving in her, feeling the solid flesh melt into the dream, congruent bubbles in the foam, floating in the formless ocean of being as One…

Maria.

It was her gift and the revelations of love to a soul and body that had grown and hardened without the nourishment and waters of love. No father, no mother, no sisters, brothers, grandparents, no young girls to have crushes on, no older women to fantasize about, no tenderness from aunts, no temptations for the adolescent from servant girls in the household. The patronizing, watchful, instructive care of the monks.

Maria.

I didn't know drought till I stood with palms extended in the pouring rain.

Maria.

And then in the night, for the first time since I had been in residence, there was a commotion upstairs and voices from the room above where the old widow was lodged. There was a groaning and a shout and then footsteps and voices. The ashram was awake.

Maria, instinctively, with great acumen wiped the make-up from her face with the end of the sheet, jumped out of bed, dragged on her nightdress and pointing me to my bed fled upstairs.

I heard voices. Shanti, Bhavnani and then Maria. Silence. Maria then came rushing into our room, took some equipment off the dresser and ran upstairs again.

She must have returned to our room after half an hour carrying a surgical tray of blood-stained syringes, pierced bottles of spent fluids, stained cotton wool, blooded lint and other stuff to dispose of from the sick room.

'The old girl should be all right,' she said. 'That bitch Shanti, I really hate her, men. Did you hear what she was saying to me?'

That was all.

No trace of what we had done or what I had experienced. She pulled the curtains and shut out the moonlight and went to her cot and slept.

The old widow died the next day. Dr Majumdar was called but she had died in her sleep and all he could do was ascertain that she had had a heart attack in the night and despite being conscientiously given the prescribed drugs, had passed away.

The relatives were informed and after a fierce argument with Shanti and Bhavnani, took the body away to be cremated. Her son very plainly said that no one from the ashram or from the Vishwadeep Foundation would be welcome at the funeral. They would be treated as legal trespassers if they attempted to attend.

Shanti and Bhavnani didn't seem in the least perturbed.

Swamiji's health deteriorated to the point where he was no longer able to be taken to preaching sessions. When, after two months of rest and convalescence Shanti dragged him out of bed to preach in the compound of the ashram, the coaches from the pick-up points returned empty and there were just six sari-clad women and one seemingly demented man in the audience.

The old man was carried to his chair and despite Shanti and Bhavnani asking him to hold his peace, he began his discourse: 'People, all people are afraid of death, so they celebrate life and they invent gods...'

A second coach arrived late. It was empty. Shanti stepped out to the gate to welcome or to berate the latecomers but ended up arguing with the coach driver. He must have been late and the devotees had dispersed in despair, she asserted. She came storming back to the meeting under the banyan tree and put a hand on the old man's shoulder and asked him to stop speaking. He stopped and closed his eyes.

'Yes, yes, take me to my bed,' he said, aloud.

'We have to stop this now,' Shanti said to the scant audience, 'Please come back next time.'

She walked off, her silver spittoon in her hand.

There was to be no next time.

Guru Vishwadeep was taken back to his bed by Maria and Bhavnani and from then on was incoherent. He stopped speaking. Every time Shanti came into the room he would grin and laugh at her and say nothing. He was mocking her, I could see it and Maria and Bhavnani could see it in his eyes and in his contemptuous but hesitant 'Hih, hih... hih!'

It was as if some realization he was reluctant to articulate had struck him.

He was, in the next two weeks, most certainly unable to deliver any discourse. He wouldn't answer questions which Shanti, Bhavnani or even the doctor asked him. He would talk to Maria. He told her he had come to new realizations but these were not to be shared with the people around him.

Bhavnani called me into the tiny ashram office and said they had no use for my services any longer as the swami had no more pronouncements to make. I was about to leave the office when Shanti rushed in and with no regard to my presence said 'It's through, the will is validated by the court, meri jaan, we have the whole Poona estate!'

Bhavnani looked at me. I shouldn't have heard that. He asked me to leave. I said goodbye to Shanti in the traditional fashion with folded hands and backed out of the office.

I went back to our flat. Rahul was lying in bed with a pile of books. He was reading something called *Civilisation and its Discontents*. I told him there would be no more money coming in, I had been dismissed, and the Guru was exhausted, there was no more work to do.

'Well, my old friend, materialistically, using the word in its non-philosophical sense, with your loss of income, this is a disaster for us. But if we think of materialism in the philosophical sense, like Hegel or Marx did, then the end of your task is a great benefit to humanity, because I have been reading the translation notes you leave about this room, the evidence of the idealist nonsense spoken by your Guru.'

'I don't know what you are saying, my boy, and I tell you I don't bloody want to know. I have lost my job and we are fucked. That's all.'

'No, my dear patron, that is not all. Your Guru talks a lot of idealist nonsense. Bishop Berkley, Kant, even back to Plato. It may all be true, but today I am a materialist. If I kick a stone and it hurts my toe, I know the stone will be there if I kick it again. Who knows? Tomorrow I may turn.'

The argument was nothing to me. Would I see Maria again? I had left a note giving her my address. Perhaps she'd come. I waited six days. Of course she didn't come and I was thinking about her every hour, every minute—no, constantly. I didn't know where she lived or whether she had a phone number. My only contact with her was at the ashram and I knew that's where she'd be.

I got to the ashram. There were half a dozen cars and a white van parked in the compound. There were the widows sitting in postures of despair on the lawns where he used to lecture and on the veranda. The swami was dead. I asked one of them when this had happened and she said he passed away the previous day and the prayers were still being said in the room. They were taking the body to the Ganges to be cremated at its banks.

I didn't have to ask for her. She emerged from the building as I was walking up the path. She was carrying a suitcase. She had been crying and hadn't bothered to wipe her face after the mascara had channelled down it in meanders of black. Her hair was not brushed.

'See these buggers? Soon as they can, they kick you out because they don't want to pay salaries. Bastards.'

'The same happened to me. Were you there when Guruji expired?'

'Expired!' It wasn't a question. 'My brother is coming to take me away. There, his car has come. I knew what these bastards were up to, so it was good I called, eh? They never cared about the old man, you know, only money, money, money.'

'Shanti has been with him for years,' I said, not knowing how to ask her, beg her even, to bring this talk of a death round to my desperate need to see her, to be with her again. She obviously had put the encounter between us, which she had initiated, quite out of her mind. It was nothing to her. I was nothing to her or perhaps I was just the transcribing secretary who had occupied, inconveniently, the same space and now she was moving on.

I told myself that with children, with the background she had, with the drunken husband and the big city, she was a woman of experience. I was not to make a fool of myself and allude to our night together. I wouldn't be able to piece the sentence, the plea, together. But I had to.

'Where are you going to live? Can I take your address and some phone number or something?' was what I found myself saying.

She thought this over and her eyes looked me up and down. Did they reject me?

'I don't know where these boys are taking me. But you give me your address. You were the only real person in this ashram, you know,' she said, and touched my cheek in a very motherly way.

I scribbled my address and thrust it into her spare hand. The brother had spotted her and began to hoot to get her attention. She waved her arm and leaving my cheek burning under her touch, she left me.

Shanti emerged from the house.

'What are you doing here? How dare you come here?' she asked, coming up to me.

'I didn't know…' I was saying.

'The three gold rings from his finger and his gold necklace with the solid gold Ganesha has also gone. Like a fool, I didn't check them every day, but I know they were all there before you left the house,' she said. Bhavnani emerged from the house and came up to us.

'Sir, she is trying to say I am a thief.'

'No, no, she is not saying that, she is telling you they are missing,' he said.

'I am telling him that if those things are not returned, the police will be called. Both you and Maria, one or the other. Who else came anywhere near his room?'

'So you are accusing me? Calling me a thief, madam? This is no good.'

'Don't "madam" me. You think you can get out of it? Look, I've got too much to do, but Bhavnani will take your address and you had better give him the correct one.'

She walked back into the house issuing instructions to servants as she went.

Bhavnani waited till she was gone.

'So where can I find you, boss?' he asked, trying to be casual and friendly.

'Find me? To send the police and put me in jail? After everything, working for so little money, I expected better treatment than this,' I said and started walking away.

'Nobody's saying anything, boss. She is just under tension,' he shouted.

I walked away and out of the gate. She would be quite capable of interrupting the funeral to denounce me to the police. I got the bus and the local train home.

Maria didn't write even a postcard. I waited for the post every day and nothing came. She had gone. Why should she care for me? She had been drinking that night and now regretted what she had done with me. It was, I suppose, nothing to her, but it meant life to me, it meant a revelation, an opening to the final knowledge of bodies, minds, nerves, brains, sensations, emotions—this was what it was about, and the monks had kept it from themselves through wilful ignorance, through the death-wish that pervades all faith though it masquerades as the opposite of such a wish, the wish for eternal life.

I looked for other work to keep us alive. Rahul seemed content to do nothing and to read books he bought from the pavement traders. Why did he want to read them? To confirm how twisted a human mind is, he said.

We again walked out in the evenings to the beach. It was always littered with clusters of friends or people watching wandering gypsy acrobats performing on poles, the monkey men with poor mangy beasts performing with belts and bells round their necks and the vendors of beach foods.

On one of these excursions, walking with our bare feet, kicking sand, we came across a crowd around a group of young white men and women with their heads shaved, leaving the simple pony tail of Brahmins, blonde and brown fountaining out of their heads, wearing white and ochre robes, sitting on the sand by the waves with tablas and cymbals and chanting, 'Hare Krishna, Hare Krishna, Krishna Krishna, Hare Hare.' There was a small crowd of curious Indian sojourners around them. This was entertainment, not religion, to see the white-skinned men and women wearing saris and with their hair grown and tied like Indian housewives, perform and go into the sort of trance with which only the rare mountain sadhu and women possessed in temple ceremonies were gripped.

'Shameful and pagan rites,' Rahul said, as I followed him towards the sound of the chanting. We joined the audience and watched the Krishna bhakts perform.

As we stood at the periphery of the crowd, a man grabbed Rahul violently by the neck from behind and was shouting at him.

'You, you are the rascal who was perverting!' he was saying.

There was a young woman with him and two other middle-aged men in the evening clothes of prosperous householders, two in western trousers, shirts and shoes and the other in a fresh coloured kurta.

'That's "sir", it's him,' the young woman said.

'You are coming with us to police. You have been absconding. This is the filthy fellow,' the assailant said.

He was in his fifties and wore thick spectacles. He wasn't much of a street fighting man but was agitated and flushed.

Rahul brushed his arm off and turned round.

'This is my ex-pupil. Miss Hemlata, if I remember correctly?'

'You will have to remember, you are going for arrest,' one of the other men said. 'You bloody basket.'

'I think you should approach this in a calm spirit and ask this intelligent young woman exactly what I was saying in that lecture on that day. I remember it clearly.'

'The judge will hear it. My daughter will convey nothing to you,' the irate father said. 'Come with us now.'

'I plan to go nowhere with you, sir. It's not necessary. Don't waste the time of the police and courts and interrupt your walk.'

'I will interrupt you! I will tear you up, you bastard!' the father shouted.

The crowd had now turned away from the Hare Krishnas who had stopped playing. One young girl and a haggard looking older man of the Hare Krishnas were standing and craning their necks to see what the commotion was about.

'I'll tell you what I was saying that day. In fact I have been living for the moment when I could make myself clear to

Miss Hemlata herself. I was asking her if the human body's purpose is to live on and for that purpose the fittest have to eat to survive. And if that is so, then is there any purpose to this survival?'

'You shut your dirty mouth,' the father shouted.

'No, sir,' said Rahul. 'I am asking all of you, what the purpose of surviving is? Do flowers just live on and die to shed their fragrance? Or do they attract bees so that they can spread their sex and more flowers can be born.'

'You see this filthy fellow. Talking muck and fuck,' the daddy said, and realizing what he said turned to his daughter. 'Shoo, go, go, go, we will bring him, you go to the car.' The father's companion attempted to lead young Hemlata out of earshot.

She looked hesitant, but obeyed and as Rahul saw her leave he said, 'So now it's safe to talk?'

The Hare Krishnas shouted. 'It's more than safe. It's music! Go for it, preacher!'

'Preachers are out to impose their views, my dear. I am not. You know our greatest sin? Not giving way to sexual impulses, not even greed and hypocrisy, but self-denial. It destroys every moment, every day and in the end it destroys your life.'

More people joined the crowd now, curious passers-by. More of the Hare Krishna gang were standing up and listening.

'Our self-denying impulse is necessary for civilized behaviour, or this at least is what we keep telling ourselves. If we gave way to our impulses, we have been taught, life and the world will descend into chaos. But it's not so. The first thing the parent teaches the child is to postpone its wants. If you want a chocolate, not now. If you want to piss, not now. If as a teenager you want to fuck, not now. "Not now, not yet" has become the slogan of our civilization and it is the most harmful slogan ever pronounced and enforced. Not now, not yet!'

It was then that I spotted that bastard Bhavnani. He had joined the crowd and, with his bulging eyes was taking it all in. Where had he come from? Why?

'Young lady, ask yourself, what is it you want to do?' Rahul turned on the Hare Krishna woman. 'You are holding cymbals and if you were not listening to me, you would be chanting "Hare Krishna". Listening to me, chanting, are those the only alternatives? No, you need to look deep, just look at the tip of your consciousness, what do you really want to do? Don't suppress it. Say it–you, young lady.'

He had fixed his eyes upon her and she said 'Me? I want to throw these cymbals away, take off my clothes and be one with the waves and water.'

And as she said this, she took her ochre sari off, unbuttoned her blouse, deftly removed her knickers and threw them on the sand and to the amazement of the Indian crowd, almost all men, she ran naked into the sea.

The crowd turned to Rahul as though it knew that he had cast some hypnotic spell on her and it wanted to read his features to see the expression an achieved hypnotic command generated.

There was no smile and no satisfaction on Rahul's face. One of the other Hare Krishna people picked up the cymbals she had discarded and her knickers, blouse and sari. She saw him from where she was now, almost neck-deep in the water and she shouted.

'You can take it all and fuck off. All of you. I don't want to play anymore. I am free.'

One of the others stripped off his ochre gown and in his Y-fronts waded into the water and swam towards her. He was going to make her see sense and retrieve her. She spotted him coming and began to swim further out to sea.

'No, get away. Get away!' she shouted.

The crowd had now turned to see how this game of cat and mouse would end. Another Hare Krishna came up to Rahul and was about to say something to him. Rahul looked sternly into his eyes and the man turned away.

Bhavnani was watching all this and came and touched Rahul on the shoulder.

'How are you?' he asked and then turned to me.

'You know I came to find you. You left no address. We are very sorry if you misunderstood what Shantiji was saying.'

'There was nothing to misunderstand, Bhavnani sir. She was calling me a petty thief, or a big thief even, gold and all this…'

'Is this the clown who accused you?' Rahul asked.

Some people were still curious about Rahul and were standing at a distance, staring.

'The memsahib did, not him,' I said.

Bhavnani looked apologetic. I couldn't make out whether he had come here to apologize or whether he had come to press the charges of theft and had changed his mind.

'No, no, secretary sahib, the suspicion has shifted from you, first day only, to that Maria, the nurse. She has definitely taken all the rings and everything. And now she has disappeared.'

'I don't believe she was a thief,' I said. 'She loved the old man.'

'We all loved the old man,' he said. 'Can I have one small word, secretary sahib?'

He motioned to me to walk with him out of earshot of Rahul and the crowd.

The Hare Krishna girl had now been persuaded by two of her group to come back onto the sands and they had covered her with her sari to preserve her modesty from the staring and excited crowd.

Bhavnani ignored them.

'Your boy, your boy is like Houdini, hypnotizing!' he said.

'He might be, so what? They have taken his job from him.'

'Such hypnotizing power? Beautiful.'

'There is no such thing as hypnotizing power, sir, and Houdini was a man who escaped from ropes and chains and from boxes in which he was thrown into the sea, not hypnotizing,' I replied, 'but you can see he is very persuasive.'

'I have been thinking something. Our ashram. No guru, no audience. I am saying what about finding another… someone…different. You see these people, these white people…so many are coming to India. They are looking for the heart of India, but they can't understand, for example, what our swami was saying. He knew nothing about white peoples.'

'So? Rich Hindu widows understood and flocked to you.'

He detected the flat note of scepticism and accusation in my voice.

'Not only them, secretary sahib. Others also were coming. But now foreigners are coming looking for real spiritual help.'

'Really?'

'I have seen it everywhere and please don't misunderstand, your young man speaks very well to them.'

'How do you know? You only heard him once, just now.'

'He made that girl take off all clothes and go in the sea.'

'He didn't make her,' I said.

'He definitely made her,' he said.

He asked if I would speak to Rahul and said he would have no problem convincing Shanti. She would trust his judgement and if she heard him speak she would know that this was their new guru.

'Speak? Words?'

He nodded.

'What else? But his name. It can't be Swami Rahul. He was thrown out of college with that name. Choose one more, different.'

I told Rahul about the conversation and the proposition.

'It will pay the rent as the Westerners say,' he said with a grin. 'We have to find our niche.'

I told him about the change of name.

'What do you think?'

'Bhavnani, the dog said it ought to be regal, like "Raja" or something.'

'It should be Saket.'

'Why Saket? What's that?'

'It's a place and a pun—"saket to me", as the Americans say.'

He was talking about preaching to Americans wasn't he?

'It means heaven and that's what they are coming to find on earth. There's no such place so they may as well find me.'

He grinned.

NOSTALGIA. THE SMELLS OF YESTERYEAR. The memory of a time which seemed, when it was around me, like a trap. These things the aunts had preserved. I opened the other cupboards in the house. There were my school and college notebooks full of adolescent ramblings which at the time, I thought in vain, hopeless yet very weak conceit, set me apart from the unphilosophical companions I was thrown together with. There were old clothes, old pens and photographs.

Why had they preserved my old clothes? Trousers and kurtas and even a jacket I had inherited from my grandfather, with moth-balls in its folds.

Diamond was shown in by the part-time cook. I held up the single pair of shorts in the collection. They must have been from when I was thirteen years old, a white cotton pair with pleats and two side pockets, designed as uniform wear for my school, worn with a white shirt and a red and yellow diagonal-striped school tie.

'My last school shorts. Growing up I remember being the last boy to wear shorts in my class and coming home and telling my aunts that I wanted long trousers because boys wearing shorts in our class were being bullied.

'We went out that very evening and bought three lengths of white cotton from the neon-lit clothier's shop and my aunts bargained with the masterji, the tailor with the measuring tape round his shoulders, for the extra price of making one pair "express", overnight, so I could pick it up and change into it on the way to school before eight the next morning.

'Sure enough, he had them ready and he was waiting outside the wooden doors of his tiny shop in the alley off Dastur Meher Road and I got off my bicycle and proudly changed into them. I stuffed the pair of shorts I changed out of into my school bag. Souvenir, I suppose.'

'Why did you care? Did you have knobbly knees?' Diamond asked.

'Not any more knobbly than the others, but my classmates would all boast about how if they wore shorts their sexual equipment would hang out of them. We were a pretty vile lot.'

'Look at this,' I said. I had come upon a crimson-covered exercise book. 'Family history. It's supposed to be my history exercise book, my final year at school. Have a look.'

She leafed through it.

'Robert Clive, the First Maratha War, The reforms of William Bentinck, See You Later Alligator, Teddy Bear, Crying in the Chapel, A Little Bit of Soap... what's all this?'

'I got beaten for it, caned. My sister, my beautiful sixteen-year-old sister, wanted to keep a Song Book so she grabbed the nearest piece of bound paper she found and scribbled the lyrics of Bill Haley and Elvis Presley songs which were on the "hit-parade" of the radio charts of the time, in my history project book. I didn't know. I found it on her bed and took it to school and the history teacher had a great and sadistic time when I submitted it.

'"Dhondy, come here. Right up here. Which viceroy of India is famous for having passed a law which specifies:

'Baby, let me be,
Your loving Teddy bear,
Put a chain around my neck
And lead me anywhere...'"

'The class laughed. I didn't know what he was saying. He held the book up to the class and read the titles of the songs.

'"*Cry me a River*', probably your essay about the Marathas

when they crossed the Ganges, eh, or was that *'See You Later Alligator'?"*

'I didn't laugh. I took the book from him and looked at the pages he had slashed his pen over. The whole horror dawned on me. I couldn't say it was my sister who had defaced the book. I didn't want to mention or indicate having a sister in front of my starved, obsessive, filthy classmates.

'"I think you should be rewarded, my songster nightingale. So bend down with your buttocks in the air."

'He rose from his chair, picked up his cane with one hand and positioned me as I leant against the master's table and raising his arm gave me three strokes on the back of my upper thigh. Then three square on the bum. I blinked and tried to grin, though the corners of my mouth twitched involuntarily downward as I resumed my seat towards the middle of the class. The rest of them were hushed, possibly stunned by the severity of the execution, except for my cheeky little bespectacled neighbour who wrung the finger of one hand and formed his lips to silently say "oooooppppph".'

'Did you forgive your sister?' Diamond asked.

'No, I waited for her to come home from college and tried to kill her. I pulled out my penknife but she ran into a neighbour's house and sought sanctuary till my aunts came home and cooled me down.'

'That was Zareen?' Diamond asked.

'How do you know her name?'

'Praful told me. He said she was very beautiful.'

'I suppose she was,' I said.

'But she was surrounded by nasty friends, wasn't she?'

'Not at all. All sorts of girls would flock around her, mostly from our neighbourhood. The only thing people said was that she chose friends who were not as good looking as herself so that when they went around together, she would be the gold streak in the ore. Not true, she loved her friends for themselves.'

'Praful said your aunts accused the friends of stealing things.'

'Why would he tell you that? What things?'

'She was given some frilly knickers and bras brought from England by your uncle and they went missing, didn't they?'

'Why was he, or why were you, talking about that?'

I recalled the incident. It caused days of weeping and gnashing of teeth in the household. My sister waited for her new and special underwear to come back from the dhobi in the wash but neither the knickers nor the bras were there. Shera said they hadn't been sent to the dhobi, they didn't send precious things to the alcohol addict of a dhobi. Shera had hand-washed them herself and hung them up in the yard to dry and assumed that Zareen had already taken them off the line.

There was a hunt for the missing knickers and all the drawers were turned upside down. Then the accusations began. It must have been this girl called Damyanti, Amy said, she always looked like a thief.

Zareen was asked to recall which of her friends had been in the house in the previous two days and who had gone to the lavatory through the yard where the clothesline was. Which of them was carrying a bag?

The truth was that all her friends would have carried their college bags and no one kept any account of who went to the lavatory. The aunts narrowed their investigation. It had to be Damyanti or the Goan girl called Innocent.

Zareen argued, protested, raged, cried for two nights when the aunts said those two girls were banned from the house. There was no way her friends were thieves. They appealed to me to corroborate their suspicion which had turned to conviction. Zareen appealed to me to help plead the innocence of girls I knew as acquaintances if not friends, girls who had teased me about my unattractiveness, but girls who meant no harm and could do none.

'So which did you do?' Diamond asked, 'did you take your sister's side and the girls'?'.

'I was a coward, I stayed neutral. The two friends were banned from the house for months and Zareen was miserable and sulked.'

'That was terrible and the girls didn't even steal the pants and the brassieres!' she said.

'What? How do you know?'

'If I tell you, you must promise to do nothing. Nothing. Nothing changes.'

'Okay, tell me. That was years ago, how could you possibly know?'

'Because I found them. Before you arrived. Weeks before. Praful kept them in a drawer. He was very much in love with your sister and you know yourself she didn't pay any attention to him. She treated him like a servant asking him to go and do this and that, even deliver notes to other boys and parcels and things for her to other girls. He told me himself.'

'You are saying he took the underwear?'

'He's still got them, knickers, bras, almost new, and his mother tried to throw them away ten times.'

'Underwear? Praful? The filthy bastard!' I didn't want to think about it.

'He was in love and you can be excused if you are in love.'

'Maybe, let's excuse his unthinkable intentions, but he knew that those girls had been blamed and he was hanging around the house knowing all the time… fuck me!'

'You said nothing would change. You won't tell him I told you. Please, you promised.'

'I suppose I did. But why did you tell me? It's not why you came.'

'No, I came to ask you, if you go to the ashram tomorrow can you look out for Saffy, my daughter? I mean seriously this time. Look.'

She produced a picture of the little girl. Blonde, dressed in white, staring into the lens without a smile.

I said I would look out for her but my mind was still elsewhere.

'You say he's still got them? The items?'

'Yes. He locks them up to keep them from his mother but I discovered them when he opened the drawers so we could hide the rum bottles from his mum in there. The old lady looks quite innocent to me. But you know, they don't get along.'

'They never got along. When Praful was young he sold his mother's sitar to some second-hand dealer and that tore the household apart. It was always like that. His father was a qualified doctor but had become very ill by feeding himself prescription drugs or injecting himself with morphine or whatever. He had stopped practising and hung around the house and the rumour was that his license had been taken away after he'd killed a few people by mistake.'

'She's still got a big photograph of him and she garlands it every week and prays to it with her Hindu trays of incense.'

'Does he ever take the—my sister's things, the stolen items—out and... '

'You promised you wouldn't do anything about it and you'd forget it as soon as I said it. I shouldn't have told you. You see, even if he uses the underwear, it's only your sister's stuff he's kept all these years. He hasn't collected women's underwear as an obsession, like. That made me think it's like true love and he swore he'd never touched a girl till we... till he met me. He's been very kind to me. You promised.'

'I didn't promise I'd ever speak to him again,' I said. 'Maybe I'll tell my aunts that the mystery of the missing underwear has finally been solved. And I'll write to Zareen who is happily married with three kids and tell her and next time she comes to Poona she can confront him and retrieve them.'

'Oh, please! God, I shouldn't have told you.'

'No, you shouldn't have. You don't understand the Indian brother thing. We are brought up to have zero tolerance for any insult to our sisters.'

'Of course I know that. He calls his sister a whore.'

'Well, she ran away with a Muslim and converted to Islam. Where is she?'

'In Bombay or Toronto or Melbourne, they don't know.'

'Sad. She was very pretty too, in a thin dark sort of way.'

Diamond touched my hand. 'Please find Saffy for me? You see how they treat me at the gates? And that fucker husband of mine. I bet the big cheese is buggering him and making him believe it's the release of energy that will lead him to self-realization. And Farrukh, I am haunted by what they might do to her. You don't know the devil. He would do anything with anybody or to anybody in front of anybody and make up a perfectly reasonable-sounding, even positive justification for the evil. Isn't that the definition of the devil?'

'I don't think the people in the ashram are that far gone,' I said. 'Yes, maybe your husband has moved in with him, but I think they have a nursery for children.'

'I don't sleep at night. Every moment is torture. I want nothing out of life but Saffy back. Nothing.'

'I can see that,' I said.

I said I did try before but this time I promised I would make it my mission.

'They would have changed her name,' she said.

I WAS AWAKE AT FIVE in the morning and cycling to the ashram a half hour later, without a shower or shave and, as prescribed with no deodorant. The streets of Poona were as dark and deserted as they were when, as teenagers, we crammed chemical equations and tried to crack mathematical differential equations and integrals late into the night and met in these same deserted streets to cycle down to the relative bustle of the railway station around which the cafes stayed open all night to serve tea and buttered bread to travellers and the restless.

The dawn was breaking as I was allowed through the gates and put through the sniff test by artificially merry sanyasins and directed into the ashram.

The place was awake and bustling with activity.

'We should give you some breakfast in the anapurna,' my guide, the 'year of fire', said.

'The canteen?'

'You could call it that, but that's not moving on. Try and understand the meaning of the Sanskrit. We don't change names for nothing, you know. It is a part of awareness.'

'Yes, of course, so let awareness come to me, don't translate. In my school they were against what they called "spoon feeding"—which meant giving you the answers. I can find things out for myself, but tell me, is there a children's section. I mean we looked in last time, but can I actually write about it, I mean go in?'

'That was just a play room. There's a regular school,' she said. 'Of course it's run on the best lines of educational advance and we don't call it a school.'

She was about to tell me what they did call it when I interrupted and said she should let me find out, test my monastery Sanskrit, but she could take me there.

'I can't today. You know you said you wanted an interview with Bhagwan and we said he wasn't giving any? He heard about you and he and Shantiji are seriously thinking about granting you that interview after the lecture this morning. I wasn't going to tell you, but they didn't tell me not to.'

'That is great news,' I said. 'Why make an exception for me?'

'Your aura,' she said. 'The Bhagwan picked you out from yesterday's lecture and asked who you were. He misses nothing, you know.'

'Was there something to miss? I mean about me?'

'Your aura. I got it as soon as I was assigned to show you around.'

'Never heard about it before,' I said.'I didn't even know I had one.'

'It comes alive in this special place,' she said. She meant it, she believed it.

'I'd like to see the Inspiration Institute,' I said. 'That's just "the school" in fancy Sanskrit, isn't it?'

She ignored the sarcasm.

'The lecture starts soon, Bhagwan may be looking out for you.'

'That's very flattering, but I don't really think I need the lecture. Is there a way of dodging it? I mean go to the school?'

'It's your loss, amigo,' she said. She was American, blonde, thirty years old perhaps, and it now crossed my mind that her main dedication in the ashram should be to lose weight.

Some of the children in the 'school' were dressed in their own clothes and others wore absurd crimson gowns.

They were being supervised by two sanyasins. Around fifteen children were playing quite happily with what looked to me like rather advanced toys and puzzles, technically state-of-the art learning devices with electronic torches on alphabet boards and little plastic-cased computers.

I had already asked if Ma Agnivarsha could identify the girl called Sapphire. She hadn't given me an answer so I was straining to identify her from the photograph I had seen. I was sure that she was aware of Diamond's agitation outside the ashram and the contents of and accusations in the leaflet, though she would not be aware of my connection with her.

Instead I went up to several children in turn and pretended to be interested in their activities. There was a little blonde girl playing on a rocking horse and I approached her. Could she be the one?

'Horsey ride? What's the horsey's name?'

'Don't know,' she shouted.

'And your name?'

'Kavita, the poem,' she said.

Ma Agnivarsha smiled benevolently.

An older woman in a white sari walked into the nursery. She came straight up to me.

'Are you the reporter from UK? Mr Ingleburger?'

'Yes,' I said. She took my hand.

'But you are Indian?' she asked.

'Yes,' I said.

'I am Shanti, the general manager of the ashram and the Bhagwan's secretary. He is interested in interviewing you.'

'I thought I was interviewing him,' I said.

'We do things differently here,' she said. 'He likes to turn tables.'

'I see,' I said. 'That'll be just as interesting.'

'No tape recording. You can take notes as you answer.'

I said that would be good and she indicated that my guide and I were to follow her.

We walked the fifty yards to the house which appeared to be guarded by four 'sentries', one of them a white guy in the crimson uniform of the ashram and the other three Indians in light blue shirts and trousers, the sort of uniform airmen wear.

They didn't appear to be armed. So the Bhagwan lived in a guarded and walled bungalow within the precincts of the ashram. The wall, not very high and probably easy to vault over, looked as though it had been recently constructed. The bungalow, circa 1950s in the imitation American style, had been given a lick of colour.

We walked to the small veranda and as we approached the entrance, the same white Mercedes driven by the same white blonde chauffeur in white livery drove through the gate and stopped at the front door. The Bhagwan, in the same white robe, his black and white beard flowing, stepped out of the house and went in.

'Wait here, we'll call you when he wants,' Shanti said, and hurried away.

My guide led me to the garden which had been planted with beds of roses, gladioli, poppies, pansies, carnations, all very well cultivated. A sanyasin was even then working away at them with secateurs and a can of spray.

In about ten minutes a sanyasi came to summon me in.

I was shown through the house to what must have been one of the Bhagwan's studies.

'You mustn't sneeze or fart,' he was saying when I interrupted him.

'Look I know all that. If I have to, I'll rush out and won't hang about to say why I'm going, right?'

'You kidding?' he asked.

'Look it's unlikely, or maybe not so unlikely,' I said, 'India always disturbs my tummy and smelling the flowers could easily have brought on hay fever.'

He didn't know how to take it, but it was too late to reject or debar me now. We were at the door.

The Bhagwan was sitting on an array of large white cushions which filled half the floor space of the room. A couple of crimson rugs were spread in front of him with pastel blue bolsters on which I was to sit or recline. I was shown in through the door and the Bhagwan indicated the rugs and cushions with a regal sweep of his arm. He called me Farrukh. So the Ingleburger disguise had been blown. How? I didn't know.

'You know it means angel face in Persian?' he asked.

'Yes, I was a baby when my parents gave me the name, so they couldn't have foreseen how it would turn out.'

He smiled.

'Faces can be transformed by emotions, by your karma even. Have you read a book by Oscar Wilde called *A Portrait of Dorian Grey?*'

'I have,' I said.

'There you are.'

Next to the Bhagwan was a two feet high pile of glossy magazines and he had one open next to him. I could see they were editions of *Playboy*. I looked at them and there, next to the pile was a paperback copy of my book *Poona Company*. It was no coincidence. They knew who I was and what I had written. He didn't allude to it and neither did I. He wasn't even looking to detect the surprise in my face.

'What are you reading?' he asked.

'At present? Nothing serious. I brought along *St. Mawr and the Gypsy* to read on the plane. D.H. Lawrence.'

'Yes. Now Lawrence was a yogi,' he said. It was a statement, not a challenge, but he wanted me to ask how he had reached that conclusion and so I did.

'He was in touch with nature, much more aware than mortals going about their business. He was once writing to another great novelist E.M. Forster after he read one of Forster's books and he said, "you should not have glorified those business people. Business is no good."'

'He had just read *Howard's End*,' I said.

A flicker of his deep eyes told me that he didn't appreciate me knowing or remembering the occasion of the quote when it had evaded him.

'Lawrence thinks love is universal; he is a prophet,' he said.

'I suppose. He is unique among writers in trying to bring out a mystical dimension of love…'

'The power play of sex,' he said. 'I only needed to read one of his books, you know. You have to guess which one.'

'If I was to guess I would say *Lady Chatterley's Lover*, but I actually think you've read much more than one.'

'So, young man, you are calling me a liar? But you are right. I have read more. I was testing your perception.'

'Did I pass?'

He nodded and picked up the magazine he was reading and leafed through the pages.

'I am going to read you a joke. Because a joke is never a joke.'

This was the most peculiar interview I had ever had or conducted. He began to read.

'Wing Kee frequented a Greek restaurant near his laundry. Mr Photopoulos and his sons and friends who ran the restaurant were always amused when Wing Kee ordered his food because, perusing the menu, he would say he wanted "flied lice" and the whole Greek company would break out in laughter. Kee got fed up of this and determined to take elocution lessons to correct his pronunciation. A few months later, he returned to Photopoulos's establishment and the Greeks gathered round with grins to hear his proverbial pronunciation.

'"What'll you have Wing Kee?" Photopoulos asked.

Wing Kee's chest swelled up with confidence.

"I'll have the frrrried rrrice—you flucking Gleek!"'

Bhagwan didn't laugh at the joke. He looked up at me and put the magazine down.

'You see what that says?'

'A bit of racism?'

'What it means is that you can work at changing your nature, but what is in your karma will always emerge in one form or the other. You can purge the poison from one part of the body, but it will enter another.' He smiled and gently nodded his head. He expected me to be amazed by this philosophical insight into the 'meaning' of the joke and I could see his disciples giving him the satisfaction of being wowed by the pronouncement. I wasn't. It was a revelation of sorts. The man traded in placebo spiritualism.

Nevertheless, I faked it. I nodded. 'Yes, I see. Great!'

He read another joke and explained it in the same way and I knew then that he was rehearsing, trying these out for a lecture or recording that his disciples would treasure.

My stomach rumbled and I was hoping he hadn't heard it. I was suppressing, with all the will power I could summon, a long and satisfying fart, knowing that pushing the wind back up myself would make my stomach hurt.

'I know what you want to ask me,' he said, 'but the agreement was that I was interviewing you, so let me put it as a question. Do you wish to know why Indians are not allowed into the sex therapy sessions we conduct in the ashram?'

'Yes, I was curious about that. Why ban Indians?'

'Well, what I tell the world is that Indians are brought up in an integrated way because of their poverty. Even if they are rich today, their genes have not absorbed the habits and hopes of materialism, so the dislocation in their sex lives is not complete. With Westerners it is the opposite. They need the sex therapy. You see D.H. Lawrence, your favourite, realized this. But he went wrong in saying that men have to assert their power over women. My doctrine is that they have to work it out, couple by couple, Adam and Eve by Adam and Eve, as though they were the only fucking creatures on earth. Each couple will find their own pattern of inequality. Indians don't need this working out. You see?'

'I see,' I said. I had opened my notebook and was scribbling the quote down as fast as I could.

He gave a little sneer.

'You don't see at all. That's all bullshit as you know, but the world believes it when I say it. The real reason for not allowing Indians into the sex sessions is because the ashram would be flooded out with Indian men wanting to fuck white girls, sick and needy white girls even, anything, and pretend to be devotees, pupils, bhakts, sanyasis, anything for a bit of white pussy. They would travel thousands of miles and give up their lives to be part of the sex sessions. You and I are both Indian men, we know that don't we?'

I can't say I was shocked.

'Why don't you say that openly?'

'You are an idiot, Farrukh. How could we continue to play the great game?'

'I am writing all this down and your manager said I could use whatever you say. I mean publish it.'

'Of course you can. When people read it and question me about it, I can give them another lecture about how this seemed to be what I said when it was filtered through your dirty brain, but it wasn't what I actually said. You know that truth is elusive, you can hold it only for a little while like water in your cupped hands.'

'I talked to one of your sex therapists. He said what he and the others were doing here was illegal in Europe and America.'

'Have you started asking the questions?'

'No, I just wanted to know what you would say about that.'

'What is legal is not the same as what is good. Do you read Karl Marx?'

The interview or encounter was getting absurd.

'I've read some.'

'The fellow puts economics, philosophy and history all into one and makes gold out of it, but it's still lead, base metal, because he forgets or leaves out the spiritual impulse, the prompting of the blood. Man does not live by bread alone.'

I scribbled all this down. It was good stuff.

'You are a Marxist, aren't you?' he asked and stared steadily at me and I got the impression that he had pulled in his bulging eyes and by some trick of the features they now appeared hooded and yet piercing.

'I am not a communist and I hate Stalinistic nonsense.'

'I said Marxist, rationalist, an "everything-can-be-explained" fellow, someone who denies the spiritual side of themselves.'

'I have never thought of myself as such.'

'That's why I called you an idiot, Farrukh.'

So that was the way he operated and he no doubt wanted to demonstrate that modus to me.

'It's your flaw, if you think about it. You know why I agreed to see you? I don't see many reporters. The Indians have been trying to get interviews with me for years. I say "no".'

'Because they don't need the interviews or the...' I was going to say 'crumbs of wisdom' but checked myself. 'They are not as dysfunctional spiritually as the Westerners?'

He smiled.

'Right. They don't come here to learn or to surrender. They come to conquer. Like you. You say you want an interview but really you want to get information about some little girl who may be called Sapphire, don't you? And maybe cause some trouble?'

'I don't know what you mean.'

'So you are not only an idiot, you are a liar, Farrukh. Good, good, good. Now we see face to face.'

Did he have his spies in town following me? Had they reported Diamond's visits to my house? Or, more sinister, was Diamond playing some sort of double or triple game?

'You must go now. You can come back to the ashram any time you want, but try and get in touch with yourself, young man. Define your objectives.'

I stood up.

'My objective was, is, to write some articles about you and the ashram. The world is curious.'

'I lead so many people astray, why do I do it?'

'I didn't say that.'

'No, I said it. But when you find the answer, please come back and tell me. I'll talk to you then. But don't say it's because I want or need the ten or fifty Rolls Royce's or fifteen Mercedes that my followers have given me. I can only ride one car at a time. It's their need to give, not mine to take. Now fuck off.' His eyes twinkled.

I left him smiling and I returned the smile as I left.

DIAMOND WAS NOT PLEASED. I had to tell her that my memory for baby features is not good and I couldn't swear that I had seen Saffy in the nursery though I was about to go and ask each one of the girls their names one by one before I was interrupted by the managerial woman.

'Could she be called Kavita now?'

'She could be dog's crusty arse, for all I care. That pimping bitch Shanti knew what you were after.'

'You may be right.'

'How do you mean?'

'Saket seemed to know that I had spoken to you or met with you. I don't know how.'

'I know how,' she said. 'They are watching me. They have plainclothes Indians following me ever since I went to the police.'

'What did the police do?'

'They have to have been bribed. The inspector sat me at a table and when I started my story, he was very interested in every dirty sexual detail and kept making me repeat everything I had already said until I realized that he was not interested in the investigation, he was just getting off on hearing me say these things. He tried to make me say what I had gone through in more and more explicit terms. I got it when he grinned. I was crying. I walked out.'

'So they know you came to my house or I went to Praful's. He did say I had the run of the ashram, though, I can go back when I want. I can write what I like.'

'How fantastic for you. And I'll never get Saffy back. These people are evil, you don't know.'

'They seem deluded, but a conspiracy of evil is difficult…'

'It's a conspiracy of silence, don't you see? They all know what goes on, that Shanti fetches women, men, children, whatever the monster wants and they all know and wait for the call. To be anointed. I know. I was there. It happened to me! And they have you fooled. There's nothing to interview him about. There's nothing to write about, except what I say, what Praful wrote for me, my "pamphlet" as you call it. He lost his job when he tried to get the newspaper to tell the truth. You have no idea how powerful…'

She broke off. She must have realized that she was getting increasingly hysterical.

'I'll try again tomorrow,' I said.

'It's too late. They'll whisk her off somewhere now that you have blown our cover. Thank you very much!'

We were sitting in Praful's tatty front room with the torn and dirty curtains and the sofas with their springs sticking out of the sides.

She got up and stalked off to their bedroom. I left.

Why was I getting involved in this? It had nothing to do with me. She had no right to say I had blown 'our' cover. I wasn't aware we were under cover.

I was going through the rickety gate when Praful came bicycling down the road. My first thought was to confront him about the underwear, but the matter was stale. It was a twelve- or fifteen-year-old story. And now that he was settled with Diamond, he would commit his sinful nostalgia to the bin. The image of him sitting with my sister, running her errands, playing innocent and all the while using her underwear for his dark and shamefully secret gratification...

'Did you find the child? Di said you would locate the babe,' he said.

'I didn't,' I said

'You told Di? She's disappointed, yeah?'

'Yeah.'

'Come and have a rum, yaar,' he said, wheeling his bike through the gate.

'Why didn't you tell me that she was being followed and watched?'

He looked exasperated.

'For god's sake man, look.' Praful dropped the bike and I stepped outside the gate with him. 'Look down the street. No one. She is not being watched at all. No one. Nothing.

She turns round on the street and accuses some passer-by of being a Bhagwan spy or working for Shanti or any nonsense. We were nearly arrested the other day. She made a scene in the street.'

'Really? Then how did that… the Bhagwan know that I was nosing around the nursery looking for Saffy?'

'They saw me talking to her when I was trying to get in there to report on it and she was screaming her head off outside. They stopped me going in as a reporter. They must have seen you taking her leaflets. They are not stupid, but they are not scared of the likes of Diamond. What can she do? She is a powerless Israeli or Jewish-American renegade. No government will help her. She tried the Israeli Charge D'affaires in Mumbai. They just laughed at her. These bastards pay off all the media and the politicians. Basically we are fucked. They don't need to follow us around. They have twenty Rolls Royces and property and those girls who work in the nursery are probably PhDs in childcare from German and Swedish institutions. The doctors who drugged her and forced her to have an abortion may be idiots but they are actually top gynaecologists and paediatricians from Europe. You don't know what she is up against. You don't know what you're up against. Try writing the truth, even writing up the interview you did with him and send it to England and see what happens.'

'I think you are being just a bit paranoid there. I can bet you the magazine I am reporting to won't be scared off by anything these people can do.'

'Great! Good luck. Write about Di and Saffy and what's happening to them.'

'I have no idea if any of it is true,' I said. 'I need to verify it independently. Not that I don't believe her, but the editor will need some sort of corroboration with this kind of story.'

'Where are you going to get corroboration? Her husband? The Bhagwan? That bitch Shanti who runs the show?'

'I'll find what I need,' I said, because he was becoming challenging, belligerent.

'Come on in,' he said, lifting his bicycle to wheel it indoors.

'I promised the aunts I would help them with Japanese flower arrangement. Must go. Will call you and Diamond when I've got some leads to Saffy.'

I pulled the rattling wooden frame of the six-foot gates behind me and I heard Di greeting Praful at the doorstep.

THEY ALLOWED ME BACK INTO the nursery the next day. I was amazed. I thought they'd be suspicious. I asked some of the girls their names. There was no Sapphire and the photograph that Di had shown me didn't match any of them.

I had nothing to lose. 'Was there a girl named Sapphire here? I mean is she here now or will she be…?' I asked the girl who was, gently and with great expertise, directing the activity of the children.

'Sapphire? No. The parents change their names, you know, which is part of our, or the Bhagwan's idea of the rediscovery of the self.'

'Rediscovery? Two-year-olds? They haven't even had a first discovery,' I said.

'How can you say that? Even the newborn has had past lives and okay—I can see you look sceptical—if you don't believe in multiple births, you at least believe in contemporary science and genes and chromosomes. So the kids know who they are, even if the particular entry hasn't yet floated into the conscious mind!'

'And even so, they want to change their names and identities?'

'Why are all of us here, Mr Dhondy? Because the world is sick. Where we come from is sick. If ever there was a way of cleaning oneself out, it's here, under the guidance of the Bhagwan. Get rid of your spiritual and mental toxins! Absorb new energies.'

A child came up. He had spilt all the contents of his water-colour paint box, the mixing water and all, on the painting he'd been doing. He was fearful and had brought the large wet sheet of paper to her. The streaks of the spillage were indistinguishable from his efforts at painting, but the angel of a girl said she'd dry the painting in the sun and give him another sheet and she stared deliberately at the wet sheet and said she could see exactly what he had been trying to do and that they could almost certainly save his creativity.

The boy was mollified if not satisfied. Already another sanyasin was mopping up the mess the paint-box spillage had left.

I gave up the quest for Saffy.

I asked Agnivarsha if I could see a sex therapy session and take notes.

'I thought you'd never ask, you've lasted three days,' she said. So she did have a sense of humour! 'Other journos ask within the first hour.'

'So? I'm lazy, or not that randy or whatever, but what's the answer?'

'Bhagwan told you why he doesn't let Indians into sex sessions. You're Indian.'

'He didn't say anything about reporters. I don't want to participate. Just observe.'

I caught her smiling to herself.

'Do you go to sex therapy yourself?' I asked trying to put her on the defensive.

'Those sanyasis and sanyasins who admit that they need sex therapy wouldn't be given the job of taking people like you round the ashram.'

'I can see that. And I take that to mean that you think the sessions are reserved for loonies?'

'We don't use such words in the ashram,' she said.

'I have heard the Bhagwan use worse,' I said.

'And so have I,' she said, 'but he is beyond our mortal calculations and regulations.'

'So no sex sessions for me. But tell me, is there an age limit. I mean a lower age limit?'

'There isn't a written regulation, but we use our common sense. Obviously children and vulnerable young people aren't encouraged to go.'

'I thought the point of it was vulnerability, like fractured people going into therapy to be healed. Have you witnessed some sessions?'

She looked at me to see if I was getting any sort of satisfaction out of this questioning and decided I wasn't.

'Yes, of course I've been. Psychotherapists and analysts who visit us are very eager to learn and I've shown them round. It's not all orgies, you know. It's very boring, modelled on yoga exercise classes where individuals and partners are asked to do things with their minds and bodies and emotions to music, except that here everything is allowed. One of our therapists who went too far was warned and then expelled.'

'How do you mean went too far?'

'He declared that he was in need of therapy himself and began using the sessions for his own ends. The Bhagwan had him removed.'

I was about to say that the man was challenging the Bhagwan's exclusivity, but knew it would get me evicted.

'I met the man and got his side of the story,' I said.

'I expect you did and reporters are free to. You'll meet all manner of lunatics who say all manner of things about the ashram, so we invite you to see for yourself. Of course if journalists go away and write rubbish and sensationalize the spiritual purposes and activities of the ashram, we warn them off.'

'You mean threaten them with lawyers?'

'No, Mr Ingleburger, or is it Dhondy, look, what we do is squat on each others' heads in a vast pyramid and then close our eyes and begin to chant and project the energies of truth to overcome the energies of negative reporting all over the world and poof! By magic the malicious copy gets erased from every sheet on which it is printed.' She acted out the closing of her eyes and grinned.

'So you do use lawyers,' I said.

'And anything else that Aunty Shanti can pull and she has pulled stunts I tell you on the East German government, so don't be complacent. Friendly warning,' she said, still smiling.

'Can I write what you've just said?'

'That we use meditation and prayer? Of course.' She was enjoying her own answers. 'You don't have to go to a sex session to get laid, you know.'

'Oh my god,' I said, 'They do get rid of inhibitions here, don't they? It normally takes me hours of hard work and a lot of drinks to get a woman to say anything like that to me.'

'Don't flatter yourself. I wasn't propositioning you, just stating a fact. There's your friend Diamond who has been round the maypole a few times in company.'

'You mean Saffy's mother?' I asked

'I wasn't aware she had a child,' she said. 'We show all the journalists our kitchens. Would you like to visit them now, Farrukh?'

WE WENT TO THE BEACH for our evening stroll and the Hare Krishna girl who had cast off her clothes approached us and said she had left the 'ritual trip' and had actually come to the beach looking for Saket who was 'so cool' because he spoke the most cogent sense she had ever heard from the lips of a human being.

She was gushing. She said she had come every day in the hope of finding us and here we were at last! It had perhaps been four or five days. She had three friends with her and she called them over. She had come running when she spotted us. They came and I noticed they were all barefoot.

Rahul smiled.

'We've just come for a walk,' I said.

'I wanted to ask you a few questions. I came to India looking,' she said.

Rahul seemed interested in talking to her and her three male companions. I didn't recognize them as the Hare Krishnas I had seen her with.

'What had you lost?' Rahul asked.

'I don't know. That's just it. Is there anything to lose?'

Rahul smiled.

'Do you believe in God?' he asked.

'I've been thinking about that. No, I don't think I do.'

'Good start. But you did believe once.'

'Sure, was brought up a Baptist.'

'The age of existentialism begins. God is dead. Now what?'

'I thought you could tell us.'

'Most of the stuff you read about finding yourself is humbug, but that doesn't mean that there is no such quest. It might even mean that if you set off West from Spain looking for India, you've gone the wrong way but you might ultimately get there if you keep going.'

They laughed.

'Or,' he said, 'You may find an alluring chunk of real estate and decide, to hell with India.'

They laughed again.

'That's so true,' one of the men said.' Can I ask an impertinent question?'

'Impertinence is in the brain of the insulted. I was trained to take it as it comes. Ask away.'

'Who the fuck are you?'

'What do you Westerners say? Have you got till Christmas?'

'We've got as long as you've got. Shall we sit on the sand?'

'That's all there is,' said Rahul, and as I watched him practising this first inckling of his power over these people, he squatted down. They sat in front of him, an audience. Several walkers on the beach came and stood around out of curiosity.

'The obvious answer is the best. I am an out of work philosopher. She was here last time when some deluded soul wanted to get me arrested to cure his own illness—how do you say it—hang-ups?'

'Hang-ups is right. Hey, we all come to India to get rid of our hang-ups.'

'Can it be done?'

'That's what we wanted to ask you, Guruji,' she said, and folded her hands. Rahul nodded, solemnly. The Indians who had gathered round in growing numbers seemed impressed. I hadn't squatted down with them and now I saw Shanti and Bhavnani approaching.

They came up and stood respectfully in the gathering and listened. Bhavnani kept raising his eyebrows to indicate to me that they had come there with a final and alluring invitation. When I acknowledged his presence he motioned to me to step aside.

'This is a miracle,' he said.

'What?'

'That we find him lecturing to white people. That is what we have been debating. No widows. Only white people. They will come to listen, they will come to learn. Swamiji could not attract them. But, sir, here—has he taken a name?—this Guru will certainly have a big hold, a big following. He is too good.'

I told him the name Rahul had fabricated and he rolled it round his tongue, repeating it five or six times.

'Saket! Great, great. And you are bringing him. You can have your own room, not like before. Saket can have the swami's room and we can have talks in the garden. He is willing, no?'

'He said he'd do it. He thinks you are offering him a sort of lecturing job and he can do that standing on his head.'

'Much more, much more, and Shantiji has forgiven you.'

'Forgiven me? I need to forgive her for calling me a thief.'

'Let by-gums be by-gums,' said Bhavnani.

'... the hero walks on the beach and he has heard of his mother's death,' Saket was saying as we rejoined the crowd. 'He is appalled that he doesn't feel anything about her death. He has entered a state of indifference. He stabs an Arab. He doesn't expect to pay any social penalty for it because it is such a random act that the normal trail of motivation can't be used to connect him to the deed. He has liberated himself and finds that this liberty leads to the prison of license.'

They were listening as though their lives depended on it. Some of the audience had settled down, squatted behind the young white girl and her friends.

The crowd was thickening and now people began to gather in greater numbers and the people at the back started pushing those in front of them till the circle around the squatters forced people to trip and fall. Someone fell over one of the young white men and the squatting audience stood up. There was a lot of shouting. Saket stood up too and Shanti took charge. She grabbed him by the elbow and firmly backed him out of the crowd.

'Let's get away from these stupid people,' she said.

There were people running behind us now saying, 'who is he, who is he? Is he a saint?'

We walked rapidly to Mr Bhavnani's car. The whites were following, shouting to us to wait.

Shanti was quick. She released Saket's elbow and turned and went straight back to the young white people. She talked to them for a few minutes and then came back to us.

'I told them there would be a lecture tomorrow evening at the ashram and gave them the card.'

We drove to the ashram and Saket was shown his room, the swami's room.

Mr Bhavnani said we must go and fetch our things and that he would drive me.

I was conscious that if we removed our belongings it would have to be when the landlord was at his gambling or drinking. We owed him several weeks' rent.

He was there when we got to our room and went up the stairs but I heard him curse, as only he could, the gods, their mothers and the postman, who it seems had been the bearer of bad tidings. We waited till, soon after his tirade, he left and we heard him go, banging doors.

We packed the books and the bedding and Mr Bhavnani helped carry our bundles down. We didn't own much then.

Bhavnani's attitude to Saket was immediately respectful. He started calling him 'sirji'. Saket tolerated this while we packed and made our getaway but once we got to the car, with Bhavnani holding the back door open for him and saying 'sirji, sirji', leaving me to pack our bundles into the boot, Saket started with a sour smirk.

'Are you giving me the royal treatment?' Saket asked as we drove away passing the unsuspecting landlord on his way a hundred yards down the street.

'Much more than royal, sirji,' Bhavnani said.

'What can be more than royal?' Saket asked mischievously, 'except the Divine?'

'Everything is possible,' said Mr Bhavnani, not quite understanding what Saket had said.

'If you agree, then stop all this "sirji" business and call me by my proper name.'

'How can I do that, sirji, you are our guru,' Bhavnani objected.

'Then call me guru!' Saket said, and after a pause continued. 'No, call me Bhagwan, God. Why not go all the way?'

'Of course, Bhagwanji,' Mr Bhavnani said.

'No "ji", just Bhagwan,' Saket replied looking out of the window, "ji" is for some Punjabi director of these stupid Hindi films.' Turning my head in the front passenger seat, I caught a glimpse of him. He had a faint, self-satisfied smirk on his face. I knew him well. He had entered the game.

THE DOORBELL RANG AT ELEVEN o'clock at night. My aunts were asleep and I, reading in bed, thought I had better get to the door before the ringing woke up the household.

I ran through the rooms and took down the barricades my aunts put up each night against possible thieves—three bolts, a padlock and a wooden beam across the door which slotted into metal holders on either side.

'Coming, coming, coming!' I said, to forestall the caller ringing again. I thought it must be Diamond.

'Me,' said Praful, as I undid the padlock and opened the door.

I hadn't been to his house since Di told me about the stolen underwear. My instinct would have been to challenge him about it across all these years but I'd promised never to mention it or let it get in the way.

'Is that bitch with you?' Praful asked. He looked sweaty and disturbed and his aggressive tone was just in his voice because he looked limp and defeated.

'If you mean Diamond, I haven't seen her. Left you and run away, has she?'

'More than that. She's stolen my mother's diamonds and the gold cup my father won as a hockey trophy.'

'When did she do all this?'

I asked him to step outside onto the veranda in the dark and I shut the front doors lightly behind me because I didn't want to wake up the aunts. We conversed in the dark. I could smell the alcohol on his breath.

'The police are at my house now, at night, taking finger prints,' he said. 'My mother is going mad and cursing all white people. And me.' His voice was pleading, defeated.

'Sure it was her?'

'Who else? She's buggered off, yaar, taking everything.'

'Where do you think she's gone?'

'Mummy discovered the missing jewellery this afternoon and started screaming. The bitch had smashed open the locks. I didn't want to believe it yaar. I went everywhere looking and I have come six times to your house but the masis must have been at work and you were out so she couldn't hide here. Are you sure she didn't come to you? Look, yaar, the police will search all suspects...'

'You think I'd hide her and lie to you, you son of a bitch,' I said.

'Stay cool, yaar, I need your help, Farrukh, boss. How could she do this? Was she lying about everything? About everything?'

'I don't think she was or could have been, because if she wanted to get sympathy and worm her way into a household to rob it, she wouldn't have chosen yours, would she? Be realistic. Your house and your mum don't exactly give the impression of harbouring great and expensive treasures.'

He was not insulted but reassured. He touched my wrist.

'Thanks, yaar. But she definitely took the stuff and where the fuck is she gone?'

'Listen man, I think she was completely sincere about finding Sapphire. Tell me something, have you ever seen this girl, this Sapphire?'

'No,' he said.

'But you know she exists?'

'I believed Di. We were going to get married, you know.'

'But she has this husband in the ashram, doesn't she?'

'Yeah, yeah, but we were spiritually married.'

'Oh, I see,' I said. 'Spiritually? She convinced you of the existence of spiritual marriages, did she? Once a bullshitter, always a bullshitter?'

'Have some feelings, yaar. I came to you as an old friend.'

'You came to me because you thought she was here, Praful. I saw it in your eyes last time. You think I want to fuck her and, even worse, she wants to fuck me and that's what's bothering you, isn't it?'

'Please don't say these things. My mum is on my back. I have to find Di before the police find her.'

'Where will you look?'

'Don't know.'

'She didn't take the gold cup to drink lassi from, you know. And she's not going to walk around Main Street wearing your mum's diamonds. She's obviously desperate for money and will sell them. You're the investigative journalist. Where do stolen goods get sold in this town?'

He grabbed my hand in the dark. The one street lamp outside the Parsee fire-temple opposite cast our long shadows along the veranda wall.

'I know where—some places. I'll look. Can I keep in…I mean talk as friends. I mean no hard feelings, yaar? Yes?'

'What hard feelings! Don't be an idiot and tell me tomorrow what you find or what the police find.'

At breakfast the next morning, before she cycled off to work at her seed sales company, my aunt showed me the day's *Poona Messenger*. On the front page was the screaming headline:

KIDNAPPED! TWO GIRL CHILDREN MISSING FROM SAKET BROOD.

Two infants had been snatched from their parents and their homes the previous day. One from a car while her mother went into a shop and the other from a park under the nose of a servant who was supposed to be looking after her. The police,. the article said, were on the trail of the kidnappers. The parents were waiting and hoping for a note demanding ransom. There were no clues about the criminal's identity, but the nanny who had turned away to chat to her friends leaving the infant to play in a sand pit, said the child was snatched by a man with dark hair who had covered his face with a gingham scarf and rode away with the child on a scooter. She couldn't identify him. The snatches happened within two hours of each other and must have been well planned.

The news item appeared under Praful's byline. He must have written and submitted it before our conversation the previous night. He had said nothing about it or about being back in favour with the newspaper's editors who were accepting signed stories from him.

The article mentioned the possibility of a ransom motive several times.

I drank my tea, took the paper and walked to Praful's place. He was standing at the gate talking to a man who turned away as I arrived, crossed to his scooter and rode away, looking me up and down as he went.

'Police,' Praful said, 'plain-clotheswalla.'

'Why didn't you tell me about this?'

'I was worried about the other thing—her.'

'It's the same thing, isn't it?'

He shrugged.

'Was one of the children her daughter?'

He didn't want this conversation. He said nothing. He looked as though he hadn't slept. He was wearing the clothes he wore the night before. Lazy? But then I knew he didn't have too many shirts to change into.

'Was one of them her daughter?' I asked again, insistently.

'I don't know.'

'But your report. Surely you talked to the parents of the kidnapped girls? Was one of them her husband?'

'I never met her husband so even if he was, I wouldn't know...'

'But the name,' I said. Why was Praful fucking around with me?

'They all change their names,' he said, looking away from me and biting his lip.

'That's bullshit. In a search for kidnapped kids, they give their real names. Passport names!'

'I didn't speak to the parents. I got it all from the police report. The Saketis don't speak to me, man.'

'Not even when their kids are missing and when you might know where they are?'

'How would I know where they are?'

'God help you,' I said.

He was looking away to hide his wet eyes from me. He wiped them against his sleeve.

'I don't know what to do, Farrukh.'

'Do the police know that she lived with you?'

He nodded.

'They've taken all her things away,' he said.

'And what's all this stuff about waiting for ransom demands?'

'That's what the coppers think and they've told the parents who are going mad.'

'But you know it's not true.'

'I don't know anything. She said nothing at all to me. We were carrying on as normal. No hint of what she was planning.'

'But you know, and I suppose I know, that she has snatched them. But why two kids?'

'Revenge?'

'What about the guy on the scooter? It could actually be some ransom gang. They know the Saketis have money. Pretty obvious target. On the other hand she may have just gone AWOL, nothing to do with the kids. Coincidence.'

'That's what I'm hoping. That's why I didn't tell you anything about it last night. It might be someone quite different. And she has nothing to do with it. She's just gone off because she took mum's stuff and...I don't know...temporary insanity. She's been under heavy pressure.' His voice faltered with doubt. He knew, was convinced, it was her.

'But you and I know different. Snatching kids. You have to find her, and them.'

'They are watching the airports. A white woman and two little white girls? Not difficult to spot.'

'That's why she won't go to an airport, even if she has plenty of money left over after hiring the scooter man with the gingham scarf to carry out the snatch.'

'I think she stole a car,' Praful said, 'A blue Fiat. It was abandoned by the railway station.'

'What was the policeman asking?'

'They carried out some heat tests on the car and found it had been driven till this morning so they are trying to find witnesses from the station or from the trains that left soon after that time.'

'What are you going to do?'

'I don't know,' he said.

BUT DID HE KNOW? THE police received a curious ransom note. Praful woke me up in the early and still-dark hours of the morning to say he had bribed the police and got hold of the ransom note and had already handed it over to the *Messenger* for publication. The *Messenger* had paid him handsomely for intimate insight into the biggest story in town. It was. It sold forty thousand more copies of the paper that morning.

The ransom note said:

> *We have the two girls. Not to worry, they are being treated in best of health and very happy with everything, except crying for their mummeez. Their father must give one crore rupees each for there returns. It have to be in foreign currency of good sort such as dollars or English. Just to help, we must tell you we are not inside Poona but have gone from city and you will await next contact so we will tell you where money has to pass and then girl children free. Announce in Poona Messenger newspaper when money is ready.*

It wasn't signed.

Praful said the *Messenger*'s editor was flattered by the ransom note's demand to communicate through his paper. The real note didn't actually name the *Poona Messenger*, it just said 'newspaper', but the editor had made his little changes to impress his readers and gave visitors to the office the impression that he was the kingpin in the negotiations to free the kidnapped girls. They were now the sensational talk of the town and soon of the country.

The police followed up the trail of the ransom demand. It was postmarked from Goa and the newspapers who said they had this top secret information through a police leak, speculated that, on the principle of hiding a pebble on a beach, it would be the ideal place for a white woman and two white infant girls to disappear.

There were other lurid stories about the kidnappers not being interested in ransom but being part of a Tantric conspiracy that sacrificed children for some satanic art or purpose.

I had made a further date with the ashram and went. The Guru had issued instructions in his lecture about the kidnappings. No one was to so much as mention the missing children or to speculate about what had happened and who had done it. He had issued an injunction, I gathered, against wasting the energies of speech on a matter that was best left to the police. He had made some convoluted point about idle talk adding and subtracting from the truth till, in a chain of Chinese whispers, no communication retained its connection to what was real.

And still the presence or the absence of the kidnapped children hung over the ashram. One felt it straight away. No one mentioned the children, Diamond, her husband or her child, but the very restraint charged these silences with suspicion.

Everyone I spoke to, about the menu in the canteen or the routines of the sex therapy sessions or about the philosophy of that morning's lecture seemed to exert some effort to avoid the subject of the kidnappings or the anguish they had caused. The lecture had been about the artificial conceits of taste and fashion. The Guru seemed to confound aesthetic judgement of the deepest critical sort with the advertising industry's passing fads. Or perhaps he didn't. Perhaps he was saying that the passing fads were of equal inconsequence to the judgements of serious critics—only his own pronouncements mattered. Criticism and advertising were both brainwashing: the conspiracy of the 'enemy'. He used an example which delighted his audience. He said that the escalating price of Picassos was as absurd as wanting a brand name on your trainers. Picasso's signature and fame and the Nike logo were manipulations of the general mind.

I may have wanted to discuss this concept, but no one seemed enthusiastic about it. The children. The menace. There were more children about in the compound of the ashram that day. Their parents, devotees, had brought them in with them and my minders told me that there was a rush of requests for accommodation within the compound. Some families had pitched tents in the rear meadow of the ashram and were refusing to move them. They intended to stay away from the city. A fortress mentality was taking shape.

The ashramites and acolytes had never got the hang of India or of this city, my city, so profoundly changed now. The closest they got was sleeping on mats on the floor in dingy rooms, stalking around the alleys and smoking bidis instead of cigarettes, feeling that they had gone native enough. The Guru didn't encourage them in the idea that India and its scriptures and traditions or its religions and ethics were the fount of all wisdom. His was a very modern, very Western movement. I wrote that down in my notebook. It was the first time that I felt I knew what I would write back for readers in Britain.

A bell rang out and a council of the devotees who had brought children seeking accommodation, shelter and protection from kidnappers were summoned in order to be told that they would be vetted and allowed to set up tents in the rear meadow till the crisis passed. The ashram was in touch with the police and 'developments' were assured.

In keeping with the Guru's injunction to refrain from mentioning kidnaps or children, no actual allusions to these were made. The message was nevertheless that the ashram was most concerned about all families and would do everything it could to stop them taking flight and threatening to leave the ashram and return to Europe or America.

That night I was reading in bed in my room. The city was asleep and the only sound was that of crickets from across the open sewer that ran behind the back wall of the house.

Out of this silence came the human whistle with the clear eight-note melody we used to use in our school and college days to call each other out from our houses at night. The signal had become very popular when I was in my teens and on summer nights, as very many of us stayed awake into the night cramming for exams, we would summon each other for a break or for a walk to the railway station for tea using the little tune.

Praful, though he never belonged to the set of my friends, knew the signal and was evidently calling me. I put on my trousers and went out in my loose white night shirt, passing through the rooms where my aunts were asleep. I unbarred the front door. He was waiting for me, sitting on the steps of the sandalwood shop across the triangular junction of our street.

'I say, you are not writing about this in UK, are you?'

'About what?'

'The kidnaps. You have contacts and an agent and all this and it's big news,' he said, searching my face.

'In England?'

'Or US. If the kids are English or American, then the newspapers will pick up the story like hot potatoes, no?'

'Yeah I suppose they would be interested—"Brit Children Missing From Cult Ashram." Yeah, it would work.'

'So you haven't written it?'

'No,' I said. It hadn't occurred to me.

'Then can I do it? I need the money, yaar. One of the kids is American and the other is a Brit so both countries will syndicate the story and I can make some moolah. It's hot stuff. I was just wondering if you'd got there first. I've been trying to syndicate the breaking stories as they come.'

'Go for it, no competition. Not what I am after, though your Diamond and her story and now she's missing and... the kids...' I trailed off.

Praful looked away.

'Do you know an agent who deals with newspapers there? Your agent. This is a huge breaking story and they'll just pick it up from the national Indian press tomorrow if I don't move on it now. It's still daytime in the UK,' he said.

I shrugged. 'I can call a couple of feature editors and news desks,' I said.

'Come to my house now and use my phone and call them. It's my first break, man, please yaar, help me out.'

I fetched my diary which had phone numbers in the back and locked my house from the outside saying a little prayer that the house wouldn't catch fire for the next hour and trap my aunts who'd be mystified. I went with Praful and rang a friend on the *Telegraph* news desk and got him to agree to syndicate the news as it came. Praful had written it out and dictated it on the phone. He didn't mention Diamond or our suspicions and said that the hunt for the kidnappers had moved to Goa.

Several disciples left town with their children and infants in their arms and were photographed and interviewed by television reporters at the Poona railway station.

'We know the ashram is safe but the Bhagwan has taught us to find the physical and mental space where the energies are not troubled,' one of them told the reporters.

'Energies Troubled by Child Kidnap' was the headline over the story in an East Coast daily in the States.

Praful filed stories every day using every detail and conjecture which he got out of the police. Though very many other reporters, mostly from Bombay, had moved onto the patch, he was still seen as the journalist who broke the story and was closest to it. He came and went from Goa and reported on the impossibility of the search for white children there, again using the simile of losing a grain of sand on the beach and commenting on the improbability of the Indian reporter distinguishing one blonde child from another.

He was milking the story dry. When there was no further news, he filed a piece about the incompetence of the other reporters in the pack that had despatched itself to Goa. He picked up the hint from the US newspaper and claimed he had conducted his own research to prove their incompetence. He had shown them several photographs of white children which he had taken on the beach and found they couldn't match two photographs of the same child taken from different angles. His little experiment, together with several of the photographs he had used for it, appeared in the foreign press.

There was no sign of Diamond and the police called at my house asking if I knew of her whereabouts. From their questioning I knew that she was still very much on their list of suspects but they said nothing to the press about it and Praful wrote not a word about her. The acknowledged motive was ransom and the kidnappers had, presumably through fear of being traced, gone silent.

The trickle of 'returning' devotees turned into a flood. The trains to Bombay from where they would return on flights to Europe and the USA were full of crimson people. They were still devotees, but they wanted to put a vast distance between themselves and the city of kidnaps.

I WOKE UP TO THE sound of the whistle signal. It was a shrill whistle, the same tune that we used to summon each other but delivered an octave higher. I wasn't sure whether I had dreamt it or not so I waited, half-awake in bed. And there it was again. 'Ray, Ti, La, So-La-Ti-Soh (lower) Ray!' The household was asleep. I got into my shoes, pulled on a shirt above my underwear and went out. I knew.

At first I didn't see her as I went down the steps of the veranda and into the street. She was standing in the shadow of the wall, away from the light of the streetlamp and she was holding two little girls by the hand. Both girls had little knapsacks. I thought of the story of Paddington Bear and how my heart went out, when I first heard the story, to the abandoned bear sitting on his luggage at a London railway station with a notice round his neck asking any kind passer-by to 'please look after this bear'.

She didn't have to ask whether she could come in. I had no option. We went through the house on tiptoe. It was as though the little girls, wrapped up in coats and wearing scarves even in the warm weather, had been instructed in the art of keeping their silence and had learnt their lesson well.

We had to pass through the room where my aunts slept, one of them snoring loudly. They would wake promptly at six to bathe, dress, have their tea and breakfast and cycle off to work.

In my room, without a word, we took the shoes, coats and dresses off the two little girls and put them into my bed in their slips and knickers. Diamond folded their clothes away, an instinctive motherly action.

'So we can stay?' she whispered.

'I'll have to tell my aunts.'

'They'll go to the police. They've been reading the papers and watching TV.'

I shook my head to reassure her.

'Not if I say. But why, why all this?'

'Because I'm mad.'

'Does Praful know you are in Poona or that you were going to come here?'

She bit her lower lip. It meant he didn't know.

'I thought for a while that he was in it with you.'

'He was, but not for the last twenty-four hours. I don't want him to know where I am. He was urging me to give myself up.'

'I may urge you to do the same thing. What you are doing is very, very serious.'

'You think I don't know that? That's why I have to get away with it.'

'What does getting away with it mean? Where does it end? You can't.'

'It means not being caught and thrown into jail. It means getting my daughter back.'

'And these two?'

'I'll exchange if they see sense and guarantee me safe passage with her.'

'Safe passage to where?'

'I was born an Israeli. I can ask for asylum in my own country and take my daughter to a kibbutz. I'm also an American, by marriage.'

'It's not going to be that smooth,' I said.

The little girls were asleep.

I pulled the cushions out from under the bed. She could sleep on them. They say the troubled get no rest but as she lay down she fell fast asleep.

I left the three of them there, tiptoed round the house past my aunts' room to the front room where I slept on the sofa, keeping an ear out for the time they would wake up to their individual alarm clocks which went off in the same room seconds before or after each other. Both my aunts were convinced that only the tone of their own alarm clock bell could wake them. They weren't similar bells. One was a whirr and the other a pair of sprung and pounding hammers on a steel hemisphere. This fancied inability to wake up to each other's alarms was a feature of their existence with which they acquainted their guests, strangers and anyone who would listen.

I heard both alarms that morning and as they woke up and went to switch on the electric kettle, their proud new possession, to make morning tea and brushed their teeth I rose in pyjamas and told them about the intrusion in the night. Both of them sat down in their nightdresses, continuing to brush their teeth as I talked.

'That woman, that Praful's woman? She has taken two children? You think we are stupid? We know she is the one who has done the kidnapping. Where are they?'

'Asleep in my room.'

'So you let them in? Those poor children.'

'The children are okay.'

'What has gone wrong with you? How can they be okay when they have been snatched from their parents by this woman?'

Diamond was standing in the doorway. She heard.

My aunts put their toothbrushes away and rinsed their mouths.

'I realize I shouldn't have turned up here. I had nowhere else. Your nephew was the only one who showed me any… interest. I am sorry, very sorry. I'll go.'

She turned away and Amy, surprised at this voluntary capitulation, shouted after her.

'Wait, my dear, where will you go?'

'Into the street. I have nowhere to go. I know you think I am a very bad person and I probably am,' Di said. There were tears on her cheeks. 'I am so sorry, aunties. I'll get the girls and you can forget we ever disturbed you. Forgive me. I beg you, forgive me for thinking there is kindness…'

'No, no, no wait,' Amy said. My aunts looked at each other.

Di hesitated in the doorway.

'Suppose we don't know that this... our nephew has hidden you and the girls. We don't have to know. You can stay in that room and just be very quiet and use the back bathroom. But then what is going to happen?'

'How many days?' Shera asked.

'My darlings, thanks,' I said. 'Till we can work something out. Maybe I can return the children to their parents and get Diamond out of here, out of the country.'

'I am not leaving without my daughter,' she said.

'As long as we don't know what's going on,' said Shera. 'Or the servants,' said Amy.

The aunts went about their morning routine and before they left Shera came to me and said they had to go to a seed merchant's conference in Sholapur, away from Poona for two nights.

They had packed their small suitcases days before. The entire staff of the seed firm, the proud establishment behind the slogan 'Pocha Seeds Satisfy', was being given a trip away by coach to discuss the modernization of seed selling in India. The proposed conference had caused a lot of excitement throughout their firm and farms. The bosses, it was rumoured, were thinking of diversifying from flowers and garden vegetables into fruit and grain.

'This way we don't even have to know that those people and the illegal children are here.'

They went and we passed the day discussing what she could do and talking nonsense when she was tired of discussing it. I got the children to play in the yard, taught them how to cut and eat mangoes, got an old spinning top out of a drawer and tried to make it spin, cooked some chappatis, with the girls helping to knead the dough, stirred up an egg curry and ate it, played charades and went to bed. Dia repeastedly told them that they would son be back with their parents who had asked her to look after them. The house was ours for two days.

Di woke up with red eyes and a red and streaming nose. I thought she had been crying but she rubbed her eyes, went to the wash basin and splashed them with cold water.

'Hay fever,' she said. 'I have it bad.'

I gave the children fried eggs and the previous night's chappatis and went out to the corner chemist to get Di an anti-allergy pill.

The chemist was very friendly.

'You are now a famous author, my friend, everyone knows you.'

I bought the pills.

'Tell me something, you live in London, no?'

I said I did.

'Tell me, are there lots of dirty immigrants spoiling our name there?' he asked.

'Is there a name to spoil?' I asked.

'I have heard the Britishers think we are all Pakistani?'

'No, they don't,' I said. 'Some rude people use the word "Paki" as a sort of abuse for any subcontinental person.'

'That is fantastic,' he said. 'Paki?'

He was savouring the word. 'I am going to use it to abuse fellows also,' he said. 'Wonderful! Paki!'

He gave me another pack of anti-allergy pills.

'I only need one,' I said.

'Keep it, free for you, my gift, you have taught me so much,' he said and as I turned away to go, 'tell me, my dear, how do you get to London?'

'Difficult. They are not giving visas,' I said, 'but train for a few years as a nurse and apply. They are always short of nurses. Too many chemists.'

As I left the shop, Praful was walking in.

'Mother's urine sample,' he said holding up a bottle I didn't want to see.

'Some problem?' he asked.

'No, just aspirin,' I said. 'Any news?'

'Nothing. I mean the police call all the time. Nothing. If you are at home, I'll come round later.'

'I am leaving town for a few days. Going with the aunts to some seed conference that their firm is holding, expanding the town's industry.'

'Their firm? That's a story, yaar. I can report that for national papers. I'll come with you. Where is the conference?'

'I think it's a closed shop,' I said. 'Trade secrets.'

'Your aunts will tell me,' he said.

'They've already gone. I'm just picking up my things and taking a rickshaw.'

He sensed that I was dodging him. He shrugged.

'I need the money, yaar. Tell me where the conference is? Okay, okay, give me the lowdown when you're back. Something, anything, my old amigo!'

'I thought you were making some money out of the kidnap stories.'

'They don't want any more, it's gone quiet.'

'Then make it up. Come on, you are a journalist. "White woman spotted in Somalia with two blonde kids. Description by coconut seller fits."'

'Please don't joke, yaar, the bitch has used me and left me and it's killing me.'

I took the hay fever pills to Di. She was bathing the girls, pouring cold water from a bucket over their blonde hair. They chatted away to her. They seemed to have no resentment towards her and treated her as their guardian and friend. They'd been kidnapped, seized, but manifested no hostility towards her, me or their surroundings. Surely this was a strange place and a strange experience? Or were these girls used to being taken from place to place and to befriending strangers and accepting wandering, isolation, secrecy and no routines? Is that what their parents' spiritual quest had got them habituated to?

The girls and Di slept in my aunts' beds and I slept in my own.

A few hours after I had gone to bed, having tried to read without being able to concentrate and dozed off, I felt Di getting into my bed next to me and snuggling up to my back.

'I want to do something for you,' she whispered. 'Anything you want!'

I turned towards her. She had one arm gently round my waist.

'You've been very good to me and I have nothing to give you,' she said.

I could see her face clearly in the half-dark because the light of the night came through the dusty bamboo blind, the wall of my room.

'I've done nothing and I can't take anything from you,' I said.

She looked hurt.

'You mean I can't be nice to you, even if I want to—for myself, I mean.'

'Do you think it's right?' I asked. In response to her closeness, my arm was now gently round her waist. She was naked.

'Right? It's completely right to be nice to someone who's been so good to you.'

'I've done nothing really and you...'

'Shhh,' she said. 'If you are worried that you'll get stuck with me and have to love me and keep me and all that, forget it. It's not why I am here...like this. It's not asking you for anything—a simple and pure and even longing offer. If you want me to be nice to you—anything—I want to do it for you. No strings attached.'

'That's very generous, Di, but you've been through a lot and we are friends so I don't know...'

I was aroused and she felt me against her. She gently rolled me onto my back and climbed on top of me and resting her weight on one hand, slipped my erection easily into herself. She was very wet.

As though she wanted to stick to her word, after I had come, and gone soft and slipped out of her, she rolled off me onto her back and, as we lay exhausted, she got up, kissed me on the forehead and wordlessly left.

The police banged on the door.

Diamond came running and woke me up and I opened it to them. Apart from that front door, there was no exit to the house. When I opened the door I could see that there were squad cars in the street and the police were out in numbers.

'Madam and the children,' the inspector who confronted me said. I thought 'madam' was good.

On turning round I saw that Di was standing behind me in my aunt's dressing gown. The two girls were standing in their nightdresses on either side of her. Di had her hands protectively or possessively on their shoulders.

'Inspector Saheb, I am here. No one else is to blame.'

'These are children you have taken?' the inspector asked. He must have wanted a confession for the record. They couldn't have not been the children, could they? And he must have had photographs of them.

'Yes, they are,' she said.

She came forward and pushed me aside gently, firmly, signalling to me that she would handle this on her own and confronting the police.

The constables behind the inspector seemed eager to rush in and make vigorous arrests but the inspector, seeing that she had decided to cooperate, gestured to them to stand back. A policewoman was summoned and she searched Di, I assume for weapons with which she may harm herself or the children. Two policemen came and took charge of the children.

'Going back to daddy-mummy,' one of them said, as he knelt down and the child rushed into his arms as though she had been waiting for just these words. The other child was more reluctant, scared. She clung on to Di's nightdress, but Di detached her fingers gently and delivered the girl, lifting her up, into the policeman's arms. He put her down. The inspector, or he may have been a superintendent or some other rank, took charge, shouting instructions to the men and cars in the street.

'You will also have to come with us,' he said to me. 'Aiding and abetting.'

Diamond was handcuffed by the policewomen and two of them led her away protesting that she should be allowed to change into her day clothes. They were having none of it. She was led out of the house in my aunt's nightdress and into a van.

The children were spirited away into a car across the street and a policeman came and tried to put handcuffs on me. I was about to submit when the officer intervened and said it would not be necessary. He addressed me by name and looked me in the face with searching curiosity. It was as though he was trying to understand what made a person of my sort turn into a kidnap and ransom merchant.

I was led away to a police car and I could see, as I got in, that there were five or six people, men and women in crimson costumes arguing with some policemen, shouting in English that it was their right. The women were shouting 'My baby, my baby' and 'Thank God!'

And out of the corner of my eye, skulking in the back of the car from which these white parents had emerged, I thought I saw Praful.

I could have been mistaken. The allergy pills. Of course. The chemist. Praful knew Di suffered from chronic hay fever. The chemist would have told him what I bought. He would have come to his own conclusions.

Why had he led them here? Jealousy? Reward money from the parents? But I told myself as I was driven away that I had caught the glimpse of a shadow and surmised that the silhouette was his. It may not have been at all.

SAKET AND I STAYED IN the Bombay ashram for six weeks. In that time there were no sessions or lectures from Saket to the old devotees who came and sat under the same tree in silence before their Guru's empty chair with only a pillow on it. No words were said. The chair and the mats were placed under the trees and the dwindling crowd would gather each morning, sit under the trees and meditate or think about their stocks and shares.

Saket was quite content installed in the Guru's room and I had my own room on the ground floor at the back. Saket had renamed me Govinda. He wanted, he said, a break from the past. I was the first person to be renamed by him and I accepted it. I wasn't to know then that he would, in the years to come, make a business of this changing people's names.

I kept away from Shanti and Bhavnani. I was aware that they didn't want me there and I had been forced upon them by Saket who was their golden goose. I had nothing to do and neither had Saket, except for his trips to Poona with Bhavnani and occasionally with Shanti who accompanied them to the site of the new ashram which they said was being constructed there under Saket's supervision.

They would go by car and return the same day or the next. Saket told me it was a grand estate in the rich part of Poona which some widow had left to the ashram in Bhavnani's name. I knew which widow. I knew the story. I was there when Shanti told Bhavnani that the plot had worked and the court had signed the papers and she had slipped and called him her 'jaan'. I couldn't quite remember. She may even have said 'jaanji '.

Saket would view the dwindling band of widows sitting before the empty chair under the tree in the suburban Bombay compound and call them idiots.

Shanti, more than Bhavnani, knew that Saket couldn't be the successor to Swami Vishwadeep and take on his spiritual congregation. He was a joker they had found and they would build a new pack around him.

I went with Bhavnani and Saket to our old haunt, the beach and, attracted by Saket's flowing beard and the long white robe which Shanti had given him, a crowd gathered. There were some hippies who recognized him from the previous encounter and came running to him shouting, 'Speech, speech'. They were brazen fellows.

Saket looked like some kind of imitation Christ by the waves, looking out over the choppy Arabian Sea.

'Tell it like it is, Master,' one of the hippies said.

Indians had gathered when they saw three white men and two girls scantily clad in shorts run towards us.

It's never difficult to gather a crowd in India.

'None of that "master" shit,' he said. 'You've been reading Kahlil Gibran. It's rubbish. Pay no attention to it.'

The hippies laughed.

'You got it, that's what he reads. Wow!' one of the girls said.

'Then think about the difference between entertainment and enlightenment,' Saket said.

They waited.

'Entertainment makes you believe the itch has stopped. While it lasts. That's why it's addictive. You need more when it stops. People watch soap operas every day. Enlightenment gets under your skin and kills the cause of the itch. Now which is better?'

Mr Bhavnani started distributing cards from a pack he held in his hand. He was giving them to the hippies and any foreigner who had joined the growing and curious crowd. Not the Indians.

We didn't allude to it on the way back to the ashram after sunset, but I was sure Saket knew what was going on.

He called me to his room that night.

'Govinda, I'm going to play,' he said.

The hippies brought their friends.

Saket was not given the same spot under the banyan tree that Swami Vishwadeep used to preach from. This was a different tree, a different chair, new mats.

He looked, after weeks of having done nothing except travel to Poona, grateful for the role he was playing, grateful for working for his gradually exalted status.

And that brought the distance, bought the distance I felt, from me.

Who was this child I had saved from being murdered? Who was the boy I had given up my own life to educate and send confident into this world? Where was the renunciation I had been taught to understand, absorb, live by and surrender myself to?

I felt the alienation in every gesture of his now.

Shanti and Bhavnani were openly saying to me that I seemed to have no role in the ashram to come.

'What arrangements have you made, my friend?' Mr Bhavnani asked me one day at our breakfast of dosas and tea.

'Arrangements for what?' I asked, though I knew very well what he meant.

'For when we have to leave these premises and go into Poona.'

'I can come with you to Poona. I can serve Saketji. Do translations,' I said.

'But he is speaking in English. There will be no need for translations. You hear him every day. The audience is building.

They are wanderer people, but rich. They are willing to come to Poona when this place closes down.'

'He wants me to be with him. I have been with him since he was a boy,' I said.

'He is now no longer a boy. He is our Guru. We are the boys. You are the boy. He doesn't need you anymore.'

That was all he had to say. No theft of jewellery, no subterfuge, just simply the discarding of the unnecessary.

'I'll talk to him tonight. See what he has to say about all this,' I said.

I went to Saket's room that night.

'I thought you'd come, Govinda,' he said. He was sitting upright in bed, writing.

'I am glad you're here. I want to read you tomorrow's lecture.'

'Pleased to hear it,' I said, squatting on the rug by his bed. 'Are you finished?'

'No,' he said, looking me straight in the eyes. 'It's you who are finished.'

Then he began to read.

'You have debts in life. Don't repay them. There is no such thing as debt. You don't owe anybody anything, because the action you are supposed to be grateful for was something they could not help doing. We are all children of the circumstance and the waves of universal happening. We now realize that the flap of a butterfly's wing and a zillion zillion such occurrences are the causes that make the effects that we call happening. Be grateful to no one. Your parents did what they had to do. Your teachers did what they were paid to do. Your priests stumbled in their darkness. You may be the result, you are the children of light, but as the children of light you have no use for gratitude. It is the effect's tribute to an imagined cause.

Jesus would have said treat gratitude as a sin, it is only the passage of those who have, giving to those who have nothing. The receiver is part of the flux and has nothing to be grateful for. Gratitude is the burden of the past on us donkeys tied to the harness of the future. Gratitude is attachment, leave it by the wayside. Gratitude is sentiment and not real emotion. It is the prompting of the mind, an acknowledgement of a weakness and dependency in the past, a call to subservience in the present. Leave it behind. Be the Sufficient Self...'

'I know what you are saying,' I said, interrupting him for the first time ever.

'No, you don't, Govinda. You don't know what gratitude does to the one who receives it. It makes him arrogant, believing it to be his due. Do you know why God is inactive? Because he believes that human beings ought to be eternally grateful to Him.'

'I can see that,' I said.

'Then see it in yourself. Your lifelong expectation of gratitude from me has paralyzed you. It has made you lazy and dependent.'

'You were coming round to saying I should leave the ashram?'

'For your own salvation, something you've stopped pursuing and something it is my duty to force you to do.'

'Duty? I thought you didn't believe in duty.'

'Call it my last weakness then, my last act of gratitude.'

He then took the papers on which he had been writing and from which he read me his sermon and tore them up. He scattered them on the other side of his bed. So had the sermon been written only as a farewell note to me?

I sat there for a few seconds. He was staring at me. Then I got up and left.

I went to my room and packed my simple things: three sets of clothes, a toothbrush, a ping-pong bat which I had carried with me from the monastery and two pens. Then I walked with my plastic sports bag out of the ashram and into the suburban Bombay night.

I WAS INTERROGATED IN THE police cell for three days and nights and then sent to the local jail. I didn't see Di, but was repeatedly told by the interrogators who walked into my cell at all times of day or night to question me, that she had confessed that we were in the kidnap together and that I should now confess to my role in the crime.

I told them the truth, only altering one fact. I said that she had arrived in the dead of night with the two children and that I had concealed all three of them from my aunts who left for their conference out of town without any knowledge of the fugitive and her victims having taken shelter in their house.

The police also told me that they had spoken to my aunts who professed to know nothing of Diamond or of the two children. My aunts had, on my telling them where I had left my passport, gone to retrieve it.

The questioning was harsh and not very well conducted. The two interrogators in charge of extracting a confession simply repeated that it would be best for me if I told the truth and ignored my protests that I had already told them all I knew. They asked about demanding ransom. They said the written English on the ransom note was in the style that a person educated in England would use. I said it wasn't, it was very bad English.

How did I know?

I said a friend of mine, a journalist, had shown it to me.

The note, they said had not been made public and so no journalist would know about it. I must have myself written the note to be presuming to make any judgement about the quality of its style or grammar.

I said the note was leaked to the journalist by a policeman who took a bribe. It was the only time the interrogator came close to assaulting me. He stood over me and lifted his palm as though he was about to slap me—and then relented.

'We are not listening to accusations against police officers. You are here in interrogation. You are not interrogating the police force,' he said.

'You are stating the obvious. I happen to know I am here. Now can I see a lawyer?'

'You can see nothing. You are a kidnapper and a blackmailer and you are making love to a foreign woman who may be an Israeli spy.'

This was a new tack. The interrogators had a technique of trying to catch me out by making wild statements and asking questions out of the blue: 'So what did you do with the jewellery?' and 'How many months were you in Mahabaleshwar with her?'

This one startled me.

'She has confessed herself.'

They went through the whole routine again and on the fourth day I was removed from the police cell and taken to what I took to be a remand wing in Poona Central Jail.

It was then that a lawyer was allowed to see me. My aunts

had hired him having heard from the neighbours what had taken place.

He was called Cyrus Bode, a young man in his late twenties perhaps. He introduced himself when the warders brought him in.

'They won't let us use the advocate-client rooms,' he said. 'Some nonsense. I would have to apply to the courts and that might take weeks, so I hope you don't mind my seeing you in this horrible place. Not that the private conversation cells are any better.'

'What am I charged with?'

'Nothing yet,' he said, 'but they could get nasty. What have you told them?'

'Only the truth. Nothing more.'

'How did you meet Diamond? By the way I am representing her and have seen her several times.'

'How is she?'

'She's okay. My question.'

'I met her outside the ashram. You know I am doing a story for a British magazine.'

'Yes, that's fine. Did you tell them about meeting her at Praful's after that?'

'No.'

'Why not?'

'Because it gets complicated.'

'Why does it get complicated?'

'Have you talked to Praful? Where is he?'

'He left town. We think he took the money and visa and ran.'

'What money?'

'The kids' parents. I believe he went to them and asked for a reward if he gave them information about their children which would lead to their recovery. They would have given the earth, those people.'

'And they did?'

'The British kidnapped girl's mother is French and she belongs to an influential French family connected to the French government and part of the deal was a Schenghen visa, a permit to enter Europe for Praful and money when he got there. That's a surmise, because he got a passport and he bought a ticket from the local travel agent. We imagine he's in Europe by now. Beyond questioning by the police. They shouldn't have allowed him to escape.'

'Escape?'

'Yes, he was, according to Diamond, in the plot with her.'

'The kidnap plot? And why did the interrogator say she was an Israeli spy?'

He smiled cynically and shook his head.

'They are idiots. Di is under threat of a very, very serious charge. Kidnapping is worse than rape and close to murder. I am trying to get the Israeli embassy to say that she was on some diplomatic assignment for them. They always protect their own and have been known to not stick to the strict truth. If I can pass her off as some sort of diplomat, I can whisk her away to stand trial abroad. These idiots have taken my submission as an admission that she is a spy. Welcome to India—or the Third World.'

'What can they charge me with?'

'Sheltering her. Not reporting the presence of a criminal to the police. That sort of thing.'

'This nonsense about the ransom note? That I wrote it?'

'We are allowing the police to feel that they are piecing together the story. Praful wrote the note, of course. Di didn't know anything about it, but he told her that he was setting up decoy tracks to give her more time.'

'Why didn't she go to him? Why to me?'

'She stopped trusting him. He drinks and she knows. He was acting weird and obviously wanted to make some money out of it. She wants nothing except her child back and she came to you because she thought you had connections with the ashram and would be a discreet and intelligent go-between.'

'She told you this?'

He nodded.

'I suppose they could do me for spying for Israel.'

'I think not,' he said.

THE JAIL ROUTINE WAS MISERABLE. I shared a cell with five others and we slept on mats on the floor. We were exercised three times a day in the yard and fed daal and hard chappatis made of muddy grain.

Bode came to debrief me once in the week I was there and then again, accompanied by a police officer and a deputy superintendent or governor of the jail to tell me that I was free to go. There were no charges being levelled against me. He brought me some clothes my aunts had sent and drove me across the Bund Garden bridge that crosses the Mulla-Muttha river to take me home.

'Where is Di?' I asked.

'It's a matter of confidentiality. I am not free to say,' he said.

'I'm not asking for vital statistics, just where she is or how she is.'

He was being officious.

'I can't discuss one client with another,' he insisted, 'But I can tell you that they dropped all charges against you because of testimony that others gave.'

He wouldn't explain himself. I presumed that he meant Di, who may have said she forced her way into the house.

My aunts were relieved. They were waiting on the veranda, watching the street for my arrival. They had stayed away from work that day to receive me, they said.

'You see, I told you, you should stay away from these people.'

'Which people?'

'These foreigners.'

'But living in London I can't stay away from them. I mean what will I do for sex?'

'Why do you talk such rubbish? You know what I mean. No one said all foreigners are bad, but some of them—we don't understand their ways.'

'I'm learning,' I said.

They were resigned to suffering my irony. The jail didn't supply us with newspapers and they had kept the lot for me. The local and national newspapers ran stories about the kidnapped children being found and the kidnapper being heroically captured by the police in a house in a Poona cantonment. Some of the reports gave my aunts' address. The reports said Diamond was in a maximum security women's prison out of town and the prosecution were preparing the case against her. One or two reports quoted Cyrus Bode and his contention that she somehow had diplomatic immunity.

Israel didn't have a consulate in India, but a spokesman for the Israeli Government said it had no comment to make on

Diamond except to verify that she was entitled to travel on an Israeli passport which she had not been using.

The next day a crimsone called at the house. A young man in his crimson uniform, he came in a car driven by another devotee and rang the doorbell. He asked for me as I answered the door and I asked what he wanted.

'Bhagwan would like to see you. To speak to you personally. It is a very great privilege,' he said.

'I've done my interview,' I said.

'He wants to discuss these events of the past few days. The kidnapping and all that. You do know that the ashram used the influence we have with politicians and the police to have you released?'

'No, I didn't know that, but if it's true, I am grateful to the ashram. To whom shall I address my thanks, though? "The ashram" is a bit of a collective noun isn't it?'

He smiled.

'Tell Bhagwan himself. He is the ashram and the ashram is him.'

'You guys never go off duty, do you?'

I WENT THE NEXT AFTERNOON as appointed, taking care, as I had been reminded, not to use soap when I bathed that morning or any aftershave lotion or anything else with perfume.

They were expecting me at the secure gates and, after putting me through the routine of sniffing me from top to toe, I was led through the ashram grounds to the chief's house and into the same room in which I had first interviewed him.

Saket was, as on the last occasion seated on the floor on cushions. There was a white mattress and more cushions for me to sit on and he indicated, with a rather royal gesture that I should seat myself on them. I did.

'Farrukh sahib,' he said, 'do we ever know what motivates us to do things? We can only say that the strongest impulse is the cause. "I hit him because he abused my mother sort of cause."' He grinned and his flowing locks shook with his head.

'But we all know that more complicated actions have more complicated causes.'

'I must thank you for securing my release, Bhagwan, I was told...'

'Don't call me Bhagwan, you don't believe in God and since it means "God", that reduces me to nothing.'

'I can stick to "sir" I said. 'So thank you, sir.'

'Good, now your friend Diana...'

'Diamond,' I said.

'Yes, of course,' he said emphatically, as though he had made a major blunder in alluding to her by the wrong name.

'You see how the subconscious works? She called herself Di and I always said to her it was an unpleasant command. The Western girls don't notice that it's the same sound as "die!". I have even got a disciple called "Live".'

'Livia?'

'I suppose so,' he said.

Why were we talking rubbish? What had he called me here for?

'We are thankful to you for persuading her to give up her victims and surrender, poor child,' he said.

'I don't think I persuaded her at all, though I could see there was nowhere for her to go.'

'But you took the poor damaged flower in,' he said. 'And she expressed her gratitude.'

I didn't know what he meant but his faint ironic smile irritated me. Was this the beginning of some subtle blackmailing tactic?

'She wanted her child back, that's all,' I said.

'Yes, her child. A daughter called Sapphire. We know about that.'

'I thought you saw to it that she didn't get her child back. Isn't that where it started?'

'I don't know where it started. As a Parsee you will be thrown to vultures when you die. Do you get nightmares about that?'

'No, I don't think about it and I have no fear of vultures. I think we should eat them at Christmas or Parsee New Year and then they can eat us when we die and we get a merry circle. Now tell me where her child is. What have you done with her?' I realized that was not the respectful way of address to which the fellow was accustomed, but he was not in the least disconcerted by my words or tone.

'There is no child,' Saket said.

A new conundrum?

'The child was with Di's husband in the ashram,' I said.

'There is no husband,' Saket said.

'Where have they gone?'

'Nowhere. There never was a husband or a child. Only in Diana's head.'

I didn't correct him this time.

'Yes, Diana's head. She wanted to be called Diamond and made up hippy parents who gave her a funny name. There were no such parents. She didn't know her parents. She was brought up in a home. She came here alone. Searching for something.'

'But you expelled her from the ashram. I saw her trying to get back and your people kept her out.'

'For her own good, Farrukh Sahib. She was fantasizing about many things, writing leaflets about all sorts of lurid imaginings. You remember we talked about D.H. Lawrence? Well, he was a very bold and straightforward writer, but if he read the leaflets that your Diana wrote, it would make him blush. The world knows that Bhagwan pronounces but he makes no idle and petty judgements. But still, I can tell you, they were filthy things.'

'She showed them to newspapers, some of the things she said were investigated,' I retorted.

'What is investigation if it's done by a fool? That reporter, Praful Surti? Shameless. He took in this poor demented creature for his dark and dirty sexual pleasures. What can you think of someone who takes advantage of a woman with delusions?'

'I thought your sex clinics and therapies were for ... well, people with problems or delusions or whatever you want to call it.'

'The object here is cure. To heal. Not exploit. The therapy is the only one in the world and supervised by true psychiatrists, not frauds like Freud and Jung.'

'Yes, I met one of them.'

'At the Vijay cafe, of course,' he said. He was right. Had someone been watching me? Following her?

'Don't we all live in our own reality? The enclosed fantasy we create from impressions and then our only contact, our only path to knowing, if it is shared is language, words?'

He paused, the accomplished charlatan. 'And we have so carefully taught ourselves how to misuse these. To deceive ourselves with those same words and create worlds for ourselves we cannot share with others because they are dreams, fantasy fabric, disturbances in the ether. Diamond, Sapphire, Ruby, Emerald—and all of them mean "I am desperate, I am human, I am lost, help me."'

He smiled benignly. Even this was a pose.

'I have to think about what you've said,' I found myself saying.

'What I've "said", yes, words again, perhaps my attempt at fumbling towards you with what is real.'

'And perhaps some tactically placed thoughts to... how shall I put it... distract or derail me?'

He laughed. It was genuine.

'I like it. You the railway engine, me the terrorist tampering with the tracks.'

'Why did you call me here?'

'You begged for the first interview. This one is given freely. I would hate you, Mr "angel face", to write something in your London newspaper which would be so outrageously untrue that it would make a fool of you and end your career as a writer. Truth exists, even though Dostoevsky, with whom you are no doubt familiar, doubted it.'

Always the steel of threat concealed in the glove of polite, even engaging if trite, philosophical discourse.

'I am most grateful for your concern and will, seriously think about, even investigate what you've said. Can you tell me where Diamond—or Diana—is?'

I stood up.

He looked with that intense commanding gaze at me, still reclining on his cushions.

'Yes, I can,' he said. 'The poor child is being examined and helped in a secure psychiatric unit. She faces some very serious criminal charges. If the doctors conclude that she performed these acts while not of sane mind, there is a chance that the Indian penal system will show her some compassion. I will personally see to it, please don't worry.'

He raised a hand, more in dismissal than reassurance. I left.

So that was the game: Diamond was Diana the fantasist. Crazy, not guilty. Just crazy.

I WAS ON THE ROAD again twenty-eight years after we had set out from the Taptavan monastery. Saket was right. There is no place for gratitude in this wide world. It is one more form of attachment. And now having nothing and only the sky for a roof, I began to think about the things I had long forgotten, about how to detach oneself and not care about hunger and how to absorb pain as part of process. There was nothing else to think about.

I could have got myself a room and resumed my life as millions in the city did, looking for the next meal, the next rupee.

I didn't. I walked that night and the next day and the day after that. I walked out of the city and went south. I slept by the roadside and scavenged for food with the dogs of the villages I passed through, waiting outside the cafes and tea shops to see if they would throw me a crust.

I walked for weeks and then for months till my slippers were worn and torn on my feet and the clothes I had were tattered with washing and wear.

I was going south and followed the coastline. I was passing through Goa, walking along the shoreline when I came upon a boatman talking to three white teenagers, travellers by their appearance. They were asking him if they could hire him and his considerably large boat, with a fishing crew of four, to sail them down the coast.

I stopped and listened to their encounter. The boatman didn't understand what they were saying. They may have been German or Scandinavian and were trying their accented English on him.

'He doesn't get it,' I said. 'Do you want me to translate?'

The travellers turned to me. 'We have money, we showed him,' one of them said.

'His craft looks fantastic,' another said.

'He doesn't know what you want,' I said. 'His boat goes out to catch fish and comes back. He doesn't go down the coast.'

'But he can take holiday. We pay,' the first one said. He told me how much he was willing to offer and that they wanted to go towards Cochin in Kerala along the coast. They wanted to know how long it would take.

I explained in Marathi to the boatman and I mentioned the sum of money they had mentioned to me. His eyes lit up. He had never had such a proposition before.

He talked to his crew.

'I think you've offered them much more than they would expect for such a trip,' I said.

'Ah, we are bargaining upwards for a change in India, eh? But that is our budget. Does he want to take it?' the first traveller asked.

'I think he will,' I said.

The boatman asked me to tell them that he accepted their terms but would like to see the money first.

I explained.

The travellers looked at each other.

'We will give him only one third of the money to start,' the first one said. 'And you explain that we don't carry any money. We carry cheque and will pay more when we get to Cochin and then more when we come back to Goa and go to the bank. We carry not much so he won't find temptations to murder us and throw us in the sea.'

I translated the message as clearly as I could, omitting the bit about possible murder.

The expedition set sail that evening. The travellers said they would pay me to join them on the boat and be their translator.

On the slow and exhilarating trip, my first at sea, I made friends with Jan, Jacek and Daryush. They were Poles and the first two were painters. Daryush was a photographer by trade. They spent their time during the day sketching scenes from the boat and the coastlines where we anchored and the nights staring at the stars, strumming a guitar and singing.

We became friends and they told me that they were spending time absorbing India and then they intended to spend some time in an ashram. Daryush said he had heard of this Guru of Words, a teacher called Saket in Poona to whose ashram a friend of his had gone. He asked if I had heard of him.

'No, I haven't, not this one,' I said. 'But then India is full of gurus,'

'I believe this one is quite remarkable. I want to go and listen,' Daryush said.

The round trip took two months. The boatmen told me that the mechanical trawlers which powered their way away from the coastline and used machines to trawl and haul their catch together with the refrigeration plans that had come to the West coast had killed their primitive fishing industry. They were lucky to have found these travellers and this assignment.

The travellers and crew became fast friends and by the time the round trip was over, Jan and Jacek had mapped out a business strategy for Yeshwant, the boatman. He would use some of the money he had earned on this journey in fitting a toilet and adding some comforts to his hardy wooden boat without ruining its character. They would then help him get business as a tourist vessel from the tourist trade of Goa. They asked me if I wanted to be part of the package as translator and facilitator.

Yeshwant pleaded with me. I was indispensable, he insisted.

Which is how for four years I became a tourist guide on the *Samundar Rani*, the Ocean Queen.

Jan and Jacek's sketches and Daryush's sumptuous photographs of sunsets and off-shore views, were plastered all over Goa as advertisements and the lad helped Yeshwant design a half deck, tiny cabins, bunks and facilities on the capacious boat which had been built to carry miles of net and tons of fish.

Between trips I stayed in Goa and over these years saw the crimson people arrive and infest the tidal tourist population. Of course I heard of the guru as the Guru of Sex as the Prophet of the Last Word, as the Swami of the Senses, as the God to end Gods, as Supreme Friend and, some said, Supreme Rogue and The Devil.

I managed the accounts of the *Rani* and I knew that Yeshwant, with all the effort and enthusiasm he put into his little industry was not yet a rich man.

One day a young man, an Indian, came to our Samundar Jetty from where our boat and now several other tourist fishing boats set out. He said he wanted to speak to me. He knew my name. I was summoned by the people from whom he was making enquiries and I went out to meet him. Did he want to book a trip? How many people? We were booked for the next four months, unless it was a single day trip and…

'Will you be my guest for tea at the Taj,' he interrupted. 'I want none of those things.'

I went that evening and he said he wanted to buy the *Samunder Rani* and its business. He called it its 'franchise'. I told him it was up to Yeshwant to sell or not. The young man said that I must know that a single boat was not going to make anyone's fortune. He was going to buy a fleet of these tourist boats and turn them into sea-going hotels. Would he want to retain the crew, I asked.

'Good God no,' he said. 'We shall have colourful youthful and multilingual crews.'

'So Yeshwant won't run his own boat?'

'When he hears how much I am paying for it, he won't want to run anything, he'll just want to take the money and run.'

I said I'd speak to him. The young man wanted an immediate answer but would wait till the next day to find out if Yeshwant was in principle agreeable and then place his bid on the table.

The bargain was sealed the very next day. I was out of a job. Yeshwant had never dreamt of getting three times what he estimated his business would bring in the next ten years at the rate at which we were operating. Of course he gave me some money.

I took it in cash and set out back for Bombay on a train.

As I slept on the train in a first-class compartment for the first time, it began to rain and a banging on the train window woke me up.

The train was moving at speed now through the dark countryside and behind the silhouetted desperate knocking figure at the window, the lightning bolts flashed. It was a nasty night. The person at the window had somehow leapt onto the foot rail or some other foot hold when the train paused in the wilderness and was now begging to be let in.

'Bhai sahib, please! Brother, for pity's sake. God will bless you, just till the next stop. I will die here. I beg you.'

I unbolted the heavy door and held my hand out to assist him in. The rain came in with him. He was drenched, his wet hair over his forehead. He came in and as I turned to bolt the door behind him, he grabbed me by the throat from the back and dragged me into the coupe compartment. Another man appeared in the doorway armed with a machete. He too was soaked, but his eyes gleamed. He must have been on the other side of the door or crouching on the wooden ladder of the coach.

The first man commanded me to be silent. 'Not that there's anyone to hear you, you disciple of a donkey,' he said. The man with the knife opened my canvas case and went through the contents. He found the bundle of money, the bagful of notes which Yeshwant had given me as severance and in gratitude. They couldn't believe their luck.

'Where did you get this? Are you a thief, uncle?' the man with the knife asked.

'No, I am a beggar,' I said.

The train slowed down and came to a stop. In the distance I could see the dim lights of a small town. The thieves tied my legs and my arms behind me with my own sheet and with some wire that one of them was carrying wound round his waist. They took their loot, jumped out of the coach and disappeared into the night leaving the door of my coupe open. It swung shut as the train moved and banged to and fro all the way to Bombay where a station porter in his red shirt found me.

TO GET OBSESSED WITH SURVIVAL and where the next meal was coming from would have lured me slowly into the jaws of concern, self-obsession and death. Ask not what the connection between these is—it was now as clear to me as the bright morning sun that woke me as I slept on the pavements of Bombay.

Yeshwant's fishing trade had been displaced by the trawlers and now business had moved into his small enterprise, put temptation his way and swallowed it. Yes, I was fated to be out of the current of change.

I took up residence in a temple by a filthy creek just north of Bombay and was employed, in exchange for food and a place to sleep, to sweep the temple and remove the detritus that pilgrims left—leafy wrappers of food, overripe vegetables which they brought as offerings, discarded rubber slippers, used sanitary pads, stubs of bidis and even locks and whole heads of hair which some ritually shaved on the plinth of the temple and, their ablutions done, left there for me.

I lost track of the years. The panditji, the priest of the temple had a transistor radio which he kept switched on most of the day. I occasionally heard on the news some talk of Saket and his ashram, some mention of Poona and the happenings there.

In a discarded newspaper, I read that a minister of the central government was journeying to the Taptavan monastery in the Himalayas to pay tribute to his guru who had departed this material sphere. The minister was calling upon fellow Jains to charitably endow the work of the monastery. The writer of the article then listed the statistics of Jain wealth.

So The Enlightened was dead. I couldn't put the memory of him or of the monastery out of my head and that night I found myself walking north on the routes out of Bombay. I might as well have a goal, I may as well resume and direct my wanderings. I had had enough of pushing that particular temple broom.

It took me twelve days to reach Taptavan. I had no money and had, in the guise of a saddhu, with ash on my face and a wooden staff which I availed myself of from a pile of a villager's firewood, the ability to beg food. I hitched rides in trucks. The drivers would stop for me and gain merit, dropping me at their watering holes and perhaps forfeiting that merit by spending their break from the road with some lady of the night.

I would get out of one truck and go up to the other truckers at the tea stall or at the pump, those going my way and beg a connecting ride.

The last twenty miles I walked.

I got to the monastery and found it much changed. There were metalled and cement roads leading to it and cemented milestones by the side of the road telling motorists or travellers how far it was. An arched gateway had been built and half a mile below the monastery, at the side of the stream across which I had escaped with the boy Saket, was an artificial meadow in which several cars were parked. There was a road bridge and a wooden footbridge now across the stream we used to perilously cross. Prosperity had come to Taptavan. Or was it corruption?

I climbed the last steep stone path, still unmodified, to the doors of the old fortress-like structure. There were other routes to the top now and one for cars. Hardy and dedicated pilgrims took the stony way. There were hundreds of them now, city people, one old man with a servant holding an umbrella over him as he climbed, and monks with the uniform I had worn all those years coming and going in pairs from the monastery.

I climbed steadily and two monks passed me by. One of them looked steadfastly in my face. He stopped in his tracks. His companion stopped and looked back at him as I passed. He was thinking.

'Are the ceremonies over?' I asked his companion.

'Two more days,' he said, and turned to his companion who was still searching my face.

'Chandrika!' he said.

'The name is Govinda,' I said.

'No. It's Chandrika. You have returned?'

The voice was not familiar but now I knew who it was.

I thought he was going to ask me about Saket, Rahul, the boy with whom he had played coonjis, but he didn't.

'Govinda, sir. A saddhu, a beggar who repents being alive, yes.' I fell into the role easily.

A flicker of doubt crossed his face and he passed me, resuming his path down the mountain.

There were crowds of pilgrims in the courtyard of the monastery. This courtyard, more or less as I remembered it, was built of stone by some king of the mountains in the era of Buddhist construction. It was square in shape and owed nothing to the Hindu architecture of earlier and later centuries. It had pillars along cloisters which led to the dark inner chambers without windows.

I sat at the back of the crowd as the bells were rung and a ceremony of chanting, lasting an hour or more, was conducted by fifty monks.

The front rows of the congregation sat on mats and were very distinctly the rich. Crowded at the back were the villagers from the hills around, peasant folk who had looked to this monastery for generations as some link to a destiny beyond scraping a living on these mountain terraces.

Towards dark, I walked along the stream and down to the village which was now alight with electricity. That I was dressed as a saddhu, a Hindu holy man, didn't seem to bother either the monks or the devotees. All religion was one, all renunciation equal to the blessedly unquestioning. As I walked through the village main street, accessible now to cars, bicycles and hand-drawn rickshaws, with here and there a cement and brick structure between the older wooden stilted buildings, I was offered food by a shopkeeper.

'Guruji,' he shouted after me, holding out neatly folded chappatis and some cooked vegetables on a brass platter. I turned round and accepted his charity.

'You can sleep in our doorway,' he said. 'My wife will get you blankets and a pillow. It gets cold.'

I accepted. His doorway was a small wooden veranda, a few steps up from the street.

I was asleep when a car drove up in the early hours of the morning. It stopped and Harkishan, my charge when he was a boy, Rahul's companion, the monk who had spotted me, stepped out. I sat up in my blankets. The street was deserted and the night dark but the headlights of the car stayed on.

'Chandrika, I have someone who wants to meet you.'

I didn't know if I could keep the pretence up any longer.

'I understand that you don't want to acknowledge me, but you took a young man away from here and I know that and only I have known it and dreamt it all these years. Chandrika, I told nobody that I had seen you go. The Enlightened and the other monks said you had drowned and that the young boy Rahul had left the material world. I knew where you had gone and until tonight, I told no one.'

'And who have you told tonight, Harkishan?'

'His mother. Wouldn't you have? Why would I live with the lie? She came from the city and she sought us out, the companions, she said, of her son who died at the age of seven. She wanted to see us. All these years she has mourned for him. She is a widow and came here a month ago and The Enlightened repeated the lie about Rahul and his instructor having been taken into the hereafter on some appointed day. She asked him what they had done with the bodies, but he said that the Infinite had taken them into itself.

Today I told her. She is in the car, Chandrika. Come with us, please. If you still have a heart.'

I climbed out of the meagre moth-eaten blankets the

shopkeeper's charity had lent me. I didn't know what I would say or do.

There was an old woman in the car. I couldn't see her features in the dark. Harkishan opened the front door for me and I sat next to the chauffeur. He got in the back seat with the old lady.

'We should drive away from the monastery. Mataji, I will get you a room in the tourist hotel in the gorge.'

He instructed the driver to move on and he pulled out a mobile phone, dialled the hotel reception whose number he seemed to have stored and identified himself. The monastery obviously did business with this hotel. He explained that of late he had been the hospitality secretary in charge of the comfort of rich pilgrims.

'Saddhuji, talk now, speak to me, tell me the truth. I can't believe what I have heard. Tell me it's true.'

'Not now, Mataji, wait till we get there and you can see whom you are talking to. Chandrika has agreed to tell us the truth.'

'So tell me now, my heart will break,' she said in Hindi. 'Just tell me again he is alive.'

I didn't reply.

'No. Wait till we get there,' Harkishan insisted. I thought she was crying and I fancied that he put his hand on hers in quiet reassurance.

The hotel was an old large and very elegant colonial house. A young man in a crumpled suit was waiting for us in the oak-panelled lobby. There was no signing at the desk. The young man showed us up the grand wooden staircase with its worn carpet, to a suite overlooking the front garden. This was to be Mataji's room and the young man said another one at the back of the house had been allocated to me. He looked me up and down. I wasn't the sort of guest his hotel was used to entertaining.

Mataji was an old lady with a gaunt face. She wore an off-white sari and the rolls of fat on her stomach hung over the edge of it showing her huge navel like a key hole. I could see in the deep hooded eyes the features of her son. What was I to say to her?

Water and glasses of lassi were brought as we sat down in the lavish hotel suite.

'Why do you say he is alive? How could he have lived? The astrologers and The Enlightened, they have told me over the years that he will be reborn…' All this in Hindi.

'Maybe he has been,' I replied, also in Hindi.

Harkishan interrupted.

'Just tell the truth. Please.'

'The truth may not be what you want to hear.'

'How can truth be something to avoid?'

'If it destroys faith?'

'Was yours destroyed?' Harkishan asked. It was a goad and an honest enquiry.

'Yes,' I said. 'But there is no reason to destroy that of…of someone who has believed all her life.'

'Chandrika, she is going to leave all her money to the monastery. If I think I am going to hear what you have to tell us, then that would be a mistake. A mistake for the world. It would be fuelling the lie.'

'So you have lost your faith too?' I asked. 'When was that?'

'What do you think?' he asked. 'I have spent the last ten years ferrying rich people about, taking their money, seeing them make fools of themselves in return for the meagre hope that their souls are separate from their bodies and life is not just the machine that breathes, the muscle that pumps and the chemicals that can form thought patterns.'

I smiled. So this meditation leads to the same questions?

'Alive?' she asked again.

'The Enlightened instructed me to kill him when the stars didn't do it of their own accord. I'll say this for him, he actually believed that the stars had a mandate to kill your son, but some miscalculation prevented it. So he thought I should step in and assist faith. He was destined to die on his seventh birthday and that should be achieved one way or the other.'

'You took him away,' Harkishan said. 'And then? Where is he today? What did you do? Is he alive?'

'Does he ask about me?'

I turned to her.

'No, he doesn't ask about you. He knew nothing about you.'

'But you were with them when they came to take him from me?'

I hadn't seen her that day or she me.

'I was. I believed what they told me at the time. Or I half believed it, if one can do that.'

'They held me down when they took him. I was persuaded to give him away but my heart said no. And they told me that was wrong. Was it wrong?'

The old woman looked from Harkishan's face to mine. Perhaps she suspected that we were in a lying conspiracy ourselves. He spotted the doubt in her face.

'My story and your story that you saved him can only be believed if you tell us where he is and who he is. If he's...'

'Yes, he is still alive. Very much so.'

The old woman got up and rose slowly to her feet trembling. I stood up too and she embraced me. She was crying and shivering. I held her.

Then she went back to her sofa and sat down, exhausted with sobbing.

'Did you look after him?'

'Yes,' I said. 'I didn't want to murder him and then there was nothing left to do but look after him. I realized that I had lived a life of nonsense and realized it was not too late.'

She let out a little cry.

'Then me, what about me? I counted the days till he was seven and then I was grateful that he was dead. My husband said so and I pretended to believe it and told myself that all my life. All my life. Look at me now. I am finished and everything I thought and lived by has been swept away and not by him being dead, but by my child being alive and the knowledge coming to me that he lives! His life destroys mine, don't you see?'

I did see.

'No, it's not too late. Chandrika will tell us where he is. He will take us to him, won't you?'

'Yes, but he doesn't know that he had, and has, a mother. He was told another lie that he was given up to the ashram and that he must believe that his parents don't exist. The child is told that all parents are but instruments of the wheel of destiny that is bound to our births and rebirths.'

'Tell me, Chandrika, Govinda, why did you come back to Taptavan?' Harkishan asked.

'I don't know,' I said. It was the truth.

'Fate brought you back,' the old woman said.

'I don't believe in fate. Not since I knew that those who are destined to die don't die.'

'There was a mistake. That can happen.'

'There was no mistake about The Enlightened instructing me to murder your child.'

'He was my Guru. He was my husband's Guru. How can we believe this?'

'Then believe what you like,' I said. 'Believe that your son is dead.'

I stood up. I just glanced towards the door. Harkishan jumped between me and the door.

'No, you are not going anywhere. We believe you! She believes you. I saw you leaving with Rahul, companion of my childhood, I saw you save him from the water and take him away and never return to Taptavan.'

'I want to believe you,' the old woman cried as though she was demented now. She grasped her white hair with both hands as though she would tear it out in a theatrical gesture straight from some television soap.

'I want to believe you. How could I have believed anything else? Where is he? Who is he?'

Again Harkishan interrupted.

'I can see that Chandrika is reluctant to speak now. Mataji, your son is alive. The miracle has been confirmed. Before you go to him or he comes to you, you must think of what it could mean. We can sleep now and talk in the morning.'

'But the saddhu...'

I knew what she was going to say. 'No, the saddhu won't run away. What you will hear from me you will have to trust and it's best that you begin to trust me now!' I said.

The old woman looked at Harkishan and he nodded.

'I will stay,' he said. 'I must think too. This is the first time I have heard why you left Taptavan.'

IN THE MORNING WE SAT in the gardens of the Himalayan View Hotel. Outside my hotel door I found a track suit with the hotel's logo, left for me to change into, presumably because the hotel didn't want to acknowledge to their other guests that a half-naked saddhu with tangled hair was sharing their space. The hotel also provided me with a toothbrush and shaving kit.

I shaved my straggly beard off, bathed and shampooed my hair, strands of it going white, and tied it in a ponytail using a piece of sash I took from the window curtains. In the dark blue track suit and pony tail, I looked like an American tourist of Indian origin out for my pre-breakfast jog.

I joined Harkishan and the old lady who now, instead of her white sari wore a plain cream one. She looked at me anxiously. No need for preambles.

'I took him to Delhi and sent him to school and looked after him as an elder brother would. We didn't have much money, but he was so clever he got scholarships everywhere and then he went to university and spent all his time reading and teaching me, getting me to read all sorts of things in English and Hindi and Sanskrit. To this day he reads everything, even foreign languages. Philosophy, novels, poetry…'

'Is he married? Does he have children?'

My hand flickered asking her to be patient.

'No, he is wedded to something else.'

I didn't quite know how to tell them.

'What does he do?'

'He began to lecture and then got thrown out of one college and then... how to put it...he picked up disciples. He has become quite famous. He preaches and the newspapers have written about him.'

'What does he preach? Not this...my God!' Harkishan had stumbled on an inspiration.

'No. He has his own religion. There's a lot about sex.'

'Saket!' Harkishan said.

'Yes.'

'Rahul is Saket?'

'Yes.'

'I don't believe it.'

'Who is Saket? Why is my Rahul Saket?' the old lady asked. She hadn't heard of him.

'He chose the name. Partly as a joke. That's what he is like. They call him Bhagwan, even,' I said.

'So what does he do?' the old lady asked.

'He has become a guru,' Harkishan said.

'That is so wonderful, God takes away and he gives back.'

'I don't know if you'll like what he has given. Rahul, Saket runs an ashram in Poona now where a lot of foreign people come and he doesn't believe in the old religions.'

'In the end all religions are one,' the old lady said.

'No, no, Mataji. They are not. They are very different, in their beginnings and their ends. And this fellow, Saket, we studied his writings and lectures. He is a Satanist. He mocks all religions and says one has to make one's own good and bad,' Harkishan said.

'Worshipping Shaitan?'

'No, nothing like that. Harkishan is going too far with all this. He talks philosophy without God. Jainism and Buddhism don't have gods either.'

'We have to have gods. We all have gods,' the old lady said.

This wasn't the time to start a philosophical discussion. Harkishan was deep in thought.

'My God, he could have been anything else,' he said with a note of despondency.

'I have to meet him. It doesn't matter what he is. He is my blood. It ran cold the day I gave him into someone else's arms.'

'My arms,' I volunteered.

PRAFUL RANG THE DOORBELL.

'They've taken her away.'

'I thought you'd gone to France.'

'Don't be silly, yaar, why would I go to France?'

'There's the Louvre, Mona Lisa, the Eiffel Tower, Sauvignon Blanc from the Loire, cassoulet…'

He looked blankly in my face.

'What's funny, they're putting her in the madhouse,' he said.

We were standing on the veranda. I was surprised to see him.

'They've had her certified, as suffering from schizophrenia.'

'I saw you in their car when they came here to arrest her. You told them she was here, didn't you?'

'Yes. The chemist told me about the hay fever medicine so I knew—and they were closing in, so what else could I do?'

'What do you mean? You took their money, reward money for informing on your "spiritual" wife.'

'I thought we'd need the money. To hire lawyers, to fight them. They are vicious people.'

There was a bench on the veranda and I asked him to sit down.

'So you didn't take the money and run?'

He was aghast.

'What? What do you think I am, a snake?'

'I saw you skulking in the car. I didn't know what to think, except that you led them here and collected the reward.'

'I did. What else could I do? That chemist, my dear, may have gone for the reward if I didn't. He is a bastard, he has seen you with her and started asking me if my wife has run away with the great writer from England. He started giving me a sermon on how unfaithful white women are and that I was well rid of her. He said he could see you didn't have hay fever and started putting two and two together. He could have gone to the police to claim a reward. I had to go to the parents of the children before he did. Money, we'll still need the money!'

'What about her lawyer, Cyrus Bode?'

'He is a son of a bitch. He was the one who suggested they put her in the mental hospital.'

'I want to see this Bode,' I said.

We went to Bode's office together. His clerk said he was in court but would be back for lunch. We waited. He didn't seem in the least surprised to see us or even to see us together. He invited us in to his shabby little office on the first floor and sat us down.

'I understand your concerns, but it was the only way to keep her out of jail. She would have gone down for a very long time for kidnapping. The British and US Consuls had sent their lawyers down to work with the police.'

'But you know and I know, Cyrus, that she's not insane.'

'Insane is not an accurate word. But what you know and I know is not material. If three psychiatrists, doctors whose qualifications are recognized by the court certify that she committed acts for which there was no *mens rea*, no culpability or intention to commit a crime, then the court decides on a different basis. The scales of justice, weighing crime and punishment are put aside. Think about it like that.'

'And she was happy to plead temporary insanity or whatever?'

'She was not at all happy, but that helped our case. She kept insisting that she has this husband and this little child and that she came with them to India, but we proved that she came alone, went to the ashram alone etcetera. The husband and the little girl are part of the schizoid fantasy.'

'So Sapphire doesn't exist? How can you know?'

'I am an advocate, I don't have to testify but we had ten people from the ashram to testify that there was no husband and no child and that the women she shared her accommodation with witnessed many episodes of this illness.'

'These bastards would say whatever their Guru or those vipers around him get them to say. They drugged her and forced her to have an abortion...' Praful was saying.

'Yes, yes, yes, all that was brought out. She started screaming and had to be restrained. Look, I know you gentlemen are very friendly with her and we are all acting together in her interests. I am applying to get her deported and then she can be free. You must help me by keeping quiet and withdrawing from this case.'

'How much have they paid you?' Praful asked.

'You are the person who takes rewards and bribes, Mr Surti, not me. I get my professional fees and not a rupee more.'

Cyrus's lips twisted in an evil smile and he nodded ever so slightly, knowingly.

'She wasn't lying. There was a husband and child and they must have smuggled them out of the country. I am going to prove it.'

'And then what? Prove that she is not crazy and get her sent to jail?' I asked.

We were walking down Main Street and he paused and looked in my face, thinking this over.

'If Cyrus gets her out, that's best for her.'

'And best for you, I suppose. She can join you in London and you can fuck her joyously,' he said.

'Don't be ridiculous. You said she was your spiritual wife.'

'She may have been, but you have contaminated her. You have raped her, seduced her with your fancy talk and writing books and shit which betray the neighbourhood that brought you up...'

The rage gushed out of him.

'She is a filthy bitch. I saw you looking at her and her looking at you. I didn't need no fucking chemist to tell me you were buying her pills. You know what? I asked him if you'd gone into his shop to buy condoms! I knew she'd go to you. And I knew you'd try and take her from me, because you've always thought that I am a punk and you and your sister, you thought we were dirt, didn't you? All those years.'

This was more than jealousy. It was as though he believed or felt deep down in his gut that I had taken some meaning of his life away.

He spat in my face and immediately winced, blinking and leaning back to get away from the expected blow. But I didn't hit out. My arms were by my side. I didn't move for a few seconds and then I wiped the spit from my face with the end of my shirt. He was backing away and then he turned and ran, not like the prematurely balding thirty-year-old that he was, but like a child fleeing in panic.

THE MENTAL HOSPITAL IN POONA is in a part of the town which is named after the institution. The district is charmingly called 'Yerawda' a perverted Anglicization of the Marathi words 'Yed wada' which mean madhouse. In my youth it was an isolated end of town, across the river. The British had built a jail and mental institution in close proximity to each other on desolate land and now, as the town expanded, it had become very much part of the city with industrial development, military and air force encampments, housing developments and lately shopping malls, hotels and clubs.

The mental hospital, though much reformed by changing and liberalized attitudes to mental disorder, still presented a grey stone exterior and barred windows which gave it an inescapably medieval, forbidden look.

I turned up at the secure gates and made my enquiries. I expected to be kept waiting for hours and my expectation was well rewarded. In the end an administrative officer of the institution came out to the small, bare, grey-walled waiting room and went through an explanation of the visiting procedures but nevertheless told me that the patient I wanted to see was still under criminal investigation and so I was denied permission to visit her.

She asked me what relationship I bore to the patient and went on to say that very close relatives or indeed husbands and wives could gain access as they would be deemed exceptions to the exceptions.

I thought for a moment of confusing things further by claiming to be Di's husband, the one she was insisting against all evidence that she had, the one whose existence had been taken as part of the schizophrenic hallucination. I didn't.

I took a taxi to the dissident's cafe. Vincent, the expelled sex-therapist was, as I hoped, there, sipping coffee and reading a dog-eared paperback.

'You know our friend has been certified,' was the first thing he said. He showed no surprise, as though he had expected me to turn up at some point.

'I tried to see her but they wouldn't let me,' I said.

'That's not a problem,' he said. 'A senior practitioner there is a mate of mine. I've been feeding her stuff she wants to use in her practice—she's my disciple—and she can get round the system there any time. I can call her now and you can go straight back and she'll get you to Diana.'

'Why did you call her Diana?'

'That's Diamond's name, isn't it? I don't give a shit, she can call herself Diabolical if she likes.'

I sat down and ordered a coffee.

'Tell me, does she have a husband and child or not?'

He smiled and blinked repeatedly, as though that would help him recall the right answer.

'To tell you the truth, I don't know,' he said. 'See Our Beelezebub, the great and reverend Guru, always isolates the people that he is using in his own little experiments. Once he has chosen them to have his little ways, he doesn't encourage them to mix with the other devotees and people in the ashram. And then the two Sparrow Hawks, Aunty Shanti and the Pimp, enforce this isolation.'

'So what she says, what she wrote in the pamphlet about being used in all sorts of crude ways for sex by Saket is true?'

'You are quite hot on this category of "truth" aren't you?'

'Please, no games about "truth" and imagination and crap. I mean it's either true or not true and you either know or you don't know,' I said.

'Oh we're back in court are we?'

'Just tell me what you know. I mean is she telling the truth? Is she crazy?'

'You are talking to the world's expert on there being no such thing as "crazy".'

It was exasperating.

'I know what you mean, but I know that you know what I mean and what I am asking you.'

'I am absolutely sure that I don't know what you are asking me. But since you are an "evidence" man I'll tell you that my pal the doctor, the female shrink in the hospital, interviewed ten people from the ashram, "normal" people who swore that Diana arrived with no husband and no child. There was also a medical examination and there was no evidence of an earlier abortion, even though she insisted that it had taken place. Not that one can be certain about abortions and miscarriages. So Mr Evidence, shall I call Ms Shrinkji and get her to give you access to your woman?'

I nodded and he asked another crimson expellee on the next table to lend him a mobile phone. He made the call and said yes, I should take a cab back to the hospital at six that evening. There'd be a change of shift and she could smuggle Di to a room where I could meet her. He said if I drove up to the gate around six she'd take me in.

'Look I'd love to tell you that the ashram is bullshit and they've contrived and connived and sent her husband and child away in a private plane across borders so no passports are stamped and their presence is never detected, and that I was there when Beelzee screwed your lady, but you are a truth and evidence addict, so I'll stick only with what at this moment I strictly know.'

I thanked him.

'You couldn't give me a small loan, could you?' he asked.

'Sure, how small?'

'Five hundred rupees? More if you can afford it?'

I gave him a thousand, which at the time I could afford.

'I'll give it back,' he said.

I made a gesture to say 'whenever' and I left the dissidents' cafe.

I went back to the hospital. The doctor, the woman he called Ms Shrinkji, who said her name was Dr V. Heblikar, took me into the building and through several dark corridors. I could hear the clashing of cymbals, the accompaniment of harmonium and tablas to which Marathi devotional songs were being sung. The voices sounded melancholy, distant, clear, without hope...

Di was in a room by herself. Her face was puffy and her hair unkempt and bushy and as I looked into her eyes I could see they were glazed over. She was heavily drugged. Ms Heblikar took me in and then left the room telling me I had ten minutes and no longer and she would be outside.

'I only found out this morning. Where you were,' I said.

'They won't give her to me,' she said.

'Was it horrid going to court? They kept me in the cells and asked me all sorts of idiotic things,' I said.

'I can't remember anything,' she said and she grinned as though she found this loss of short term memory funny. 'But every day I ask that Sapphire be taken away from that bastard and from the ashram because she is in danger. That person will stoop to anything to satisfy his lusts—men, children, animals, anything. You don't know who he is. Get me the fuck out of here. I must get to her.'

'Look, Di, the ashram insists that no husband and no child exist.'

'Ah, they've bought you out?'

'No, nobody's bought me out. The fellow, the Bhagwan himself called me and spoke to me. I think he was anxious that I'd write about you and the children and your motives. The American child you picked up...was involved...so the US press would be very interested. Especially if it came from me because I was there when... when they came for us.'

'You've gone over to their side,' she repeated.

Then she walked past me to the door and went out. I tried to stop her but I saw that she had encountered Ms Heblikar outside who took charge of her with a firm, steering hand on the small of her back.

'Ah good, the time is actually up,' she said leading Di away with no attention to me.

She walked Di down the corridor where two male attendants stopped her. Ms Heblikar told them in Marathi to escort Di back to her ward and she then turned and came back towards me saying she'd show me out.

'Tell your friend Vincent that the hospital has read his report and they have checked his credentials etc. and everything is okay.'

'Which report is this?'

'She was his private patient in the ashram clinic, wasn't she? He was treating her for what he is calling chronic dissociation?'

MATAJI AND HARKISHAN CHECKED INTO the most expensive Poona hotel. They wanted me to stay there too and to go to the ashram and invite Saket to 'finally meet his mother'. I declined to get a room at that hotel. Even in the Himalayan luxury resort, I had taken the blanket off the bed and slept on the floor. It was the habit of the monastery and the discipline of poverty and I had grown to like it. I felt uneasy in the 'seven star hotel' as they liked to style it.

I got myself to a traveller's lodge near the Yerawda jail and said I would think about being their intermediary. I told them I was not sure whether I had been permanently dismissed from the ashram. I was sure that Shantiji and Mr Bhavnani would like to see me dead, because I always posed the threat of reminding Saket of other times and loyalties, other uses for his glibness of mind and tongue.

I told them I didn't even know if the final lecture on gratitude, being a sentiment for which no one should have any use, was a ploy to tell me to get out of his life because I was of no further consequence to it, or whether I had mistakenly and over-sensitively taken a philosophical treatise as a personal dismissal.

Harkishan said I was the only living witness to his removal from his biological parents. I was the agency of his adoption into the monastery and I was, through those circumstances, the only person capable of providing the evidence Saket would need to believe that this was his mother. Surely he would want to be reunited with her, a man who had never known a parent or only known a caring, but poor, surrogate?

I didn't sleep much that night. The smell of kerosene pervaded the cheap guest house and was very oppressive. It was a warm night. I washed in the morning in the one basin provided for the fifteen clients of the bedbug-infested hotel.

I called on Harkishan and Mataji who were waiting for me. I had made my decision. Eight or more years had passed. He had become something and somebody I didn't know. Perhaps I had too. Why would I want to face Saket and invite him to where his mother was? Why would he leave the ashram on my invitation?

'Because Mataji has decided that she will not leave her fortune to the monastery after all, but she would give it all to her only son. You go and tell him that.'

'His ashram is already rich,' I said. 'The Americans and Europeans are flocking in. They are the only ones allowed, even though he seems to be making exceptions for rich Indian donors like top businessmen and film stars. He's already got several, dozens, of Rolls Royces and Mercedes parked in the ashram. Don't you read the newspapers?'

'He will want to see his mother.'

'Of course he will. Wouldn't anyone on earth? But will he listen if I tell him?'

'Who else can tell him, my son, but you. Go tell him. Tell him his mother repents believing the lies that self-deceiving people told her. Say she is repentant for having denied her own womanhood by sacrificing her child.'

'No, no, don't say all these things,' Mataji continued. 'I will explain them to him myself if I can stop crying. You are bringing me a grown man. This is a stranger, but he is from this!' She held both her hands to her belly. The apron of fat with its staring belly-button wobbled. 'From here. A woman never forgets that, Swamiji.'

'There is another way,' I said. 'Why don't you and Mataji go to the newspapers and tell them the story? There is a local paper here and from there it can become universal news and you can say I am here with you and was a witness to the whole of his life. Shanti and Mr Bhavnani always pay attention to newspapers.'

Harkishan thought about this. Mataji looked at him for guidance.

'You are afraid of him,' he said.

'Yes,' I said.

'You brought him up. You taught him how to read.'

'No, no, he knew how to read before he was five. Yes, I taught him English. I had to learn it myself, but we both spent years doing nothing but reading.'

'Then go to him and tell him the truth,' he said.

I didn't reply.

'We should do what the Swamiji says. Go to the newspapers,' Mataji said.

THEY DID. THE *POONA MESSENGER* had the biggest scoop of its existence:

'God Has A Mother' was the headline. The desk clerk at the inn where I was staying showed it to me. I knew it was to appear. It was an article with the byline of Praful Surti who had come with his photographer team to the hotel and heard the story from my own mouth, substantiated by Harkishan who testified that he had grown up in the Taptavan monastery under my guidance and in the company of Rahul who had later become Saket.

This Surti interviewed Mataji who said all she wanted was to be reunited with the son she had lost.

The story was carried by every newspaper in India and some newspapers and magazines abroad.

Then the ashram and Bhagwan issued their own statement:

A group of confidence tricksters has come forward to claim that they can now reveal the parentage of Bhagwan Shri Saket and a woman of the appropriate age has come forward claiming to be his mother.

Bhagwan wishes it to be known that he has no mother. The gang that has made these claims of acquaintance with Bhagwan Shri Saket are criminals or fantasists. Perhaps, in their deluded minds they believe in some 'bullshit' theory of reincarnation and that's why they have made up the name of some monastery where Saket was supposed to have been imprisoned in his youth. They should tell the truth and attribute their memories to some previous life…

I recognized the style. This may have been a press release from the ashram, but it was a transcript of a lecture that the man himself had given to an assembly. I knew the pauses for effect, the cadences, the conceits, the insertion of 'bullshit' to impress the Americans.

The report, the retaliation went on:

Think about it. A mother, at a ripe old age wants to confess the sin of having given her infant away for the sake of some astrological belief. There is no excuse today. We now know that the constellations that the Greeks or Persians or Sanskritik astrologers drew in the sky are not perfect pictures at all. One of the stars in the picture of The Crab is one billion miles away. Another is ten billion miles away. The light from the latter is ten times further away and by the time it reaches us, by the time we see that star, it may not exist.

The rebuttal, familiar to me from all those years ago, this talk of modern astronomy trumping flaccid astrology was on radio and in the *Messenger* and Surti was on the trail of the story. He came to see Mataji and Harkishan again and asked for their reaction.

'Everything we said is true,' Harkishan said. 'There is more—ask Chandrika here. He brought him up and has witnesses. He was thrown out of a college where he was lecturing, for obscenity.'

I stopped him. 'Mataji wants to find her son so she can give him her large fortune.'

This made Surti sit up.

'A fortune? How much is involved?'

'What can we leave behind but ashes,' Mataji said. There was some studied guile in the old woman still. She wasn't one to spell out to the press an inventory of her worldly holdings.

'A fortune?' Surti repeated. 'This is the big news.'

I had blundered. Harkishan looked at me as though he wished he could use psychic powers to make me vanish.

'Her spiritual fortune,' I said.

Surti knew I was backtracking and also that no one would be willing to speak openly about this.

The story as he wrote it was a masterpiece of twist:

The woman claiming to be Bhagwan's mother and her advisors, two young men who guard her as though she was their personal property, hints at the idea of a fortune changing hands. But which hand will be the giver and which the receiver? Bhagwan Saket owns several Rolls Royces, custom-made Mercedes and several properties worldwide, it is believed, are in the care of his trust. There is also land and, if persistent stories are to be believed, money in foreign banks.

Bhagwan and the ashram roundly reject the idea that a long-lost mother has returned to claim her son and are alert to the fact that claiming maternity is certainly a way into the 'sect' and the ashram's fortunes.

The item was read in the ashram and there was a rebuttal in the following day's lecture. It was printed on the ashram's presses and issued as a free sheet leaflet all over the town:

MOTHER OF GOD

MARY WAS UNDOUBTEDLY THE MOTHER of Jesus Christ. We take that on trust because very many good men contrived to tell us that. Christ acknowledged his mother, but made her no part of his church. He belonged to his Father, not the earthly one, the one in heaven and was part of him. It is where he ultimately came from and though there was the mechanism of a womb and a pregnancy involved, he did not acknowledge that womb as the ultimate source of his soul.

Today we know that the soul is an illusion and it is now logical to think that the womb is the source of life. It is this thought, logical, scientific even, because the cells of one's very being are nourished and made of what passes through the umbilical cord. Yes, logical and damning because it is the first attachment one forms, child to the womb that bore it—child to the mother—and the chain of attachment is born, perpetrated, cast. The infant takes milk from the

> breast— attachment. Hunger, thirst, passion, possession— attachment.
>
> Where are the men and women who will say they have no mother? Let's adapt the yogi John Lennon's wisdom: 'Imagine there's no mummy, it's easy if you try…'

I could hear him pause for the audience's laughter. None of the others could have written that. It was his answer to us.

Nevertheless, that evening Mr Bhavnani turned up at the hotel. We were having tea in the gardens and he came through, his bloated, belted belly before him and as he approached the table at which we sat under a garden umbrella, he bowed down and touched Mataji's feet. She and all of us were shocked.

'Forgive him,' he said. 'He is full of his philosophy because it is the only thing that filled the emptiness left by the mother's love. He will love you, he will hundred per cent love you.'

He stood up, looking flushed. He had been sent on this mission by Shanti. The hint of the fortune to be left had brought him here. He looked furtively at me and I smiled at him.

'This is Mr Bhavnani, he is like a father to Saket,' I said. He didn't get the mockery in my tone.

'No, no, no, no,' said Bhavnani, striking either cheek gently in a gesture of warding off the evil eye. 'He has no father.'

'Oh, yes, he had a father,' Mataji interrupted. 'My late husband, who made me give him up.' She held the end of her sari to her eyes and perhaps shed a genuine tear.

'We are convincing him,' Mr Bhavnani said. 'He will acknowledge you.'

'You think he will?' Mataji asked.

'I am sure, but I can't put time-limit,' Bhavnani said.

'Do I have to die before he forgives me? I have done the worst thing a mother can do. What made me do it? What made me cut off a piece of my flesh, my brain, and give it away?'

'Saket would say it was supreme non-attachment. I am sure he admires the act,' I said.

Harkishan looked at me in the same way again. This time it wasn't a blunder. This woman had given away her child because some superstition told her to. There was no sparing her.

'Mataji, are you really surprised that he has rejected you? You sent him away to die! You know in the monastery, while I was bringing him up, taking your place—yes I had to wash him as an infant and feed him milk—I often wondered what kind of a she-devil could give away her child to some belief in cold stars.'

Harkishan stood up and touched me on my shoulder.

'Don't do this, Chandrika. Go, please go.'

I left them without a further word. I thought I'd go back to Bombay the next day and went to my crowded guest house.

I was in the room I shared with four other travellers, early the next morning, sitting on my string bed when Harkishan and Mataji arrived. They were shown into the room where my room-mates were wrapped like mummies, from top to toe in stretched sheets, their faces covered in the ends of the sheets and the contours of their bodies evident. I was already awake and sitting up in bed contemplating leaving.

'Come back with us,' Harkishan said.

I packed my bundle. I found they had paid my bill. Mataji was waiting for me in the car and Harkishan indicated I should get in and sit next to her.

She touched my cheek as I did.

'He was angry with you, but yesterday I knew you were telling the truth. You were his mother, not me. You gave him milk and washed him and patted him when he cried.'

'When these infants cried in the nursery we left them alone till they quietened down, exhausted,' I said. She ignored the comment.

We drove back to the hotel and Harkishan led us into a conference room.

'I want to make you a trustee of the estate I wish to leave to him. You are close to him, the closest anyone has ever been. I trust you. You will convince him to love me or at least to acknowledge me and the wrong I have done him and then he can take what is rightfully his,' Mataji said.

'What do you want me to do?'

'Sign a paper,' Harkishan said. 'We've called a lawyer to draft the trusteeship.'

'I am a simple man, a monk. I know nothing about these things,' I said.

'There's nothing to know. If anything happens to Mataji… God forbid…'

Mataji touched my cheek.

'You are my real son,' she said.

The lawyer with a female assistant was ushered in by the hotel staff and he was introduced and began some explanation which I didn't understand. They asked me to sign ten times on different sheets of paper.

I signed without reading what I was signing.

'I can see you are not reading, Chandrikaji,' the lawyer said. 'So the bottom line is you hold the property, accounts and assets in trust till Rahul, now known as Saket, wants to accept them as his inheritance and signs the papers acknowledging his parentage,' the lawyer said.

Mataji was required to sign more papers than I was and Harkishan and the lawyer's assistant witnessed the signings.

We would go back to Bombay, Harkishan said and I could come back to Poona and try and meet Saket and bring him round.

Our car descended the Ghats and the air became hotter and humid. Mataji fell asleep in the back. The car traversed the coastal strip and we entered the stink of the city on the sea.

We didn't disturb Mataji who was clearly emotionally and physically drained.

The car stopped outside the house and Harkishan tried to wake Mataji up, gently at first and then holding her arm and trying to shake her awake. She was still and her jaw had dropped. He put his hand on her heart. He felt her pulse and there was panic in his eyes. I was looking over his shoulder.

'Mataji, mataji,' he kept saying. He fanned the flies off her face. The spittle dribbled out of her dropped jaw. She was dead.

I was now the trustee, the virtual owner of several prime commercial buildings, housing estates, a thick portfolio of shares, bank accounts and sumptuous flats.

It was outside the building containing one of these sumptuous flats that we discovered that Mataji was no more. We didn't know how long we had been travelling with a corpse. Her soul passed from her body or the movement of chemicals that we call life, stopped.

The papers we had signed would have been filed by now. As we hastened upstairs, Harkishan instructed the servants to summon Mataji's personal physician straight away. He would know what to do.

I looked around. It was not the flat from which all those years ago we had taken the fated infant. That was an older flat in the heart of the business district, gloomy, echoing, sparsely-furnished. This was a sumptuous, modern penthouse on the nineteenth floor of a seaside building with carpets, well designed furniture and curtains through which the breeze of the Arabian Sea came into the spacious open-plan living room. Such was the evolution of the styles of the rich.

The servants panicked. All of them went down to the car, the women raising a wail and holding the ends of their saris to their faces. The physician did know what to do. He was a young man and had looked after Mataji for ten years as his father had done for forty before him. He ordered the hearse and his secretary managed the funeral, scheduled for the same evening before sunset.

I found myself, adopted son designate, walking around the funeral pyre and setting it alight as was the ancient custom of Hindus, even though Mataji was not formally a Hindu. This was the funeral that the young physician and Harkishan between them had contracted, and in the end, in the metaphysics of the disillusioned Harkishan, an end was an end.

THE WHISTLED MELODY IN THE night again. Praful. Why was he calling me? I got into my trousers and shirt and went through the house to the street.

The dogs of the neighbourhood had heard the signal and had begun to bark. Praful indicated that we should move away and led me fifty yards up Synagogue Street.

'I forgive you,' he said.

'I thought you were the one that needed forgiveness,' I replied.

'You have to understand, I love her. You just used her.'

The anger had subsided. He was asking for my pity.

'Look, I need your help. Everyone's been bought off. My editor won't publish. The Bombay papers are not interested. The police just laugh in my face.'

'About what?'

'She does have a husband and a child. She was seduced and was pregnant and was drugged and aborted. I believe her, you see. She is not mad. She is telling the truth.'

'How do we know?'

'What do I do for a living? I am a journalist. Not like these other Indian journalists who copy press handouts. I check things out. I found the man who can bear witness to the truth, the whole thing, but again they bought him out. He has disappeared. You know him.'

'I don't know anyone who has confirmed Di's story,' I said.

'Vincent. The sex therapist fellow,' he said. 'He confirmed everything she is saying. He wasn't treating her for schizoid disorders. She and her husband came here not for spiritual business, but because he was crazy and she had read somewhere that this prophet of sex and his ashram cured people.'

'It's not what Vincent told me. And I think he even handed over some report to the hospital here.'

'He was paid to. You don't know this town, this country, anything can be bought. Price is all. It's contagious. Even when these goras come here and get absorbed in the culture, they acquire a price tag.'

'So if Vincent was paid to lie…'

'I paid him more to tell the truth.'

'How did you pay him? From the money you got for betraying Di and me and getting me thrown in jail? From the kids' parents?'

'No. I was doing this story about some woman claiming she was this devil Bhagwan's mother. A very rich woman. Old. The God said he wanted nothing to do with a mother, because he couldn't very well acknowledge a family—it would ruin his image and for him image is all—and he has no need of money. So the woman left the money in trust to a fellow who brought Saket up. The guy is now a trustee and billionaire. I have been talking to him and told him about Diamond and that she was sent to the asylum. That bastard Vincent, with his psycho qualifications impressed the court. He signed some affidavits to say he was treating her for schizophrenia.'

'Vincent told me himself when Diamond was there that he doesn't believe in schizophrenia,' I said.

Praful sneered.

'You don't learn do you? You don't see what's happened to this country. If I pay you to believe in schizophrenia, then you do. Listen, I took money off the millionaire monk and paid him to change his story.'

'Did he?'

'Sure he did, he said he'd sign a legal document to say she was completely sane.'

'And that would get her out?'

'It may have done, but he's disappeared again. I can't find him. They've got at him. They've probably got rid of him or kidnapped him…'

'Or given him even more money to disappear?'

'I don't know, but he's gone and I have no proof of what he told me. He wouldn't let me record it.'

'What were you going to do?'

'What this witch Shanti and her fat court jester, this fellow Bhavnani, don't want me to do. A story about forced sex and abortions, madness, selling passports...'

'What do you mean selling passports?'

'Why do you think these idiot Americans and Europeans who come to the ashram have their names changed? He changes their names to some Sanskrit bulltoss which he gets out of a dictionary and pretends that he has read their "auras" and from the energies they exude has given them their "real" Sanskrit name.'

'Sounds a harmless enough game,' I said.

'Yeah. Except that Bhavnani then offers them a new Ashram Passport with their new name and the fools surrender their US passport or UK or whatever, which then gets sold on the black market in Bombay by the immigration racketeers.'

'But then the mugs get stuck in India with silly passports.'

'They can go back to their embassies and say they lost them. That's if they really want to get out. They can't afford the truth to be told. The whole business will bomb.'

'If that's true, it should,' I said.

'You are here to write the truth. In a British weekly. They can't interfere with that.'

'You told me they could!'

'I know, but you could try. They may not find out in time.'

'So what do you want me to do?'

'Write the truth. Say Vincent told you.'

'He didn't tell me. He told me the opposite.'

'But he told me.'

He looked anxiously at me.

'But if I write it and...'

'The Indian papers are sure to pick it up.'

'And then what happens to Diana? She is not crazy, so the law then moves in and says she should be tried for kidnapping children.'

Of course he'd thought of that.

'Before that, I'll get her out of there and out of the country.'

'How?'

'Bribes. The trustee man, the new millionaire. He used to be a monk but I am sure he'll give me cash if I explain the whole thing.'

He searched my face.

'Will my editor in London believe this story? It sounds crazy doesn't it?'

'Doesn't every news story? Wars and murders and religion?'

'We've got used to all those. This is the kind of story which will be believed if it emerges from the proceeds of a court case.'

'Just write it,' he pleaded.

I DID START WRITING IT, but I was interrupted.

Three policemen called at the house that day. My aunts were at work or it would have startled them.

'We want your computer,' they said. 'You have been reported to us as a person making child pornography. With kidnapped children. You have cameras? Mobile phone?'

'Don't be insane,' I said.

'Who are you calling insane?' the chief policeman said.

'It's manner of speaking,' I said. 'It means it's an absurd suggestion.'

'Why were the kidnapped children brought to this house?'

'You can have a look at the computer, there's nothing on it. And what you are suggesting is disgusting,' I said.

'Persons who are doing these things are disgusting,' he replied.

They demanded to be shown all the computers in the house and they took my laptop away. They said they'd arrest me too if I protested and that I was not to leave town till their investigations were completed. I told them I had no camera, but they searched anyway and examined my phone.

The notes and the article I had written went with the laptop. The paranoia was infectious. It crossed my mind even as they spoke that the ashram had had the police confiscate my computer, but then reason kicked in. I could write whatever I wrote again and send it from another computer or write it by hand and send it. They could have arrested me if they wanted to stop me.

They did want to stop me. Almost immediately after the police left, Mr Bhavnani called. He rang the bell and I answered. He greeted me as though I was a long-lost friend.

'So long since we spoke,' he said. 'You must not mind my coming and interrupting your daytime.'

'Not much of a daytime. The police came round with some nonsense about collecting child pornography. They've taken away my laptop.'

'That is very terrible,' he said. 'These Indian police, they are terrible chaps. They can actually put the images or anything they want into your computer and prove anything. This is a disaster. You should never have let them take your computer.'

'It's not that easy to fabricate stuff or plant stuff in computers. They have dates and times attached to the files,' I said.

'True, true, but they can falsify their own diaries. They can say they took the laptop only ten days later. You don't know how cunning these chaps are. You have lived out of the country too long.'

I wasn't going to invite him in and he sensed that.

'I have my car waiting and I want a dear word with you, sir. Please come with me where I can be your host.'

'Say what you want to say right here, Mr Bhavnani. I have no desire to be your guest.'

'That poor lady, your dear friend, we are thinking of helping her to get released from the mental asylum and getting her back home to abroad where she came from. It is such a dangerous place. You don't know how much suicides there were of the patients taking their own lives last year and this year. It is happening all the time.'

'You are threatening to kill her,' I said.

'What kind of language are you using, sir?'

'Not the language of blackmail that you use,' I said.

'This is not the time for any temper of this sort, Mr Farrukh. If you are caring for this lady you must help her by making her see the truth. Poor child, she is heavily delusioned and some foolish people are taking her delusion stories seriously.'

'I get it. If I write any reports based on what she says, she may commit suicide. Is that it?'

'I came here to help you. And also tell you that the Bhagwan would be most happy to receive you any time and give perfect interviews as you please,' he said.

'I don't please,' I said, and shut the door in his face.

He knew that I had absorbed the threat. I waited behind the shut door and heard his car pull away.

THE TIRTHANKARAS, THROUGH THEIR MEDITATION and practice of detachment from the quest for earthly happiness, achieved their nirvana or moksha. For all the years of my adolescence and youth I was brought up in that faith and believed it with every atom of my being – till I realized that my being was itself atoms and space and my consciousness the near-miraculous product of chemical flux. Is that a realization or the adoption of a model of being, just as the duality of body and soul is to the religions of the desert?

And now six bedrooms, five servants in the house, a chauffeur and two cars and a lawyer and a family accountant who came twice that first week to advise me as to how much money I held as a trustee and then to tell me that the papers I had signed placed no obligation upon me to hand over what I held to Saket. Mataji's Poona lawyer had either framed an imperfect set of documents or Mataji had made some leap of trust, signing her estate over to me to give to her son when he came to acknowledge her if I wished to.

She believed in the process, the inescapable wheel of karma and kindness to all creatures and now she was aware that her son's karma had not condemned him to death and his next rebirth, but that she had in abandoning her flesh and blood to superstition condemned herself and lost all the merit of her previous lives. Was she making amends to regain it?

I was when I first arrived at the flat installed, by the servants who looked at my clothes and generally assessed my appearance with some derision and suspicion, in the master bedroom. I took one look at it and moved myself to a smaller room which didn't face the sea but looked out on the compound towards the next high-rise building with the expensive cars parked on both sides of the dividing wall. Even there I couldn't get myself to sleep on the bed.

The cook who doubled as the serving man knocked on the door at eight the next morning and it was the thought of his contempt for me that got me off the floor and scrambling into the bed before I invited him in with his tray of tea and a hot roti.

The rituals and even the food of the house were far from those of the strict Jain household from which we had received the child. That household would have had a Jain cook, almost a priest. This one had an old Goan retainer. Mataji's regret for abandoning her child was not her first withdrawal from the life and inheritance and traditions of her husband's family. The widow had gone some way towards assuming the attributes of merry, affluent Bombay.

The day after the funeral, Harkishan got in touch with her distant relatives and told them that the lawyer had stated that they had no claim to her wealth and property, being third and fourth removed cousins, but we, that is I, would give them a small stipend each out of moral duty. She had no siblings and her husband had quarrelled with his so they didn't care to pay their posthumous respects.

She had a nephew's nephew, a young man who came to see me. He told me he was the only one who talked to her or kept in touch and it was he who had induced her to sell the old property when her husband died and bought this seaside penthouse for half the price of that chunk of decaying central real estate which had been demolished to build office blocks and part of the new Bombay Stock Exchange. He had invested the rest for her. He very tactfully insisted that he hadn't touched a paisa of her money.

I called the lawyer after he had gone. The young man deserved something more than the tiny stipend the other relatives had. The lawyer said he knew the man and would look into what could be transferred.

Being in charge of so much wealth made me realize its worthlessness and yet as the weeks passed I began to take some of the comforts it afforded for granted. I would order a vegetarian meal in the morning and the cook filled jugs of lassi and fruit juice and left them in the two fridges, one in the kitchen and the other in the dining room.

I lay in the beds and watched television. I used the cars and the chauffeur to take me to spots to which I had never been. I went into the bar of the Taj hotel and turned back at the door. I couldn't face such a place.

And what was I doing in these new clothes that Harkishan, who had now moved into the flat with me, had bought from clothing shops in malls. I had, when I came out of my brown robes, only worn clothes from local markets—the long kurtas and coarse pyjamas of wanderers and then the shirts and trousers worn by the faceless clerical millions who rode the local trains of the commercial metropolis burdened with tiffin boxes and worries.

I told Harkishan I was going to Poona. He didn't question me. He said the chauffeur would drive me there; it would take the car three or four hours. I said I would go by train. I took a rickshaw to the station, bought a second class ticket and went.

I walked to the ashram and was admitted as a member of the public for the late evening lecture. I made my way to the front and squatted with the crowd of men, women and children, all in crimson, sitting and buzzing with talk and chanting around me. Then silence, and the Bhagwan was driven in. The crowd stood up and clapped. I did so too and as he climbed onto the podium his hands held in greeting and acknowledgement, I know he saw me and nodded, very briefly. I understood the signal. It meant: 'see me afterwards, surreptitiously'.

The lecture was about sex without love being an ideal.

'Adam and Eve were in love and they couldn't help it. There was no one else.'

It got the expected laugh. The thesis turned again to detachment but for this crowd, especially the women, he wasn't going to risk an out and out opposition. It would be throwing the baby out with the bathwater as they say. Of course love was the higher ideal but it should not become possession as in marriage and it must not become a bind to restrict the growth of one partner sacrificing herself to the other. He chose the pronoun. He got the gasps and the applause he wanted.

I dispersed with the rest of the crowd and went towards his house. He stepped out of the car and was immediately, surrounded by acolytes outside the guarded iron gates. I stood a little distance away and as he shook off his disciples with a few words and implied blessings and walked to the gates he gave me a little nod again and as I approached him he grabbed me by the wrist and walked me through the gates, up the steps of the old house and through the doors.

In the house he turned to me.'I know you not old man,' he said. 'From Shakespeare, from King Henry III or IV or something.'

He didn't smile.

'I've come from Bombay especially,' I said, lamely.

'To offer me some old woman's money? You think I need money? Look around you, my dear guardian. I could buy that old lady twenty times and her grandfather.'

'I think he's dead,' I said. 'And she's dead too.'

'Ah, yes, I heard some such thing. So enjoy it while it lasts. It is a tale told by an idiot signifying nothing. That too is Shakespeare. Hamlet. I have been reading more and more of it.'

'Why don't you take the money and give it to charity or something.'

'There is no such thing as charity,' he said. 'That's a Jewish concept. Sharing the material of the world because it belongs to everyone is Hindu.'

'So why don't you share your Rolls Royces and why do you have iron gates around your house?'

'I neither asked for a Rolls Royce or for gates around my house. These things appeared. They will continue to appear and then, because they are insubstantial, they will disappear.'

'What shall I do with your houses and your money?'

'Listen, Govinda, Chandrika, my benefactor, the one who saved my life...'

'I didn't save your life,' I said, 'I just didn't obey the order to kill you.'

'A double negative, to refuse the negating order.'

'Maybe.'

'So why did you do it, monk Chandrika?'

'You've never asked me before.'

'I didn't know the truth before and you always told me some bullshit story about why we left the ashram. More or less true, but not the truth.'

'How could I?'

'You should have. So why did you do it?'

'Because I suddenly realized that what I was being told to do was wrong. That there was a right and a wrong and that brought me, if you like, real enlightenment.'

'Good,' he said, staring in my face for any sign of insincerity.

'And then because this seven-year-old child or his fate had brought me to my senses and a new life, I began to love him.'

'You love me?'

'No. I dislike you and all this, but I loved that young boy and that young man as he grew.'

'You formed an attachment.'

'Yes, and your "philosophy" doesn't make me ashamed of it.'

He turned away and paced to the window. We stood there in complete silence for perhaps two or three minutes. The curtains weren't drawn and I could see a moon in the sky over his shoulder. Then he turned to me and his eyes were wet. There were tears down his cheeks running into his beard. An utterly silent cry.

'You loved him?'

'Yes,' I said.

'And you never touched him?'

'Not like that,' I said.

'No, I know. But you did touch his heart.' He nodded slowly. 'But that boy and that young man are dead.'

'I know,' I said.

There was no light but that of the moon in the room, but I could see him clearly and since I was facing the window, he must have seen my face.

'You must go. You know these vultures want your money, the old woman's money, my so-called mother's money. They want everything. They have everything but they want more.'

'Didn't you know that before you got involved with them?' I asked.

'As I remember, you made the deal with them. And as I understand it, if you die, the estate comes to me, whether I want it or not, whether I acknowledge that she was my mother or not.'

'I suppose it does, but I think only if you make an acknowledgement, but maybe not,' I said.

'Then, Chandrika, you live dangerously and you have been foolish to come here.'

As he said this I sensed a presence behind me. I turned. Shanti and two men had entered the room and were standing behind me. He must have seen them enter as we talked.

'Who let you in here?' Shanti asked me.

I didn't answer. Their bodies blocked my exit.

'Take him out,' she ordered the two men.

They were big men. One threw his hand across my mouth to prevent me crying out and the other grabbed me and lifted me off the floor. They dragged me out of the room into the corridor and through another room towards a back door of the house. It wasn't possible to struggle. One of them pulled out a cosh and struck me hard on both knees, on my head and in my face. They were going to kill me. I felt faint with the blows.

I was still trying feebly to struggle when I thought I heard voices and cries. They threw me to the ground and there was loud shouting, but sounds and flashes of light were all I can remember and then they must have grabbed me and thrown me into a vehicle. I was on the floor of the spacious rear seat of a large car and there were feet on my neck and on my body holding me down, or so I thought.

I felt a wetness on my face.

'Straight on, I think he'll be okay,' a voice said. 'Can you sit up?'

'Leave him on the floor. They've bashed his head in,' another voice said.

The sides of the car and its ceiling were spinning when I opened my eyes.

'You, customer,' the first voice said.

I opened my eyes again and held out my hand and felt a coarse cotton garment.

'You're going to be all right,' the same voice said. 'Just try and sleep, we have the address in Bombay.'

I must have slept. Harkishan woke me up.

The doctor had been called. My skull was cracked and there was internal bleeding but they didn't need to operate so I had been brought back to my bed. Two crimson men had delivered me to the door in a Rolls Royce. Harkishan said I was in a hell of a state. They had explained. I was visiting the ashram when intruders attacked me. The Bhagwan himself luckily witnessed the attack and called for help from the window. Six or seven stalwarts of the ashram, one of them a martial arts instructor had overpowered the intruders and the Bhagwan had ordered them to drive me all the way to Bombay.

It must have been true. Was he in on a plot to murder me? Second thoughts? Changed his mind halfway through the execution of a murder? One of the voices in the melee, now as it came back to me, was clearly Saket's. Shanti had ordered her men to carry me away and he had called out for the hand-picked devotees of his household to fight them and save me.

I didn't say anything to Harkishan.

It took me five weeks to get over brain haemorrhage and longer for the broken ribs to heal.

I WENT STRAIGHT TO PRAFUL'S. He was in his room still bashing away at an old manual typewriter. His mother let me in and led me through the rotting wood of the door frames to the room where he was sitting on a three-legged stool at an old desk with one leg made of an improvised broomstick, bent over his work, for all the world like some Uriah Heep.

'Why don't you get a computer?'

'I had one, I had to sell it to eat,' he said.

There was no arguing with that. He anticipated my thoughts as he rose to greet me. 'I could go to an internet cafe, but they'd find out and get copies of every word I write. This old typee can't develop any bloody virus or any hacking or any of this nonsense.'

'Bhavnani came and virtually said they'd kill her if I wrote anything about them.'

'Then write that.'

'I thought you loved this woman, Praful. I've known you since we were kids. What the fuck do you mean? You want her dead. You were the one who said these people can and will do anything.'

He sat down on his three-legged stool again, frowning.

'They could. They would,' he said.

'Suppose I wrote the whole thing to a friend in London and he or she put it out in a newspaper—"The Truth Behind The Sex Guru Ashram"—and they couldn't trace it to me, why would they touch her or me or you?'

'You don't know what's happening in that place, man. These fuckers think they are the Brave New World. They can do anything to the rest of the planet. Only those within the sacred acre are the chosen.'

I looked into his eyes and for the first time in our lives saw that they were green, or brown tinged with green. In all the years of our childhood I hadn't noticed that. And I had, I thought for the first time, heard him sum up a grand truth. Yes, if they thought they were a civilization apart, one that succeeded materialism and superseded the nonsense of Hindu mysticism, then they could arrogantly parade as the chosen.

The established religions didn't even count. Most of those in the ashram would have been former Protestant Christians of one sort or the other, Catholics perhaps, but those doctrines were beneath contempt. The bearded one with the locks, the smile and hypnotic eyes was the Pied Piper to the promise of the age.

I could write all that and they wouldn't care. But if I wrote Diamond's story they would kill her.

'Can they really kill her?'

'How long have you been away? Your fucking Cambridge and nonsense. India, man. You can pay two guys twenty pounds each to throw her out of a window. Where have you been?'

'I don't know,' I said. 'I think I've been in a place where truth means that the words correspond to something material out there, an object, a process—you know, nouns, verbs... what you are saying is any damn thing goes here and...'

'Yes, I am saying that. This was a decent town, you know, with progress and capitalism coming to it with factories and tractors and chemicals and jobs. That was the time you left for England. I was stuck here man, with a sick mother and a sister whom some fucking Arab, who came here from Bombay in his limousine for the horse races, offered to marry because she had green eyes. Then these bastards came with the worst idea in the world.'

'Meaning?'

'It doesn't matter what the idea is. The worst idea is the one that believes it's the only idea.'

'You know, you are becoming Saket, talking like that,' I said and immediately regretted saying it.

'Why don't you fuck off,' he said.

'Because we both want to save Di from being murdered.'

'They've told you to stop writing, so it's done. They won't kill her if no one believes her or reports her story.'

'If they can kill her, they can get her released and get her out of the country,' I said.

'Yes,' he said. 'It means we've lost. Hands up. Let's go together. He's your friend. Let's go and beg him. Make a deal. Let our Diamond go free and we'll never write a word against the ashram or him.'

'Why would he believe us? I could go back to London and write what I like. Blackmail only works if they've got the knife at your neck.'

'Your aunts?'

I hadn't thought of that.

HARKISHAN LOST HIS FAITH IN an instant as people who have witnessed a miracle gain theirs. He lived in the bedroom facing the sea and assumed, quite naturally, that the money that had come to me was also his. I was in my own way used to the use of money. I suppose rich and poor understand its values and versatilities equally. But Harkishan who had lived the life of a monk and had never had access to cash or what it could and could not do, seemed to fall under its spell.

He had never handled money and when he asked me for some I asked my lawyer how I could access it and he said there was a safe in the flat and he had been entrusted with its combination which he would give me.

There were wads of old and freshly printed notes in the safe, crores of rupees. I suppose that's what diamond merchants keep in their homes as well as having bank accounts in the country and abroad, all of whose cheque books and numbers I had and to all of which I had gained access by signing in the boxes of copious bank forms.

I took three wads of fresh notes out of the safe and gave them to Harkishan. He counted them diligently as though the sums would convey their value to him.

He began to spend the money, first on my clothes and his and then on whatever he fancied.

He went wild. He frequented the bars of five star hotels he'd heard of, using the cars that were at our disposal. He drank whiskies and cocktails and was brought home each night by the chauffeurs, blind drunk.

He went to clubs and returned one night with two women whom he escorted into the flat and disappeared behind the door of his sea-facing bedroom. It was a whole new aspect of karma for him.

He had different women coming to the flat. They bought themselves clothes and jewellery from the money he lavished on them and they brought bottles of champagne, cannabis and cocaine into the house and shamelessly drank, smoked and snorted these with Harkishan in front of the servants. I declined their persuasive and playful offers of drink, drugs and even sex.

Maria. I had not forgotten Maria.

Harkishan's women changed. He had begun by buying two girls together and now as he gained confidence, he picked up women, impressing them with the money he was throwing around. He did nothing now but sleep, eat, set out for his clubs and bars and forays into the holiday hotels with fresh girlfriends of which there seemed an endless supply.

We had nothing to say to each other now. I would give him what money he asked for without once questioning him about this rapid, almost desperate, change. He was not a stranger to introspection. He had been taught its disciplines, just as I had, but he seemed not to think about what he was doing. A man swept by a tide doesn't calculate the force of the current.

Harkishan was arrested in an opium den in a large seaside bungalow in Goa. He was with three women at the time and two of the others arrested with him were a high court judge and a prominent businessman. Their photographs were all over the newspapers and that same Praful Surti who interviewed us about Mataji's claims, honed in on Harkishan.

He sold the story to the national newspapers who at first had been more interested in the high court judge and the businessman. Surti had the best angle on the story about the dope den, being able to identify one of the sybarites as an ex-monk who now seemed to have deteriorated into a life of criminal indulgence.

The focus was now on Harkishan and the newspapers got hold of photographs of him at some religious Himalayan ceremony, his head shaved, wearing a brown robe, beads and a white muslin mask over his nose and mouth. His eyes, with their constant look of mild surprise were distinctive. The photograph of him shielding his eyes from the flash of the cameras in the opium den was printed next to the old ones.

I hired the lawyer who had processed our documents in Poona and drove with him to Goa to have Harkishan released on bail.

When we got back to Bombay we found Mr Bhavnani waiting for us. The story had triggered his enquiries and through the police and subsequently through our lawyer's office he had found us.

He brought with him a nasty young Parsee lawyer called Cyrus Bode whom he introduced to me as representing the interests of Bhagwan and of the ashram.

Harkishan and his women had imported a flashy drinks cabinet and there were hookahs and other decorations which Mataji would never have tolerated. In some seizure of taste he had bought a painting of a horse by M.F. Husain and hung it on the wall above the pastel blue sofa. Bode walked in and immediately began to look around proprietorialy.

'This is a splendid place, splendid place,' he said.

He looked at the whisky collection in the glass-fronted drinks cabinet. Harkishan didn't want to confront them and went to his room without making any excuse. I heard the key turn in his door.

The cook, seeing guests, hung about waiting for my command. I said he was to bring our guests some tea and he went to prepare it.

'Unless you prefer something else.'

'No, no that's fine, Mr Govinda. My dear friend I have known you so many years, so many years. Bode Sahib, Chandrikaji, as we used to call him, was the secretary of our beloved Guru Vishwadeep, writing, making translations, doing everything. And of course the rest of the story of him you know with services to Bhagwanji and all these things.'

'I have heard so much about you, Govindaji,' the fellow Bode said.

I invited them to sit down but they were still looking around the room, making mental inventories, and Bode walked to the glass doors and parted the curtains to the balcony.

'Yes, I've formed a good picture of you mostly through Mr Bhavnani but also through Bhagwanji who owes you so much,' he said to me.

'I thought Rahul had given up owing anything to anybody. Gratitude is a sin, or haven't you heard?'

'I am a simple lawyer,' Bode said. 'These philosophies are beyond me. And thank God. Philosophy would stop me doing any proper work. Eh?'

I indicated the sofa to Mr Bhavnani as the tea arrived in cups on a tray. Bhavnani sat down but Bode remained standing in the middle of the room, his legs apart and his hands clasped now behind his back, a pose which indicated that he was going to get down to business, to the purpose of their visit.

'Govindaji, there are three possibilities,' Cyrus Bode began.

I decided to demonstrate a calm tinged with contempt. I had guessed, even from the way he examined the curtains and looked at the Husain painting, that these two had come on behalf of the witch Shanti to make demands on what was now legally mine. I sat down and called to the cook to bring more sugar and a teaspoon.

'Number one: I have examined all the documents you signed and the transfer papers for the accounts and have in fact contacted your lawyer. There is deep, deep uncertainty as to your claim to this property and to the bank accounts and the estate of the late Mrs G. P. Jain. I think your lawyer will agree that in a few years time, because everything takes long in the Indian courts unless you pay a bribe to get things going, we can dislodge you from every rupee and stick and stone of this estate. A judge will, unfortunately agree with us that your so-called trusteeship doesn't exist and was obtained under duress by your drug addict accomplice who has just been released by the police. He no doubt exerted undue influence on the old lady.'

'I was going to watch the cricket on TV today, transmission from UK, but this is better entertainment. Carry on,' I said.

'I am glad you are enjoying,' Bode said, bowing ever so slightly, like a complimented player. 'The second possibility is that some of Bhagwan's closest disciples, people he values, including Mr Bhavnani and Shantiji whom you know, persuade him to immediately give up his stance on the bequest, acknowledge Mrs G. P. Jain as his natural mother and accept the entire estate which is only held by you till such time as he accepts his parentage. Bhagwan will say they act for him in every legal circumstance and then they will claim the money you now temporarily and mistakenly hold.'

'Bode, Bode, Bode, you don't know Rahul, or Saket, as I do. He says there is no such thing as gratitude. If your Mr Bhavnani and your Shanti got this fortune away from me, he will denounce them. He will stake his own claim and he won't do it to get rich, he will do it to teach Bhavnani here and your Ms Shanti, the lesson of non-attachment and absolute poverty. That's what your man will do, and if it comes to that, I will help him.'

I grinned as brazenly as I could, turning to Mr Bhavnani.

Bode was not disconcerted by what I said.

'These are all perfectly plausible outcomes,' he said, 'But my third possibility has still to be adumbrated.'

'Adumbrate away' I said.

'That we come to an arrangement with you. You make Mr Bhavnani and Shantiji the trustees of the estate and they fix upon you, at the same time, an agreed and generous sum. It takes away from you the burden of trusteeship and the duties that are prescribed therein and we can part friends.'

'I think you've overlooked one major factor,' I said.

'And that being?' he said in his best court advocate's questioning tone.

'That the entire fabric of Rahul being the son of Mataji who was taken away and brought up by a young monk till he was seven years old and then saved from being murdered by the same young monk by some act of conscience and an instant conversion and then brought up and educated and set loose upon the world to become Saket, depends on the word of that one person. And that one person sits here, stirring more sugar into his tea. He could change his story. None of that ever happened. What baby? What prediction? What monk? What seven-year-old child? There is not one living witness who can substantiate this fantastical story. Poor old Mataji is dead and gone and there is no DNA evidence which will conclusively prove that he is directly her son.'

Bode was thoughtful for a moment but his lawyer's instinct kicked in.

'You are on record telling your story,' he said.

'You know there's no record. The newspapers say what they want. My dear friend Praful Surti will come to court and testify that he made the whole thing up. And then there's Harkishan, my co-benefactor who will tell a completely different story. Besides, Bode, I am quite enjoying having what you call "the estate". Now can my driver take you back to the railway station or even perhaps drive you back to Poona? Or as your Guru Saket might say, will you fuck off?'

They looked at each other. Mr Bhavnani stood up. He was anxious to discuss this latest development in the scheme with Bode. I stood and stretched out my arm to indicate the direction in which the door stood.

'You don't know who you are dealing with,' Bode said.

'It should be "whom"—"whom you are dealing with". Rahul used to read out these books on English grammar to me. Even though I don't know, and never knew, any "Rahul".'

HARKISHAN SPENT MOST OF HIS days and nights in his room now, as though he were a hospital patient. The threat of a drastic change of life in jail had frightened him. His women came and were turned away at the door. The servants were instructed to let no women, no reporters or anyone else in. He had no friends, only hangers-on who had attached themselves to him for his money, so there was no need to make exceptions.

He became sullen. The lawyer said he would get the prosecution case postponed indefinitely and would have to pay bribes to the police and courts every few months when it was scheduled to come to court.

The only person who kept Harkishan's disgrace or memory in the public eye was the journalist Surti. Our lawyer asked him outright if he would take a bribe and stop writing about the case but he said it was vital to his soul's peace to pursue the high court judge and businessman who had been arrested with Harkishan in the raid. He wanted them brought to book. He assured us that he had nothing personal against Harkishan who was one of fortune's changelings but his hatred of high court judges and businessmen was a compulsion in his blood. So no, he wouldn't take a bribe to stop reporting the stories, but if we wanted to pay him something to avoid mentioning Harkishan as far as possible, he would consider it.

Apart from the fact that the postponements of the case for unfathomable reasons and with invented bureaucratic excuses was preventing the case coming to court, there was nothing much to say. So Surti began pursuing his prey, the high court judge and the businessman, for other irregularities in their conduct. The judge, he discovered, had a wife, six children, six grandchildren and two mistresses. Surti named them. The businessman had thrown a huge party for his second son's wedding in a palace in Rajasthan a few years previously and had invited a list of a hundred Arab 'friends' and associates from the Gulf states. He had purportedly received huge sums in presents at the wedding. Surti discovered and announced that there were no such Arab potentates and that in truth the businessman had made up most of the names and cash gifts in order to launder the money he had earned on the black market and on which he hadn't paid income tax.

This spilt bucket of worms enhanced Surti's reputation as an investigative journalist and with the focus of public attention shifting to these exposures, Harkishan was temporarily forgotten. We, of course, paid Surti for this obliquely delivered service.

Perhaps bribing Praful Surti, or giving him what he called 'encouragement payments' was a mistake. Our lawyer from Poona, the one who had drafted the first legal papers in haste for Mataji, now wrote to me saying he had made some grievous blunders in drafting the documents and my ownership of the estate may not be as firm in law as he at first believed. The rascal had obviously been contacted by Bode or the witch Shanti and paid off. I got my Bombay lawyer to reply. The ace we held in our hands was that without my testimony or Harkishan's, there was no claim that Rahul could pursue and they knew it.

Then they tried a new tack. The Poona lawyer signed an affidavit saying that it had appeared to him at the time that Mrs G.P. Jain was not in her right mind. She seemed under stress and was being made to sign papers under duress by Harkishan and myself.

Bode even got in touch with our Bombay lawyer and hinted to him that he could profit hugely by changing sides. But he didn't. He told us about Bode's phone calls and remained steadfast. He possibly thought the reward for loyalty would in the end be greater than the bribe for treachery. Or was that an unworthy thought? The sort of judgement that the fellow Surti would make?

But why did I want to hang on to the estate? My stratagem with Cyrus Bode was not so much motivated by keeping the money as by not wanting the witch Shanti and her dog Bhavnani to win. I was realizing I had no need or desire for—or as we would have said, no attachment to—the house, the servants, the car, the luxury. I spent no money and didn't use the car. I walked and still took the local bus and I knew that the servants thought I was the most abject form of miser. They had no respect for someone like me who didn't use money. They regarded Harkishan with all his newfound rudeness, contempt, wantonness, womanizing, drug-addiction and even criminal notoriety as the real master of the household and they treated his reclusive phase reverently as a sickness, tip-toeing past and into his room with tea and the simple rice and daal which he had now taken to eating.

I thought of giving the servants a stipend each and dismissing them, liberating them, setting them free with a sizeable pension for life. I had read in the Arabian Nights that it was the practice of merchants and potentates to set their slaves free as they prepared for their death. Not that I was preparing to pass on, but when I mentioned it to our lawyer he looked at me with a pitying expression.

'They were born to work as servants,' he said. 'They will hate you if you propose it.'

I knew he was wrong and was going to propose the deal to the cook, the maids and the chauffeur, but Harkishan stopped me.

'They need us and I need them,' he said.

'You are going to jail sooner or later. They'll feed you there,' I said, not intending it as a joke or insult but as a matter of fact.

'This money business is funny business,' Harkishan said. 'I have had everything that it could buy and it's landed me in sickness and sorrow.'

'Not having anything might have got you to the same place,' I said. 'Remember where we met? What we used to do? How we gave away our youth to The Enlightened One and a pack of lies? We'll never get that back.'

'I remember nothing,' he said. 'I smoked opium and took coke, shoke and poke to get the memory of that lost youth out of my blood. It's gone. I am numb.'

'That Parsee lawyer probably has some case and some point and he has all of Saket's money to use. They might soon snatch all this away from us anyway,' I said.

He was thinking about that when the bell rang.

The maid answered it and I heard a voice I knew, a voice that echoed in memory, asking if the 'saheb' was in.

The maid let Maria in and shut the heavy door behind her.

Maria was wearing a dark dress. She was holding a black handbag under her arm.

I could see as I searched her face that she had developed dark circles under and around her eyes, circles of loose and lined skin. She had faint hairs on her dark chin and she had lost the expression of nonchalance. She looked almost apologetic for occupying the space in what was now my front room.

I went up to her as the maid, confident now that she had admitted a known guest, went off through the kitchen.

'Maria,' I said. 'My God.'

'I was reading about you and your friend in the papers, men. And I was saying to myself, you must go and see the old dog.'

'I thought I'd never see…' I said.

'How can you say that, men. We are such good friends.'

It's what we weren't, we were never friends. I had so longed for her. I had waited for her and dreamt of her, and here she was, an old Goan lady dressed as if for church.

'Come, come, come,' I said, and as soon as she saw that I was welcoming and willing and vulnerable, she smiled and, stepping forward, hugged me.

'What a long time, yaar,' she said.

Harkishan was standing in the door of his room watching and he must have concluded that this was personal and, though he had never seen me embracing anyone before, he went in to his room and shut the door behind him.

Maria put her handbag down and her eyes began to sparkle as of old as I remembered them doing all those years ago. She was suddenly ten years younger and she bounded to the balcony through the glass doors, examining the place. I followed her. She was gazing at the sea.

'What beautiful luxury, men, you are so famous now.'

I had no words. This was an apparition made flesh—let me not be romantic about it—she smelt of cheap perfume and in the heat of Bombay she wore tights which were laddered on her dark legs. This was no ethereal floating angel, but the substantial, not particularly shapely or alluring woman who had been my first and only love—my initiation, a gift, an endowment of sensuality. Gone, gone forever and yet here she was again.

'Why did you come?' I asked, turning to try and face her.

Below us the waves crashed against the large boulders thrown onto the shoreline to preserve it against erosion. The waves crashed and dragged their white foam back across the sands carrying now the detritus of Bombay, the plastic bags, spars of wood, cardboard and occasionally the bloated carcass of a dog, back into the undulating shallows of the sea.

She was thinking about how to answer my question.

'My son,' she said. 'My son is a scientist.'

'I asked you why you came to find me,' I said.

'Yes, yes, Chandoo, that is why I have come. My son, I got him educated, men. The Jesuits gave all the help. They sent him to seminary and then when they saw what kind of boy he was, they thought he is not having the proper attitude for wanting to be a priest. No calling. He didn't get calling, but they knew he still was a good boy so they sent him to college and paid all the fees. They knew I was a poor nurse and lost my job and all this.'

'What did he study?'

'He went into science and now he's got a job in microbiology and genetics, researching. In USA, men!' She said it with such pride.

'So you want something for him?'

'No, no, no, no. He is doing fine. He gives me everything and his brothers and sisters and that no good father of his, drunken, good-for-nothing, gutter snipe fellow, smells of booze all the time, he even gives him cash, men. I tell him not to, he will only drink it up, but the boy has a soft heart. Boston, Boston. I should have told you. Earning big bucks.'

'That's so good, Maria, so good. All this, this flat, the money, not my thing.'

'I know. I was very surprised to see you involved in all this business. But you told me about the boy you brought up and everything and then I read the newspapers. I was sure it was you.'

'And it is,' I said and I turned to her and she embraced me and kissed me on the cheek.

'Now those fellows,' she said. 'Before my son got the education and the job you knew me and how poor I was. I will tell you something I used to do. I would keep all the medicine bottles and containers and the injection syringes and equipment after it had been used because I knew I could sell it to these crooks who would clean it up and sell it back to doctors as new stuff. It is of course illegal, but all nurses who were working in private were doing it and also especially in the public hospitals. They are sterilizing and using syringes over and over again and also bottles.'

'But then your son got educated and you stopped all that. He had plenty of dollars and...'

'No, no men, you are not getting it. I still have the syringes and the bottles which that bitch was using on the old man.'

Her eyes widened as she said it.

'I have kept just those. There are maybe twenty bottles and bandages and everything. And syringes.'

I didn't understand what she was trying to say. She was looking around the flat even as she spoke. I thought she was rambling. The curtains were being blown in the breeze.

'Your fellow, that new swami, has made these bastards rich. I am reading all the time about the Poona ashram with all the millionaire white peoples going there and giving up all their fortunes, men.'

'It's not quite like that,' I said.

'My son now told me that there is something called DNA technique which was lately discovered and if some laboratory looks at the syringes that I have from those days, when I was nursing Swami Vishwadeep and she moved me out and started giving him injections by herself, we can find proof.'

'Of what?'

'Of what? You know what! They murdered him, men. You know that and I know that. And now this DNA business, all of which my son and his friends know, can prove it in a court of law. Murder! I have got the bastards.'

'You really want to get them?'

'I hate them. Look what they did to you and to me. At least they didn't murder us, men.'

'There's nothing we can do though. If you give your syringes to the police, they will just buy the police off—that's what's been happening.'

'This is why I came to you, to see how we can catch these monkeys.'

'Where are the syringes and stuff?'

'In my house.'

'Have you told anyone else?'

'There's nobody to tell, men. Other people will think I am mad. I waited till I could see you,' she said.

'Don't. I mean tell anyone else.'

'I have told something to my son and he said I should find you. You are also witness to these things. Did you love the old man?'

'He had goodness in every bone of his body,' I replied.

'I liked him too. When you are bathing, cleaning and feeding someone they become like your baby, men.'

'Is that why you are… chasing these…people?'

'What do you think? I am a Catholic. They have to pay for their sin of murder.'

Standing on the balcony with the sound of the waves sloshing and smashing on the rocks I reached in myself, wanting to know what I felt for this woman. Nothing. There was no spark of longing and the memory was as if of someone else. I had dreamt so often and longed for the touch, the smell, the sound of her breathing and her moan but the dream had dissolved on looking at her. Time? Or the self-deception of the first time? In my life the only time.

I asked her if she wanted something to drink.

'If you are giving it, men. That expensive whisky looks A-one!'

There were cut glass tumblers, which Harkishan's women had bought, in the cabinet and I knew they drank whisky from these and usually ordered ice from the kitchen to go with it. I poured her a glass and must have given her too much because she said 'Arrey, arrey, go easy, men. You want to get me drunk, eh? And then what shall we do, eh?'

She grinned and showed me that she now had three gold teeth. I called for ice and she settled down to sip her drink. I could see that she was still thinking I would invite her to stay, at least for a while.

'You are looking just as handsome and young as before,' she said. I just smiled. 'You must remember that night I got drunk, eh?'

'I have remembered it ever since,' I said, 'but then you disappeared. Not a postcard, nothing.'

'I'm sorry, yaar. I felt a little ashamed, you see. Because I knew you were a holy man and I had done sinful stuff.'

'I never thought of myself as a holy man and I have thought ever since that you did very good and generous stuff.'

'That is a nice thing to say,' she said. 'Do you have a girlfriend?'

'No.' I said. I was going to add that she was the only one, but that would have sounded like an encouragement towards where she was trying to get us.

'I would like to see the sunset over the sea, yaar. It will be very soon, won't it?'

'Big and crimson every day,' I said.

She stayed and we watched the sunset together. She tried to slip her hand in mine and I held hers limply. We stood like that on the balcony and when I deftly detached my hand I could see she was uncertain and embarrassed and she asked for more whisky.

I poured her some and it must have been more than drinkers drink because she giggled when she saw it and yet she downed it as the day finally turned to night and the waters of the Arabian Sea turned black with the spark of oil lamps on the boats out at sea.

Then we went in. The servants had adjusted the quiet lighting in the room. Maria asked for more whisky. We talked of the ashram and she of Shanti and how I didn't know how cruel she actually was to the old man, how she shouted at him and even slapped him for being incontinent and wetting the bed.

'She had nothing to do with it, men. It was my job to change the dirty sheets and clean him up in the morning but she was still shouting at him saying that the smell was not good for business and that she was having to afford more and more sheets for the bed and pay big dhobi bills. She gave him two slaps also in front of me and the old man started crying. He was never complaining about anything, just going on with you—talking things which you were writing down and then giving lectures and getting money for those vultures. Can you imagine, yaar? For dhobi bills and bed sheets she was beating him? And it was his own earnings because people were coming only because of him. Pinchings even to make water come in his eyes.'

'I knew something like that was going on,' I said.

'You did love him, I know,' Maria said.

'I don't know about loving him, Mariaji. I knew he was honest and meant everything he said.'

'Does this boy you have put in his place to make them rich, does he believe all this stuff that white people are flocking for?'

'I don't think he knows what he believes. Maybe the idea of belief has gone from his head,' I said.

'That is so sinful, that is so sinful, Chandoo. I believe in Jesus,' she said and crossed herself.

Then she stood up and said she wanted to go to the bathroom. I directed her to my bedroom. She staggered as she walked.

'Too much, I am dizzy,' she said.

I waited ten and then fifteen minutes and she didn't return. I went after her.

She was lying obliquely on my bed, quite drunk, her legs dangling off the side.

'I'm sorry, Chandrix, sorry, sorry, sorry. You gave too much bhisky!'

She lurched up and rushed to the toilet. I heard her vomiting. Then the basin tap and she came back and flopped on the bed again.

'You should get inside the bed. There are other places to sleep and anyway I don't sleep in the bed.

The light of the bedroom wasn't on. Only the light from the passage and from the bathroom fell in shafts through the doors into the room. She sat up and tried to pull her dress off, but she was sitting on it. I went to her and helped slip it from under her bum and over her head. She flung it on the floor and I picked it up and folded it.

She was wearing a white singlet under it and she dragged that off. Then she tried to undo her bra and fumbled with her hands behind her back. I was wondering whether I should offer to help when she manoeuvred the back strap round to the front and undid the buckle and let her large brown breasts with splashed nipples droop to her belly.

It was then that she realized that she was half naked in front of an almost stranger and she smiled, a nervous smile.

I was staring at her breasts and she was trying to work herself under the sheet. She managed it and then took her knickers off with both hands, drawing her legs up, and throwing the knickers in a gesture of abandon on the floor.

'You are coming, aren't you?' she asked.

I shut the door to the sitting room, took my clothes off in the half-dark, keeping my underpants on and got in next to her in the bed.

She kissed me on the cheek and then she fell fast asleep.

'THERE'S NOT MUCH OF A story,' I told Tony, my editor in London over the phone. 'Obviously I can describe the ashram and what's interesting I suppose are the people who have left one way of life in Europe or America and have taken to another, quite different, routine.'

'Yes, that could be a feature if you interview say ten of them and extract a thread,' he said. 'But we have to know how deep their commitment is. Is it just a mental holiday, a temporary drop out, wearing funny clothes and rejecting the pressures of the rat race? Have they become Hindus or what?'

'There's just talk of Hinduism, whatever that is. The fellow is quite hypnotic.'

'That's the cliché,' he said. 'Expect you to get below that phrase. Surely one or two of the victims, disciples have a fascinating narrative.'

'I'm looking for just that. And on getting below the clichés, I think I can characterize his religion or doctrine in a few words even though he uses millions to spin it out—thousands come cascading over us every day.'

'I'm sure there's enough curiosity about the phenomenon to run a series for six weeks, say. Can you get dispatches to me from the frontline? I mean start writing while you're there?'

'Sure I can, but maybe I'll get back soon and work from my notes. I've got stacks of stuff.'

That's how I left it.

MARIA, HAVING LEFT THE NEXT day, returned in three. She took a plastic bag out of her handbag. In it were three syringes wrapped in tissue and seven empty bottles which had contained Swami Vishwadeep's injected medicines.

'You've kept them all these years?'

'I have hundreds. I was sterilizing and selling them on the second-hand market. Some girls don't even sterilize, spreading disease. God only knows if the bootleggers do any precautions.'

'They buy them from you?'

'Everything and anything. Old bottles, like this.' She took one out of the bag and showed it to me, its metal top punctured. 'They fill their own medicines or sell them to drug addicts.'

'Yes that could kill people! Surely?'

Maria shrugged. 'Everything kills people, men. This is India,' she said.

'Why did you keep these?'

'They were the ones the swami was injected with on the last three days. I am sure they were killing him. You can trace poison even now—and that doctor they had, he was paid heavy cash, my friend. He would not do it himself but he helped them with drugs to bring on heart failure. Then he signed the certificate.'

'We're going to the police with these?'

'No, men. What would the police do against such people? They would have bloody locked me up. No, the bootleggers only take from you if you have five hundred or thousand items. I had got rid of a batch just previously so I didn't have a full batch to sell. Then I lost my job so I didn't get any more syringes. I just kept them all these years.'

'Why did you want to show me?'

'I am sending them to US for analysis. They will be able to tell that this is Swami Vishwadeep's blood and skin and everything and that she, that bitch, was holding the syringe. She didn't even bother to wear gloves or nothing. And they will find heart attack drugs.'

'I know what they do,' I said. 'They match samples. You'll need a cutting of her skin or blood or something.'

'Teaching your grandmother? I am a trained nurse, men. You'll have to go and try something. I won't be allowed anywhere near that place.'

'I am not their most popular person either,' I said.

Harkishan understood the dilemma and suggested that we talk to Praful Surti about it. He seemed like a man who would poke about and perhaps find us what we wanted.

'I WAS CYCLING TO WORK when I noticed this fellow following me on a scooter. He was going as slowly as my cycle,' my aunt said at dinner that night. She was puzzled. 'Then when I came home I wheeled my bike from inside the compound and the same fellow was waiting somewhere outside the gate and again I noticed him starting his scooter and coming very slowly behind me all the way to this corner. Nobody drives a scooter like that. Same fellow. Shall I go to the police?'

'Did you get a good look at him? Indian?'

'Yes, of course,' my aunt said. 'I hope he's not there tomorrow. It gave me such a fright.'

'If he was out on the street, he couldn't have done you any harm,' my other aunt said. 'But of course you still don't want these fellows following you.'

'What sort of fellow? Young, old?'

'Young, loafer type.'

'Did you get the number of the scooter?'

'I tried but every time I turned round on the bike to look, he would go sideways and go zigzag on the road. I didn't want to stop and give him any extra attention as if I was scared or something.'

'I understand. I'll cycle with you to work tomorrow,' I said.

I did go with her the next day but there was no scooter following us. I knew she wasn't deluding herself.

Was it a sort of warning? For me?

The next day a couple of crimson people stopped by the house and delivered a leaflet. It said:

Dear Amy and Shera Antia,

You and other neighbours and fellow-citizens of ours in your ancient and beautiful town have been specially selected by the Bhagwan Shree Saket ashram to participate in a Ceremony of Oblivion. It is designed to bring eternal peace to troubled souls. We will let you know the time and place when all the preparations for the ceremony are completed.

My aunt Shera took a dictionary from the shelves.

'What are you doing?'

'This word, oblivion,' she said. 'It means "A state of having been disused or forgotten". Bloody cheek! And it also means being given an amnesty or forgiveness. Who are these people? We don't want to go to their wretched ceremonies. Why are they picking on us?'

'They are not picking on us,' Amy said. 'That's just their language to make stupid people feel special. They must have distributed this leaflet all over town. I'll ask Tehmi next door if they came there too.'

I took the leaflet from her. I didn't want to explain.

'Don't worry about it,' I said. 'And don't ask Tehmi, I'll go around myself and ask the neighbours.'

I went to Praful's house and showed him the leaflet.

'That is a threat, isn't it?'

'I told you,' he said. 'They are fuckers. They think they have made a state within a state. Outside the law, but notice how careful they are being? An invitation to some ceremony that they will actually carry out. But its basic purpose is to threaten you.'

He read the leaflet again. I thought of telling him about the man on the scooter, but didn't because it may have been unrelated and I didn't want him to think I was totally convinced about these conspiracies.

Praful bit his bottom lip in thought.

'Obviously you can't write any exposes, not now or when you get back.'

'No,' I said.

'Something has come up. Did I tell you about the guys who inherited the fortune of this idiot Saket from someone who claimed to be his mother, some dotty millionaires, diamond merchant family, Jains?'

'I read what you wrote, but your article didn't say she was crazy.'

'The last thing we should do is argue about the definition of crazy. Is a fellow who gasses six million people sane or is he crazy? A fellow who divides a continent on religious lines and doesn't realize that millions of people will die in the interchange—I mean is that crazy or can you call it just miscalculating and sane? This poor old person was led to believe by these ex-monks that they had brought up a boy whom she had sacrificed to the gods when he was a few days—or some cock and bull story like that.'

'Conmen?'

'Obviously, some con of some sort. The two of them are sitting pretty with moolah pouring out of their bums, man. They called me. They did have something to do with our devil. One of them was his secretary as far as I can gather. Before the terrible twins took him over. Now they are at war.'

'What sort of war?'

'The two con-monks think they've got some dope on the twins: the harridan who runs the show and that evil choothya Bhavnani who came to threaten you.'

'Dope?'

'They say they've got evidence that even the police won't be able to hide. I suppose I'll go along for the ride. Blow it. They can't do anything to me. Not more than they've done.'

'And Di?'

He shrugged.'You know better than anyone in the world that she wasn't very loyal to me. It's got to end somewhere and this is where you come in, my friend, my brother.'

BHAVNANI, WHEN HE CAME TO threaten me, had also said that the Bhagwan would be pleased to give me any audience I requested. I now, after talking to Praful, wanted such an audience.

I called the ashram and asked to speak to Mr Bhavnani and was asked to call back in an hour and to leave my phone number. I did and he called me back his voice sounding urgent.

'Er, yes, Mr Farrukh. You were calling me.'

'I called to say I got your messages. My aunts also got the message and, yes, I shall be very glad to have the interview that you promised me with Bhagwan. I will, of course, sign a legal pledge to submit the article to you before publication.'

The phone went silent and then, through heavy breaths he said, 'Mr Farrukh, you are a true journalist and a very mature person for your young age and of course you can have immediate interview with Guruji and I am delighted to confirm the same.'

'Mr Bhavnani, you are too kind. I hope I am not taking advantage when I say that I also want to speak with you and Shantiji for a bit of background to the establishment of the Bhagwan.'

'Yes, yes, yes, yes. That is no problem. No problem, Farrukhji. You have before you ask.'

He made an appointment for the next morning. I was to attend the breakfast lecture and then be received by all three of them.

I got to the gates by 5.30 a.m. and went through the sniffing and then in the enclosure, the ritual of his arrival and the standing ovation for it. I fancied that he searched the faces of the front rows and found me in the corner of the second.

'Those of you who were brought up as Christians and went to church—how boring...' (nervous titter of laughter from the crowd) '...had to sit through some man telling you what Jesus meant when he said this or that or when he told a story. When and if you read the book itself, written by followers and disciples you might come, as I have, to completely different conclusions.

'Not that I ever heard it in church but I have read the published sermons of several of these priests and popes and yes, that is the conclusion I come to. The word leads you somewhere. The interpretation leads you elsewhere. Not me. I can read.'

He smiles; applause from the crowd at this signal.

'Christ was a yogi.' He pauses. 'Anyone—and I am now asking you to pick up the book and read it again—with eyes open can see that his was a consciousness that had reached a state where it could command the material world. A man tries to step on water, he sinks. It is called Archimedes' Principle. Heard of it?'

Again hesitant and then full-blown applause. 'Christ walks on water and the priest calls it a miracle. You and I know that miracles don't come from without, they come from within and the highest form of discipline, the highest plane that the inner self can reach is that of the yogi who has attained consciousness and that consciousness is in control of matter itself. Christ can walk on the Lake of Galilee. The scientists who try and measure the specific density of water and speak about how it could have been made heavier than a human being by some asteroid or something else falling from space or some thickening by fungus life, are just talking fungus.

'As much rot as the priest who believes in miracles, which really is only an admission that you are an ignorant fool. No, the only answer is inside and the discipline of yoga. Forget the water and walking on the lake. How else can a human being survive forty days in the wilderness? Why does he go there? The priest tells you it is a trial against the devil. Have you ever heard such nonsense? Why does the devil live in the desert? I would have thought he lived in the White House or a penthouse in Bombay.'

More laughter.

And so on and so tediously on. I haven't slept and I suppress several yawns, pulling the air in through my slightly parted lips to conceal them and prevent an epidemic of infectious yawning breaking out in the front rows.

I am carrying a khaki canvas shoulder bag, a relic from my schooldays, an army surplus piece of paraphernalia I picked up from the chor bazaar, the thieves' market, when these second-hand bags were all the rage for carrying schoolbooks.

It now held my small tape recorder, my notebook and pens and a round biscuit tin I had brought, with cheese straws that my aunts had made. The bag had been searched at the gate and the sanyasin in uniform commented on the cheese straws. My breakfast, I had said. I offered her one and she declined.

I asked Mr Bhavnani polite questions about how he had discovered Saket. He gave clear evidence of not having absorbed Saket's agnostic ramblings because he said God had led his footsteps to Saket.

'It was the beach so you could see the footsteps clearly in the sand from my car to where this young man was preaching fascinating things, things I had never heard even from our former guru Vishwadeep.'

'Footsteps?'

'Yes, sir, my own footsteps were already on sand before I had walked, leading me to him, believe it or not.'

'Oh, I believe it,' I said.' And tell me, what happened to Swami Vishwadeep?'

'He was very old, very old and he became very ill and then poor fellow died of heart attack.'

'You must have been heartbroken,' I said.

'Oh, yes, yes, we were all heartbroken but then we know that God gives and God takes away.'

Again, this was the sort of statement of which Saket would not approve. Gods don't exist ergo they can't give or take away, but I didn't point this out.

I said I would really like to know about the great tradition of Swami Vishwadeep's teachings. Bhavnani looked quite blank and then said it would be better coming from Shantiji who was really a scholar though she had never developed it.

'Were you a scholar too, sir?'

'No, no, I was a manager of a cinema, nothing much. I did college, but it was waste of time since my father owned two cinemas—which of course later went bankrupt when they raised entertainment tax.'

'I see,' I said.

He led me to Shantiji's office.

She was sitting at a desk surrounded by paper: correspondence, invoices and bills, no doubt.

'You are going to do proper stories Bhai Bhavnani tells me.'

'With your consent and help,' I said.

She invited me to sit and said she had kept half an hour especially for me.

'Your rules forbid cameras so I have no photographs of the ashram,' I began. 'But you must have plenty. For a foreign audience the visual impact will be very impressive.'

'We have thousands. Very many of the sanyasis here are professional photographers, film-makers, we have all that. We can give you anything and everything. Are you connected with the BBC? We can supply you whole documentaries.'

'I have friends in the BBC,' I said. 'I can certainly explore that. But what I really wanted was a picture of Swami Vishwadeep. I mean do you have any?'

'I will have to look in my personal effects. I am sure I have some photographs, but not in these filing cabinets. Swamiji of course never had anything to do with this place. This was established after the new incarnation.'

She smiled and nodded benignly.

'Oh dear, I was hoping to take a photograph away to use,' I said.

'I'll find it,' she said.

'Thanks,' I said, just as a young sanyasi put his head round the door.

'Ma Shantiji, sorry to interrupt, but something urgent.'

'Nothing is urgent, swami. Sorry, it will have to wait.'

'Can I just tell you, please?' the young man insisted.

'What sort of urgent?'

'It's a journalist at the gate, our old friend Mr Surti. We didn't let him in. He says it's something about passports. He said he wants just a few words with you and that will fix it. That's why I intruded, I am sorry.'

She looked annoyed at the mention of Praful's name, and at the mention of passports, she frowned, uncertain. She thought about it for a moment.

'Can you excuse me just a few minutes?' she asked.

Of course I could and I said so.

It was working better than I had expected. It was arranged that I would try one or two ploys to get her out of the room and leave me in it and then, if none of them worked, Praful would present himself at the gates, be refused admission and make dark hints about illegal passports, exposure of the racket etc. and demand to see her.

She left the room. I had already emptied the cheese straws from the very polished cylindrical biscuit tin into my canvas bag and as she left and I heard their footsteps and voices receded, I darted towards her desk and picked up the small silver spittoon she carried around with her. I pulled out the biscuit tin and put the spittoon into it, contents and all, and then shut the tin tight and lowered it into my bag and resumed my seat and pretended to be avidly taking notes when she returned a few minutes later.

'Was it all right?' I asked. 'I know this fellow Praful Surti. Indian journalists have completely different values from us foreign reptiles.'

'What is reptiles?' she asked, casually. Her mind was clearly on what Praful had said to her. I knew what it was to be. He was going to ask to see her about having traced forged passports to the ashram's inhabitants. He would ask for a price to suppress the evidence and I supposed that the terms of the bargain were tumbling through her mind.

'Reptiles? Snakes and creatures low in the food chain, you know. It's a word which a magazine called *Private Eye* in the UK uses for journalists. We deserve it, I suppose.'

'That's the best name for these Indian journalists. Snakes, like your friend Mr Surti.'

'Friend is stretching it a bit,' I said.

'Now ask your questions,' she said. Then she reached for her spittoon and found it was missing. She looked under the desk to see if it had dropped and then must have concluded that she had taken it somewhere and left it. She pulled a handkerchief which she had tucked into her sleeve and put it to her mouth.

I asked her ten innocuous questions and scribbled the answers.

They were mostly PR nonsense.

'Bhagwan Shree Saket has been described as the greatest living philosopher of modern times. Do you agree with that or is he something more than that?'

And so on.

I had the spittoon and sputum.

PRAFUL WAS AS PLEASED AS a monkey with a banana. He took charge of my biscuit tin and sealed it with sticky tape and wet dough which he tested as it dried. That would make it air and water-tight and keep any dribbles of spit in, he said.

He went through a ritual of getting me to sign an affidavit saying where I got the spittoon from. He said it may prove necessary in a court if for some reason I couldn't be there to testify myself. It sounded sinister, but I signed.

We travelled together to Bombay and went to the seaside flat of the fellows he had labelled the con-monks, the inheritors of Saket's fortune that apparently Shanti and the sister-fucking Bhavnani, as Praful now called him, were after.

I was introduced to a Goan nurse, a woman with bright red lipstick and rouged brown cheeks, called Maria. Her son was going to submit the samples for analysis in America. Praful seemed very hopeful and couldn't stop talking all through the four-hour journey and through the traffic jams about how he finally had the ammunition to get Diamond's revenge. He could even threaten them with hints of having the information and get her released. Yes, if she left India she could blab about the truth of the ashram and the perverted way she was treated, but that would be better for them than being hauled up for murder and hanged!

'But do I want to get her released?' He looked at me. It was an accusation.

Praful should himself, if the stars had been otherwise disposed, have been the Bhagwan, a Saket with thousands of white followers who would shower money on him. There was somewhere in Praful and in the two 'con-monks', one called Chandrika and the other called Harkishan, an urge to test the real uselessness of wealth by having a surfeit of it.

Once in Bombay we went directly to the seaside flat. The monks came to the door to greet us. They had lived exacting lives and in that setting appeared to me like fragments of pebble embedded in elaborately carved gold. They were both naturally dark and their hands were rough through toil, their bare feet on the luxurious carpets, marked with lines which testified to walking barefoot in their youth in the mountains or wherever they claimed to have spent their time.

Our mission was to see that the spittoon was dispatched and a certain amount of ceremony attended the nurse's parcelling of the biscuit tin in several bags of plastic and then summoning a private courier company to carry it by personal dispatch to Boston.

Maria, the nurse, said they were dispatching some syringes and medicine bottles by separate parcel to her son at the same place.

They phoned the son in their excitement, not taking into account the fact that he would be asleep. He told them the approximate number of days it would take him to get a forensic report.

I told Praful I wanted to get back to Poona and he stayed on, saying there were Bombay stories he needed to report on, but from the fact that he had several times obliquely mentioned a reward for procuring the DNA sample via the spittoon, I knew that he wanted to latch on to the con-monks and extract some material recognition of our efforts.

I was only anxious that the missing spittoon shouldn't be traced to me. My aunts!

The analysis took several days and Praful returned to Poona with a copy of the report and no doubt some reward from the monks. The report was not a scrap of paper but an impressive, attested legal document signed by two eminent forensic scientists in a New England court.

'If the *Times of India* publishes this,' Praful said, 'Every newspaper and TV channel will pick it up and I'll get to the foreign press with the story that the Saket empire has been built on murder. They won't be able to pay their way out of this one. Look!'

I read the report which had been carefully framed by a legal mind. It recounted the circumstances under which the samples had been examined and that the samples submitted for analysis proved that a heart-attack-inducing drug was repeatedly administered through injection syringes to Party A by Party B. The DNA evidence was conclusive. That Party B was the same person whose spittle had been tested from the silver spittoon submitted was also beyond doubt. Other samples of fragments of bandage etc. that had been submitted for analysis established beyond doubt the identity of Party A.

'Put that together with Maria's testimony and Chandrika's presence when the old man died and you have a watertight case of homicide which will swing our Shantiji from the end of a crude rope and convict the pimp Bhavnani of conspiracy to murder. Or maybe he'll turn state's witness and put all the blame on her. I want to fuck them.'

'And Saket?'

'He knows nothing about any of this. Before his time. But those two, mon semblable, mon frère...?' Praful said.

'When are you going to write it up?'

'I am thinking. I've got a nuclear warhead, man. Now what to do with it? Deterrence and diplomatic concessions, or all out holocaust?'

His hooded eyes were shining.

'Use some threat, some hints to get Diana out first,' I said.

'You would say that, wouldn't you?'

'Isn't it what we did all this for? And what you want?'

'Mmm, yeah,' he said as though he wasn't at all sure that that was what we did it all for. 'I'll write it. Let me think of the best way. You are not involved, so they won't get at you.'

THAT EVENING AS WE SAT at dinner, my older aunt Shera clutched her bosom and shut her eyes.

'What's the matter?' Amy asked.

Shera held up her hand to say it was okay, it was expected, it had happened before.

'She's got gas, but she thinks it's a heart attack. She always thinks the worst,' Amy said. 'I'll get you the soda.'

She went to their little rusty fridge in the corner of the dining room.

There was no soda.

'I'll get one now, from ...'

'Don't worry yourself. I'll be dead before you come back,' Shera said as I ran out.

'You see this theatre?' Amy shouted after me. 'Go, go and get it, get three.'

I was already out of the door.

I ran down Sachapir Street to the Kayani restaurant in Sarbatwalla Chowk. I asked for three sodas at the counter and the man shouted 'Teen soda batli parcel,' and the cold and frosty bottles were instantly brought.

I ran down the road and passed Praful's house. A Bentley was parked outside and Praful was being shown into the car by a chauffeur. The more curious neighbours had come out to see, but I was in a hurry and didn't stop to look or enquire. Of course the Bentley, a car one doesn't see on Poona roads, was from the ashram.

Shera and Amy were still at the dining table. I had been gone barely ten minutes. I opened the soda and Shera, still clutching her bosom with one hand, drained the bottle, stretched her hand out for the second, drank it and then belched four or five times. She began to breathe hard.

'Dadar Hormuzd ni madad,' she said, invoking help from the God of the Zoroastrians.

She belched a few times again.

'See, I told you it was just gas. You try and scare us for nothing,' Amy said.

So Praful had been driven away? I didn't have long to discover why. In the early hours of morning I heard the whistle signal. I am a heavy sleeper and am only alert to sounds in anticipation of something. I must have been that night, because the whistle, repeated three or four times, woke me.

I went to the door.

She was there dressed in a drab grey gown, the costume of the demented. Her hair had grown beyond shoulder length and was unwashed and unkempt.

'Can I come in? Will you take me in?' she asked. Her perfect teeth had turned yellow in the asylum. She had a bundle, a knotted sheet with, I assumed, her personal belongings over her shoulder.

'Of course. Come. They let you go?'

'They woke me up in the middle of the night and asked me to take my things and led me to the gate. They didn't say why. They just threw me out. I walked from there.'

'My God. Did you see Praful?'

I led her through the house, through the room where my aunts were sleeping, Shera snoring like a grand unmelodious organ, and took her to my room. She sat on the bed and I switched on the reading lamp.

'You're okay now, you should sleep,' I said.

'To answer your question, I didn't see Praful. I went to his house just now and his mother answered the door and spat in my face and started shouting about stealing her jewellery. She's a fucking mad woman.'

'I saw him leave earlier in an ashram car. He must have been the one who got you released.'

'Why did he want me released? So he could fuck me?'

I didn't know what she meant. She sat on the edge of the bed.

'They all have their own little games,' she said. 'The only white woman that little weasel of a balding pervert can get is me. Or it was me. That's why he wanted me released.'

'At least you are out of danger, Diana. It's too early maybe to ask you about your plans but I think you should get out of the country as fast as you can. Tomorrow. I'll help you.'

'That's not helping me. You think I can leave this country and leave my daughter here?'

I didn't have the heart to tell her that I didn't think there was ever a daughter and if there was she had long since been removed, sent away.

'Where will you go?'

'I have just said I won't go anywhere. If you don't want me, I'll sleep on the street.'

She stood up and went for her bundle. I took it gently from her hand.

'Don't be like that. Come on, sleep. You look exhausted and you've had—I can't even imagine it—a hard time. Just sleep, we can talk and fight in the morning.

She fell back on the bed. I took the folded sheet at the foot of it and covered her with it and placed her bundle on the floor. Then I switched off the light and kissed her on her cheek.

'You're okay here, you're welcome here,' I said, and went beyond the dividing cupboard to the other part of the long veranda to sleep on the old cushions piled in the corner.

I didn't tell my aunts that she was there that night. They went to work without noticing her presence and after they left I woke Di up with a cup of tea. I didn't pester her about what she intended to do. If she had plans she would tell me in due course.

I was certain Praful had secured her release. Did she have any objection to my going to him and asking what he intended? She shook her head and shrugged. She said she wanted a bath and could I give her some shampoo.

'Of course, Shera masi offered you unconditional baths, remember? I'll try and find Praful,' I said. 'I think you should stay in the house. For as long as you need to.'

'Your aunts? I've been in the madhouse. They must know.'

'I'll explain. They won't mind. After what you've suffered?'

There was a large truck outside Praful's house and a team of men were loading it with the old wardrobes and crates. It looked as though they were emptying the house.

As I watched, a car drove up and Praful brought his mother out of the house. She was clutching a pillow. He helped her into the car and then saw me.

'Moving?' I asked.

'I know that bitch is with you. She was set loose last night. I set her loose and I knew where she'd go.'

'She came to you first and your mother chased her away.'

'I told her to,' he said.

'And you seem to be vacating,' I said.

'Come and see us in the new house,' he said. 'It's half a mile behind the ashram.'

'You've got a new house?'

'Well, it's not mine yet, but we'll live in it rent free. Comes with the job.'

'New job?' I knew what the answer would be.

'Public Relations Chief for the Bhagwan Shree Saket Foundation.'

'Congratulations. What a great job!'

He shook his head and shrugged.

'You should go back to England, you know. You don't understand India, Farrukh,' he said, and then turned to instruct the truck driver to wait while he locked up his father's old rickety house at the corner of our street.

PRAFUL'S FIRST ASSIGNMENT AS PUBLIC relations man of the ashram came almost immediately in the form of issuing a fervent denial and keeping the peace in our, stirred up but quiescent, town.

Every year in Poona, in the month of Muharram, the Muslim communities construct 'taboots' or 'tajias', replicas of the kaabaa in Mecca, except that these are not black boxes, but bamboo frameworks plastered with silver, gold, red, yellow, green, purple, pink and other coloured silver-paper. The constructions look like towers and can be anything from eight to thirty feet in height, depending on the wealth and relative prestige of the community fielding the moveable monument.

For the days of Muharram, the taboots rest in a blocked-off street or in a recess or square in the neighbourhood of the community sponsoring it.

On the last night of the ceremonial, the town takes up its taboots, carried by the men of each community on poles, like a palanquin or sedan chair and parade it in procession round the town with drums and frantic dancing, before and after.

At dawn the taboots are taken to the banks of the river and thrown into it, breaking up into a debris of bamboo, fretwork and coloured silver paper and floating jute string. The passage through the streets, a procession of scores of taboots converging from different parts of town on agreed routes, keep the town awake that night. In preparation for the towers passing through the streets, stalwarts and stewards of the various Muslim communities scout the route carrying tall bamboo trestles with which they push the telegraph and telephone wires that criss-cross the streets strung between poles a few feet higher. It's a temporary measure to allow the tallest taboots to pass with ease under the wires and has been traditionally accepted as an allowable practice by the municipality and population.

The bamboo props are taken down as the taboots pass and the wires allowed to hang in their normal catenaries again.

Three days into her refuge in my aunts' house, Diamond asked me to accompany her to Vincent, the Dutch psychoanalyst's house. She had been told in the mental hospital that he had signed a report certifying her as a schizophrenic and dangerous. She wanted to confront him.

'Why not leave it alone? It might open a can of worms or release a genie you don't want to confront,' I said.

'I want to face the devil,' she said. 'That fucking devil. I thought he was my friend.'

I went with her. We walked through the cantonment into the city through the narrow Laxmi Road to the crowded locality in which the dissidents from the ashram, those who had been expelled, had set up a colony. These were the denizens of the dissidents' cafe where I had first met Vincent.

As we approached the six or eight houses where the exiles had set up camp, the old and faded crimson kurtas and saris became evident. These men and women may have, for one reason or other left the ashram or been expelled from it for misdemeanours, but some of them still wore the uniform.

Diamond went up to one of these ex-sanyasis with tangled blonde hair.

'Vincent?' she asked.

'Three-ninety-three. House with the red door and planets painted on it,' he said. He paused and watched us as we went towards it.

It was a building with three storeys. The front door was ajar. There was no bell. We pushed the door open and entered a flag-stone-floored, almost bare room.

Di shouted for Vincent.

The front room led to a passage at the back with rickety wooden stairs. We went up and on the landing encountered Vincent wearing a towel round his waist.

'Ah, the man of truth and evidence,' he said. 'And Diana, goddess of light. Come in, come in, come in.'

He led us into what must have been his room. There were three beds in it. The walls were crudely painted with stars and traces of constellations as the Greeks or Persians drew them. An Indian girl in a very short skirt sat on the bed twirling her long loose black hair into a single plait.

'This is...what was your name, darling?' Vincent said, absently.

'Raghini,' the girl said.

'We're done. Put it on the account,' Vincent said.

The girl didn't look pleased. She fitted her slippers to her feet and stalked out, looking Di up and down.

'I thought you'd left town with the bonanza they gave you,' I said, trying to soften him up for what I knew was going to be a hard interrogation from Di.

'What on earth can you mean, Mr Evidence?'

'I think you know what I mean. Diamond here knows what I mean,' I said.

'Yes, Diamond,' he said and grinned. He sat on the bed, naked as he was, wrapping the towel again round his waist and tucking it in.

'You lied...' Di began.

'About your name? That was your fantasy,' Vincent said.

Diana was about to launch into the half naked analyst when a fellow in a crimson kurta and jeans barged in.

He had a hammer in his hand.

'The fuckers have cut the phone, man,' he said. 'I was speaking to the States and these arseholes outside... '

'What are you talking about?' Vincent asked.

'I'm going to fucking break some heads man,' the young hot head said, and turned and ran down the stairs. Other footsteps followed him and we could hear Hot Head shouting in the street.

'Oi, fucking take that shit down!'

'Excuse me,' Vincent said, and throwing off his towel grabbed a pair of shorts from the floor and dragged them on. He went down the stairs.

'Come on,' I said to Di.

We followed and as we did three or four more dissidents, two of them in crimson shirts came out of the other houses.

Hot Head was confronting a group of six men with his hammer. The men, from their appearance, beards and one or two with checked scarves would have been Muslims. A handcart with a supply of the long bamboo props for pushing up wires, propelled by two more guys, followed them. They had already established several props to clear the centre of the road of its overhanging wires.

'You've fucked with my phone, man,' Hot Head was saying.

The bunch of wires outside the house, which were very untidily connected to a terminal protruding from under the window of the first floor had been disturbed and the bamboo trestles had unintentionally damaged two of the wires which dangled now from the terminal, disconnected. 'You've fucked with our phone and our lights. You deal with it. You put my phone back, motherfucker,' Hot Head said to the Muslim task force.

The dissidents were lining up behind him.

'Don't go on my mother,' one of the Muslims said. 'You are telling dirty things, tell it to me. Don't tell it about mothers.'

'I'll fucking tell it as I like, you cunt. Now take your stick down and fix those wires. You think I want to be electrocuted?'

Hot Head went to the bamboo prop that they had set up and yanked at it. It fell to the street. He went to the previously erected one twenty yards down the road and kicked at it and yanked it till he got it loose. As he went to jerk another bamboo loose, the leader of the Muslim task force grabbed him from the back and Hot Head turned around and swung his hammer, striking him at the side of his head. The rest of the Muslim gang rushed to his rescue and one of them dropped Vincent to the pavement as he rushed up to stop Hot Head murdering his victim.

There were ten or twelve dissidents there now, a few women among them and they joined in. The Muslims must have felt they were defending their religious rights and they fought fiercely, the propellers of the cart breaking a tall bamboo and wielding it in cracking punishment.

The traffic stopped as the fight spilled onto the street. A shopkeeper and a few of his employees jumped into the fray and tried to intervene.

'Brothers, brothers, this is no way. Stop, stop, stop!'

A whistle was repeatedly blown and three police constables came running down the pavement.

I didn't want to see any more. I grabbed Di by the arm and led her down a deserted alley and away from the fracas. She might have been arrested with the dissidents and that would have been crazy. We could hear them shouting in English and in Hindi as we fled.

A few streets away from the fray we got in a rickshaw and got home. Di was silent throughout.

The town was full of it the next day. My aunt's neighbour's cook brought the gossip. A Muslim mob had descended on the ashram with flaming torches to set it alight and had only been prevented from doing so by a cordon of police who had resorted to firing tear gas to disperse them.

The ashram issued a statement, quoting their public relations officer Acharya Surti, which said that the people who had assaulted the bamboo-telephone-wire task force had nothing to do with the ashram. They were people who had been expelled from it and were troublemakers.

The mullah of a prominent city mosque told the *Messenger* that the crimson people and these foreigners in the town were an infidel Hindu cult which was trying to disrupt the Muslim festival of Muharram. The police were quoted as saying that a dangerous religious division seemed to be growing in the city and all irresponsible statements and provocation would be treated as criminal acts and instigation to public disorder.

The next day, the day before the night when the taboots were to be taken out in procession, a spokesman for the Muslim community said that their ceremony would go ahead and any interference would be met with maximum force.

Politicians and magistrates were alerted and there were rumours that the army had been ordered by the state's Home Ministry to stand by.

The procession passed through the streets without incident. It was reported that Hot Head, Vincent and friends had been taken into protective custody by the police.

PRAFUL IN HIS NEW CAPACITY, drafted the short response on behalf of the ashram:

> The miscreants who attacked the organizers of the Muslim community ceremonies had nothing to do with the Bhagwan Shree Saket ashram. The shameful actions perpetrated by these individuals are condemned by the Bhagwan and the devotees. These were imposters who, having been rejected

by the BSS ashram continued to perpetrate the idea of being associated with it.'

There were letters in the national newspaper:

This mistaken Hindu cult, spreading through the riff-raff of the Western world is one of the bastions that the Indian fanatics have constructed against the inevitable spread of Islam, the submission of the true believer, the Salvation of the corruption of created mankind.

A.A. Sharief

Are we surprised that once again Hindu India in the shape of the Poona municipality and its police have allowed the victimization of the minority religion and protected the miscreants with police cordons? Oh, bleeding heart of the believers, when will justice be done in the land of the infidel?

Muhammed Gul Hanif

The Inspectorate of Police has now received the report of its investigation into the incident in Rastapeth, Poona. No religious feeling was involved in the incident whereby the disruption of telephone lines by an error was objected to by persons using the telephonic services.

Staff Reporter

The BSS ashram has issued the following statement:

The Bhagwan wishes it to be known that his teachings and lectures are without doctrine. To characterize any part of his philosophical considerations as deriving from Hindu texts is erroneous and is, as he himself says, 'running a race by facing the opposite way from the track on the starting line'.

The Gita is undoubtedly an inspiring book and has fulfilled an inspirational function for generations, but the Bhagwan disowns it as a source of his thoughts or inspirations. All religions have a common goal and that is to dispel the mystery of life. Some of them, notably Christianity, Judaism and Islam start from the fear that consciousness has of its own extinction. They postulate a further life after death in the company of their maker. It is a self-evidently absurd belief but these faiths enjoin the terrified consciousness to suspend itself in an act of faith and believe in the absurd. The Bhagwan rejects the notion that his philosophy of awareness and beyond-awareness, while exposing the inherent contradictions of these religions, is antagonistic to any of them.

There was a reply:

Hinduism has throughout history been all things to all people and anything to anyone. I was born into a Hindu caste but a revelation at the tomb of the Sultan of Hind at Ajmer, Baba Moin-ud-din Chishti (Peace be Upon Him) transformed my consciousness and gave to my soul the great gift of being the servant of this Sufi saint and of the last prophet Muhammad (Peace be Upon Him).

The statement by the Shree Bhagwan ashram is grievously mistaken about the nature of Islam which simply means submission to almighty. The statement seems to me to be the work of an ego which cannot submit to anything bigger than itself and though I am not certain of this, the doctrines that it puts forward calling themselves 'beyond-awareness' are the work of the malevolent power of the devil.

Ghulam Nabi M.A.(Hon)

Praful wasn't letting that one go.

A public newspaper should refrain from representing the views of fanatics in the interests of communal harmony.

We demand an immediate retraction of the inflammatory statements made by your correspondent Mr Nabi and that an apology be prominently printed on your front pages immediately. Failure to make amends will result in immediate legal action for damages to the reputation of Bhagwan Shree Saket.

P. Surti,
(Director of Public Relations
BSS Ashram Worldwide)

NO APOLOGY WAS PUBLISHED.

The carcass of a freshly slaughtered calf was found on the steps of a Hindu temple on the banks of the river under the bridge. It was deemed to be a provocation by the Muslim communities and immediately the chief minister of the state of Maharashtra, on the advice of the collector and the city's politicians, drafted in police forces from all over the state. To avoid the impression of public apprehension or panic, no curfew was imposed, but the police made it clear that gatherings of more than three people would be challenged and dispersed. Twenty-two people getting together for a game of cricket or hockey was tacitly forbidden.

There were a few incidents of provocation, but no riots took place. The precautions worked. The chief minister announced that a most rigorous investigation into the outrage—the killing of a calf and defiling the temple—would be launched. In a stroke of Machiavellian manipulation, he appointed a Muslim as chief commissioner of the town's police. The perpetrators were either Muslim bigots of some sort, or others attempting to provoke unrest in the city. Either way, appointing a Muslim police chief with a reputation for ruthless neutrality, was a smart move.

The *Messenger*, undiplomatically dismissing the conspiracy motive, assumed that the act was perpetrated by Islamic militants reacting to some political event in Kashmir, and welcomed the appointment, using the unfortunate idiom of 'setting a thief to catch a thief'.

The new Commissioner of Police Alauddin Ahmed told the press that the police intelligence networks already had information which would soon bring the criminals who had defiled a religious place, to justice.

I went to the ashram repeatedly during this time, doing innocent interviews with devotees—where they came from, why they had left their lives in America or Europe and chosen to live as sanyasis in the ashram; what they found in the philosophy of the Bhagwan; what contact they retained with their families and former lives.

The answers were surprising only in their uniformity. They said the same things about all but this last question. They were in crisis with the materialism of Western life. They had all read some Hinduism/Buddhism/mysticism and, though it set them on the path of self-enquiry, there was always something lacking. Some of them identified this as the ultimate illogic, the broken connection between where they were 'at' now in our contemporary, scientific, materialist, consumer, capitalist civilization with its conventions, pretence at old religion and new religions such as political correctness, worship of the ecosystem and the planet and the preaching of the ancient wisdoms. The Bhagwan and the ashram provided the answers. He was the bridge.

It was surprising how many of them used this metaphor. He called himself God—Bhagwan—and I put that to them. He didn't call himself a bridge.

'God is a bridge,' two of them said.

I took notes.

As to the last questions, some of them wrote every week, every day to their loved ones or relatives, telling them how amazing everything was. Others had cut themselves off from the past and said they never wanted to return to it. I asked them if they had surrendered their passports to the ashram and some of these said yes they had as they wanted to sever that escape route to the past. They were true sanyasis now and had been promised some sort of elevated status in the ashram.

So many of them had brought their wealth to the ashram and donated it. Not simply dollars, pounds and euros and what these could buy, including a pair of private planes, but the wealth of their skills as doctors, international lawyers, businessmen, designers of everything. The 'mechanics' in the ashram were actually the men who had designed, for Benz, the engines and the bodies of the cars they had brought with them.

Yes, these would be interesting if undramatic interviews. I would collect them and go back to London. And Diamond, with whom I had been to Bombay to the American consulate, had filled in the forms to establish her American citizenship and was awaiting their reply and passport, would perhaps come with me.

I was beginning to want her to. Yes, the relationship with the lying, cheating woman I had been living with in London, was conclusively not what I would return to. I would have to look after Diamond if she came with me and I searched my heart day and night to determine whether I wanted that responsibility. What would she bring to my life except chaotic charm? And wasn't this question and possibility premature? Didn't one have to settle the conundrum of Sapphire and the husband first?

One night I did what we used to do as teenagers. I cycled out in the middle of the night to the Poona race course, parked the bike and climbed over the white picket fences to the central lawns and lay down watching the stars in the black sky. I was asking myself to think back and ponder the reason I had left this town where I grew up. I had often said to myself, like the characters in Western movies, that a town was not big enough for 'both of us' and that in my case it was myself and the Indian beliefs with which everyone around me had grown. But now I realized that it was an inadequacy. I was afraid to tackle the irrationalities, the smallness, the chaos of the life it promised. I wasn't too big for the town. It was too big for me.

And what would I be doing asking Diamond to come back with me? Inviting someone who had come from what I used to regard as the ordered world to the chaos of the Indian reality and complexity and been broken by it, to go back to a life in London where I would seek work and order and to get completely away from any 'quest'. I knew I didn't do quests and wouldn't ever.

My aunts had accepted now that she stayed in their house till she 'made her arrangements' as they put it. I made no pretence of not sleeping with her in my room, though of course they maintained the pretence that that sort of thing was not happening, thought of, seen or discussed.

I had established a polite rapport with the Director of Public Relations Mr P. Surti (BA). He supported my attempt to get straightforward interviews and discussed their publication with me.

A car drove up to the house one morning as I was setting out on bike to the ashram and Chandrika and Maria stepped out. They had driven from Bombay and wanted a word with me. I led them into our own humble front room.

'You fellows have betrayed us, men,' Maria said.

I knew what she meant.

'I didn't intend to. I did what I could to help you. You know that these people had threatened me.'

Chandrika nodded.

'I knew it wasn't you, it was that reporter Surti. He seems to be working for them now as some director.'

'He made a deal with them.'

'It's a stupid deal. What does he think, I don't have a duplicate of everything? All papers, copies of samples, everything? You fellows were going to take it and put it in the foreign newspapers, no?'

'He was,' I said. 'He had nothing to lose, he said so at the time, but now it looks like he had something to gain. They've given him a nice house with a garden and a salary and they are able to keep an eye on him and swat him like a fly if he gives any sign of trying to get away.'

'He is a regular bastard,' Maria said. 'I've been trying calling him fifteen times, men. What does he think he is? So smart? He thinks he can get these culprits cleanly away? What does he think I am?'

'Can you do the whole murder in your English newspaper? That will work, won't it?' Chandrika asked.

'Please! I go back to London and what happens to my aunts here? They've already threatened me and if they can trace any connection to me, they'll… I don't know what they'll do. Praful knows who has the evidence and if it's published he will be in deep shit himself. Because he's probably told them that he is the only one who has the proof.'

'So no-go then?' Maria said. She looked thoughtful.

'I understand your case, men. These people are too evil. We are at the Marriot hotel, please come and have tea or something when you can. We are staying three–four days.'

THE *MESSENGER* WAS AFFORDED THE privilege of breaking the story. There was the banner headline and then four pages of articles and photographs inside and a gleeful editorial.

The headline said:

ASHRAM EXECS ARRESTED ON SUSPICION OF MURDER.

The ashram had been raided at night, Ms Shanti and Mr Bhavnani arrested and taken away for questioning. The police had cordoned off the ashram and no one was being allowed to leave in case an attempt was made to destroy relevant evidence. All files and records of the ashram had been seized. The new Police Commissioner Alauddin Ahmed was in charge of the operation and had ordered it.

I went down to the ashram. There were ten police cars and a heavy police presence at the gate. A little further away, TV vans were parked with Indian and foreign crews hanging around, taking external shots and trying to interview ashram members, police, local cafe owners, landlords and anyone they could find.

Commissioner Ahmed was, I was told, at the TV studios giving interviews. Saket himself was still in the ashram but no one was allowed access to him.

There was no point in hanging around outside so I went home and caught Ahmed on the evening news bulletin.

He said that his team had gathered expert evidence from scientists of international forensic repute to connect the suspects to the murder of Swami Vishwadeep. That the crime had been committed years ago was irrelevant, he said, 'justice is timeless.'

He repeated the phrase with great satisfaction.

'Why have you maintained a heavy police presence within the ashram and prevented people from leaving or entering? Surely the evidence of a murder that took place so many years ago is unlikely to exist in the ashram today?' the presenter asked.

'We are also working on a theory of a breach of public order law and religious provocation and conspiracy,' Ahmed said, nodding.

'Conspiracy to do what?'

'We have evidence now, though I can't say too much, that the great insult to religion that was done last month, by the slaughter of a holy calf and throwing the carcass into the precincts of a temple was done by certain elements to cause disharmony between the religious communities of Poona.'

'Are you saying that the ashram or devotees of the ashram were responsible for this act?'

'I am not saying anything. My job and the job of my force is to furnish proof to the courts.'

'Are you saying that the provocation was not done by Muslims as has generally been assumed?'

'Look, I can't say who the suspects are at this moment in time. We have good evidence and all this is part of the investigation. I have to be very careful in this situation because I am not saying Muslims or Hindus or anyone did this. If there is proof that a foreign hand was involved in trying to cause unrest among our own town communities, then we shall provide that proof and produce it in court.'

'Is the Bhagwan himself a suspect in any form of misdemeanour or crime?'

'I can make no comment on that.'

Not making a comment was enough. The non-comment was plastered all over the national papers. There were photographs of a very frightened-looking Shanti and a very surprised-looking Bhavnani taken through the windows of a police car. There were photographs and reports for the next three days of hundreds if not thousands of crimson-clad foreigners deserting the ashram and leaving Poona, crowding the railway platforms and trains.

Most of them didn't want to say anything, they just wanted to get the hell out. These were people who lived outside the ashram in the town and had not been caught in the police curfew but feared for attacks by people who couldn't distinguish them from the dissidents who had started the riots. Some of them scrambled out of their crimson outfits, even though they must have known that fleeing Poona as civilians at that time wouldn't in reality prevent them being identified as devotees.

I spoke to a few of them entering the railway station with their backpacks and children. It was the end of a dream, they said, the death of an illusion. There was no getting away from the material world. It was all that is the case and if the administrators of the ashram and, God forbid, the God himself, were found guilty of murder, the illusion was well worth losing.

'What about murder itself being an illusory concept?' I asked. The man with long blonde hair, looked at his wife who was holding on to their two children.

'I think we can stop talking shit right now,' he said.

I went to see Maria and Chandrika at their hotel. They weren't coming down from their suite but they called me up.

'So you blew it?' I asked.

'Blew it?' She didn't understand.

'Told the police?'

'Of course. That fucker Surti who thinks he could double-cross us, men, taking money from both sides, I am going to get him too,' she said.

Chandrika stayed silent and solemn. He offered me some tea. The phone rang. Commissioner Ahmed and his bodyguard were coming up to their room in the lift.

Chandrika went to the door and let Ahmed in. He was a tall, dark-skinned man in police uniform with distinguished service medals on his chest. He had a thin moustache curving downwards.

'Do you want me to leave?' I asked Maria in a whisper.

'No, men, you stay. I told the Commissioner that you had taken the spit sample for our analysis. I am going to tell him to arrest that bastard for obstructing justice and taking bribes to suppress evidence,' she said loudly as Ahmed walked in followed by two cops.

'Don't worry, Miss Maria, we have taken note and your fellow will be apprehended. He is at present giving out brave statements to the press saying they have engaged the best national and international lawyers and they will challenge any and every evidence the police have,' he said. 'He is boasting that nothing will be proved.'

I understood why Chandrika and Maria had stayed behind in Poona. They would be chief witnesses.

'Even if we are ready, their lawyers will make some bahana to get postponements forever and tire us out. I am going to keep applying for extension of detention and feed those two on chapattis and daal for as long as they are my guests,' Ahmed said.

'Give them some torture,' Maria said. 'Their own medicine, men.'

'Vigorously opposing bail. Murder suspects are not easily given bail, especially suspected poisoners.' He grinned. 'If they get extension, you will have to prolong your holiday in our lovely town, or go and come back but always keep in touch for moment's notice,' he said. He turned to me.

'And you too, Mr Dhondy. Maria has told me how you helped collect evidence.'

'Are you going to release Rahul—Saket—sir? He has nothing to do with it. I can swear,' Chandrika said.

Ahmed nodded. 'But he might have been in charge of the slaughter of the baby cow.'

'That is not the way he would do anything. He is cunning but a different kind of cunning,' Chandrika said. He seemed sincerely to want his man released.

'We shall see, give me two days,' Ahmed said. 'The fish must not escape the net, but the net can spring some holes. This is India.'

THE FISH DID ESCAPE THE net. Cyrus Bode went to the ashram gates to represent the Bhagwan as his personal advocate. Praful Surti remained on duty in the ashram and valiantly attempted to send dispatches out by phone and fax but the police had cut the wires and quarantined all the computers and mobile phones within the compound on the pretext of looking for evidence of the conspiracy.

Cyrus was not allowed entry and kicked up a fuss demanding to see the commissioner. He did.

Ahmed turned up in his police jeep, wearing his menacing shades and police hat. Cyrus was, apparently, very rude to him demanding access to his client. Ahmed was in a bad mood and gave his juniors the vaguest sign indicating that Bode should be arrested, thrown into the rear of the van and charged with insolence and wasting police time. Later it emerged that the police had given Bode a good thrashing in the van and then again in the police cells.

There must have been a few hundred crimsones trapped by police siege in the ashram.

On the third night of the siege, thirty Bhagwan loyalists gathered at the gate and attempted to force it open and, being challenged by the police sentries, fought them. The police whistled for reinforcements and three or four trucks turned up and battled the crimsones who rearmed themselves with staves and courted arrest by attacking the cops.

While the fight was on, smoke began to rise from two separate sites in the ashram compound. Sanyasins and their children rushed to the gates and screamed at the police to call the fire engines as they couldn't.

The fires were real and the black smoke billowed out over the night sky. The crowds that had gathered outside the perimeter restriction, which the police had imposed, could see the light of the flames lighting up the sky. The fire engines arrived.

The fight and the fire had caused a lot of confusion.

Bhagwan had got into a Landrover used for landscaping in the ashram and his driver had smashed through a hedge which separated a footpath at the back of the compound and driven away.

The police had no legitimate reason to detain the Landrover or indeed to arrest Saket, but they did so anyway. The car was stopped as it was attempting to leave the town by a road heading into the Western Ghats resort of Mahabaleshwar.

The report of his attempted escape and arrest were all over the morning papers which also said that the crimson people had deliberately started the fires despite a heavy police presence within the compound.

Chandrika hired a battery of lawyers and they turned up at the small provincial police station where the Bhagwan was being held. Their persuasion must have been effective as the Bhagwan was that very day brought before magistrates and released without charge as the police offered no evidence against him on any count. Commissioner Ahmed phoned Chandrika to say so.

The crimsones who were arrested in the fight were, it seems, the only ones willing to stand up for their adopted Guru and way of life. They were all charged with causing a public nuisance and affray and sentenced to several months in jail. The rest of the devotees from the ashram found themselves floating about the town, all of them lost and looking for exits from it.

Ahmed lifted his siege. Perhaps he had fulfilled his purpose of destroying, or at least disrupting the functioning of the ashram. He was content to send those who had fought his constables to jail and he was, as Chandrika and Maria told me, looking forward to bringing two murderers to justice. He would be at the centre of the trials and he planned to call the American forensic experts to the Indian court and attract international media attention. Not least for himself.

RAHUL RANG THE BELL HIMSELF. He had some fellow with him, but now both of them were wearing ordinary Indian clothes, a kurta and pyjama, no flowing white starched robes. He had also cut his beard from the long flowing fleece to the rounded cut of the Haji Muslim and his hair was now shoulder length. They must have stopped by a village barber and got it done and his vanity intervened to stop him agreeing to a complete cut.

'The Bhagwan himself! Come in,' I said.

He didn't cross the threshold.

'Can you call me Rahul, please Chandrika?'

'I thought I was Govinda,' I said. 'Rahul, my friend, come right in. Are you in disguise?'

'No, no, I just need some time to think,' he said.

He and his friend came in and stood awkwardly in my splendid drawing room. Harkishan heard us and came out of his bedroom. Maria had gone to receive her son from the airport in one of our cars.

Rahul remembered Harkishan though they hadn't met since he was seven, or at least he made a show of knowing him.

'Harkishanji,' he said, folding his hands in greeting.

'You are free?' Harkishan said.

'Yes, but homeless,' he said. He was looking round the room.

'Have some tea…er… Bhagwan,' Harkishan said.

Rahul nodded. 'Just Rahul,' he said.

Even in this modesty the habit of command came through. 'Bloody but unbowed' was some phrase I had read in one of the books he used to have in his days as a humble college lecturer.

He sat down.

'I am glad you are here, Harkishanji. I wanted to talk to you together.'

Harkishan shouted to the kitchen for tea but he didn't sit down. He stood and loosely folded his arms.

'I will just say what I have to and go,' Rahul said.

'Is this a lecture? Some philosophy about the sin of gratitude?' I asked.

'No,' he replied. 'I came to tell you that I realize I have no claim to the wealth you have inherited from the lady who said she was my mother. I denounced that claim and besides, the lawyers of my ashram have made a mess by finding all the articles of the will of the old lady flawed. Without the two of you testifying to what you know, I have not a whisper of claim to any of the money which is yours now. And why should I think you will testify in my favour? I never knew her as my mother. Only the two of you did and who is going to say that the infant you took from her grew up to be me?'

'There are DNA tests,' I said.

'But she has no immediate relatives alive,' Harkishan said.

'Masters, I am here to tell you that I am not going down that road. I will not spend a moment of my life trying to prove that this flat and the bank accounts or whatever it is you have, belong to me,' he said.

'Why not?' I asked.

'Because I've been used. I don't know what will happen to...those two but I know them well and I believe absolutely that they killed the old man. I should have known that from the start.'

He turned to me.

'Perhaps you did know, did you?'

I didn't reply.

'So what is it you want from us?' Harkishan asked.

'Nothing. I want nothing,' he said, and signalled to his companion to put the tea cup down and to go.

'Wait, where are you going? What will you do?' I asked.

'There's nothing much I can do,' he said. 'There'll be disciples who still want me to be...what I was yesterday. I can get some of them back, but I want to go away and think. Not think in the way I have been, a lecturing machine, layering ideas, mostly second-hand ideas or making up some obvious defiance of the same second-hand ideas. None of it was dishonest and all of it I said and did with the utmost sincerity, but it was as though I saw through a veil darkly and mistook it for the brightest sun. Now I want to come face to face, not with some deity, but with myself as the feeblest of my American disciples would say.' He smiled slyly.

'I hope I'm being clear?'

'You are,' I said and some mischief returned to his face.

'Who knows, I may decide to become a great guru or a demi-god again. You can't throw off your past, like you can old clothes and worn shoes. Your past is time's skin. If there are those who want to undertake the new future journey with me, I might find them. Or I may walk alone. By the way, this is Mahesh. He was not a disciple, just the driver of the landscaping car, but he's still here.'

He walked to the door with Mahesh following him.

'Do you have a mobile number, Mahesh?' I asked, detaining him for a moment as Rahul passed through the door and pressed the lift button.

He gave it to me and I wrote it down as they left.

Rahul, whom I had brought up. Rahul whose real mother was in DNA terms the old lady who had made me rich. Rahul who had been God to some and had built an empire with words. An insubstantial faith and with none of the fakery of the godmen, the frauds who set themselves up by performing miracles. He had professed no miracles, no divinity. Words and the ability to play on the fears of living while the great religions we follow play on our fear of dying.

I told Maria when she returned with her son, full of plans for the murder trial of Shanti and Bhavnani.

It was Maria who said I shouldn't have sent him away empty-handed.

'He was your brat, men, like this fellow is my brat,' she said. 'Why you didn't give him some money?'

I thought about it for three days and then phoned Mahesh.

'Are you still with Rahul?'

'We are in Pathankot, north India, Punjab or something. Maybe Himachal, driving, driving every day,' he said.

'What is Rahul doing or thinking?'

'He want to go in a river and sit by some temple or something he is saying. In Himalaya, high up.'

'And you are going with him?'

'I am driving, what else to do?' he said.

'Look I want to give you both some money.'

'What money?'

'Enough money to buy a house in the Himalayas and live on, if that's what he wants to do. If I offer it to him, he will refuse, but you must take it and settle him in. He's like my younger brother, I can't have him wandering about like a beggar or a saddhu or a guru who doesn't want disciples.'

'He is saying he is the prophet of love now,' Mahesh said. 'He made up one speech when we were sitting in a tea shop with plenty foreigners who are coming here by railway to go in Manali to where Tibetan persons is having for stay from run away in Tibet with Dalai Lama.'

'A speech?'

'He cut hair very short now and shave off beard because we both got lice and nobody was knowing it is same Bhagwan. He started with talking love and all this things and they were simply loving all his talks. I was gone outside and collecting every phone number of mobile from these loving foreigns.'

'The Prophet of Love,' I said. 'Look, can we speak in Hindi?'

There was a pause.

'I am not speaking your silly language. Only Tamil and little bit of Malayalam and this English. How I am going to get your money?' he asked.

'Do you have any money at all?'

'Very much small,' he said.

'Then open a bank account with it in the town you get to. Any proper bank, not some money-lender, and phone me with the bank details, account number and all this.'

He said he would. They were going up to a town in the hills and had enough petrol and a few hundred rupees to start a bank account. I assured him that he would get a transfer as soon as he phoned me.

He phoned me. He had opened an account in his own name with the Himachal Bank. He gave me the relevant details after a lot of sweat and questioning.

I asked him to pass the phone to Rahul just to make sure that he was still with him.

Rahul came on the phone.

'The Prophet of Love? Sounds stupid for someone who has read all that philosophy and literature,' I said.

He giggled at the end of the phone as he used to when he was a boy.

'Only you can say that to me,' he said.

'I am sending Mahesh some money,' I said. I waited for his reaction but there was none.

'A lot of money,' I said. 'Enough to live, though I know that the Prophet of Love will never starve. It is really your money, Rahul, and when you want it, come for it.'

'Thank you,' he said. 'But it isn't my money. And that theory of gratitude? It's all balls, forget it.'

'Done, forgotten,' I said.

A CURIOUS ADVERTISEMENT HIT THE national press:

THE PERSON, RAHUL JAIN, FORMERLY KNOWN AS BHAGWAN SHREE SAKET WISHES TO RENOUNCE THE NAME SAKET AND ABSOLUTELY SURRENDER THE TITLE OF BHAGWAN.

HIS FORMER DISCIPLES, IN THE MISTAKEN BELIEF THAT THE WORD WAS THE ENGLISH EQUIVALENT OF 'GOD' GAVE HIM THE TITLE.

SUBSEQUENTLY IT HAS BEEN UNDISPUTABLY DISCOVERED THAT THE WORD 'BHAGWAN' IN OLD SANSKRIT MEANS THE FEMALE SEXUAL ORGAN.

OF COURSE ITS METAPHORICAL MEANING IS THAT IT IS THE PLACE FROM WHICH ALL LIFE EMERGES AND IT IS IN ITS ATTRACTIVENESS THE MOTIVATION FOR HUMAN CREATION.

HOWEVER, THE TITLE AND THE NAME ARE HEREBY RENOUNCED BECAUSE, AS THE ENGLISH SAY 'WHO WANTS TO BE CALLED A CUNT IN PUBLIC—WE GET ENOUGH OF THAT AT HOME

Though I am sure he spelled it out, all the newspapers euphemized the four letter word in the final sentence, rendering it as C*** or substituting the phrase 'the female organ'.

ON THE ORDERS OF THE commissioner of police, Praful Surti, director of public relations for the BSS ashram was arrested on a charge of the suppression of evidence in a murder case.

In a twist of fate, Shanti's lawyers accused Surti of using false evidence for purposes of blackmail. Bhavnani's lawyers were pleading that his DNA and fingerprints were not on any of the incriminating syringes or medicines and that he had nothing to do with Ms Shanti and if she was guilty of murder, she was acting on her own.

The ashram, two of its houses and its congregational tent burnt down, was shut. The police were investigating the alleged act of arson. The crimsones had gone. Some could still be seen in their uniforms defiantly parading around the town but they were no longer treated as welcome guests. Rumours of the conspiracy theory linking them to the attempt to provoke religious riots in the city were believed by most people to whom I spoke.

Diamond was radiant with schadenfreude. It was as though

she had wreaked her personal revenge on the ashram and the people who had wronged her so grievously. She said she had heard conclusively that her husband and child had fled the country in the chaos. It would be easier to find them when she followed.

There was nothing now to stop me writing her story. The perpetrators of threat were in jail and to be tried for murder with the scales so loaded that they would be hoist high by the weight of evidence.

I wanted her story from the beginning. I would question her about it. The leaflet she or Praful had written was rhetorical, accusatory. I wanted her to tell me the detail of the story: her entry into the ashram with her daughter and husband, the first encounter with the Bhagwan, the steps towards the seduction or, if it wasn't a pure seduction, towards the relationship that turned so destructive.

She said she'd give me every detail but every time I raised the question she would find something else she needed to do. My aunts were now reconciled to her being part of the household and we all ate meals together and she helped them in the kitchen at nights and on weekends when their part-time cook was absent. She diligently volunteered to dust the house and sweep the yard.

In the evenings, she would watch Hindi TV soaps with my aunts and she had the use of my computer which was connected to the Internet through the house phone line.

'Who are you talking to?' I asked as she concluded one of her intense sessions of e-mailing.

'About my daughter and that man I don't want to think about. I am picking up clues from abroad—his relatives and people who used to be around him as to where he might have taken her. I guess he still works for the same firm, plodding on. Same summer, same snow, same life, same death.'

'But you have some indication that she's safe?' I asked. She didn't reply.

'So who told you that he had taken her abroad?

She sighed, but again didn't reply.

'Surely you—we—should be looking for her. I mean bending every sinew to…'

She turned to me and for the first time I saw a flash of contempt in her eyes.

'We? What can you do? Of course I know she's safe. Did you imagine I'd just cool it here and sleep with you if I didn't know?'

'That's good, but where is she?'

'Just leave it alone, will you?'

'If she's back in the States, you can surely find her. You don't seem anxious to do that, that's all I'm saying.'

'I can't go. I'm waiting for my passport.'

She was. She said the consulate had phoned her to say it was in the hands of the Washington bureau because her naturalization as a citizen hadn't been quite straightforward.

I was anxious as I wanted now to book my ticket back to London. Bhavnani and Shanti would be put away and there was no threat to my aunts any longer. I could write what I liked. I could wait till we got to England. Yes, I wanted to ask her to go with me. I did and again she was evasive. She wouldn't say she wanted to go with me.

At night, in bed, if I turned to the topic, she would get close to me, press her body against mine and say 'Sssshhh, I don't want to think about going now. I want to think of you.'

I talked about her living with me in London. I said it would be easier to find Sapphire from a base in London. I had friends and she had relatives in America and they would help. We could get the child to come and live with us.

'You just want the story, to wow the newspapers in England, destroy things here, don't you?' she once said.

'That's a nasty thing to say to me,' I replied and she was sorry.

'You don't understand. For such a clever boy, you just don't understand.'

I WENT TO THE FIRST court hearing in the case of the Indian state vs Shrimati Shanti Patel and Mr Ram Bhavnani for the murder of Guru Vishwadeep. The national press were out in force. The proceedings took a few minutes with lawyers for either side dressed in shabby black jackets bargaining with each other under the high court judge's bench on which a small man with round, thick spectacles struggled to keep up, holding a palm behind his ears to hear better and interrupting the lawyers in their arguments and taking occasional notes. It seemed very disorderly with court officials of all denominations walking around and even through the courtroom with impunity.

The defendants were both present in the box but there was obviously no camaraderie or partnership left between them. It was dog eat dog and these hounds were enemies, each trying to incriminate the other and so get free.

The procedure went through. The case was registered and the plea and was then postponed for a month.

Should I stay to see the end of it? I could send my dispatches from here and wait for the verdict. I couldn't afford to go back and return even once for the procedure of the trial. I knew more about it than anyone else—indeed had been involved in the gathering of evidence against these two alleged murderers and the commissioner had expressly ordered me to stay. The international press, already writing features about the end of the spiritual journey, the last of the hippy generation, the return of materialist reality etc., would be on the case. I should stay. I'd ask Diamond. Her personal story would give me the edge.

There were several men and women I recognized as crimsones in the public gallery of the court with me and towards the end of the trial Vincent walked in. He raised a hand in greeting and sat next to me through the remainder of the proceedings.

When the court adjourned, he suggested we go to the tea shop.

'With a bang and not a whisper,' he said. 'Murder, mayhem, sex, debauchery.'

As we sipped our tea he asked if Diamond was still in town.

I said she was and I guess he'd guessed that she'd be with me. He nodded, thoughtfully.

'Tell me, then, did you really treat her or put her under analysis or whatever it's called? In the ashram?'

'Why would I?' he asked. 'She was perfectly sane as you would, with your evidence-head, say.'

'Then why did you certify her crazy? You did, didn't you?'

'To fucking save her from jail and God knows what atrocities inside. Sure the ashram also wanted her put away, because she was writing rubbish and spreading shit about them and they wanted to stop her and I agreed that it was the only way to stop them prosecuting her.'

'You say spreading shit, so all that didn't happen? The Guru didn't screw her and screw her up? And screw the husband?'

'Of course he did. He screwed the arse off her. He screws everyone he can get hold of and he has no difficulty getting hold of them, they offer themselves up. Then he gets tired of one and moves on to the other. He's the emperor of ice cream with a harem. Except he doesn't let them hang about like a harem, he moves on. He threw your Diamond out. And there was no husband. As far as I can make out he is some schmuck in New York.'

'Yes, we know that.'

'And she didn't like being an ex-sexual experiment.'

'We know that too. Would you?'

'If I was her, I'd have taken the hint and fucked off back to Israel or America or wherever the fuck I came from.'

'Are you really entitled to talk. You got thrown out and you're still here.'

'You got a point. But I didn't hang about hoping to get back in there. I just find India, the laid-back attitude, the inefficient corruption, the disconnect between words and truth—you know your thing about evidence and "reality"—I find that's where my consciousness is at.'

'Okay, but she hung about because of her daughter.'

Vincent smiled and shook his head.

'Great,' he said.

'I want to know what you mean by that.'

'If you don't know… look you're living with the woman. Maybe you got plans. Who the fuck am I to tell you anything?'

'Tell me,' I said.

'There was no daughter. There never was a daughter.'

I could see he was not lying. All ambiguity had disappeared. And he wasn't mistaken.

'Then why kidnap two girls?'

'This is a question you should ask her. She knows.'

I knew he'd say no more.

She wasn't at home when I returned that afternoon. She wasn't there when my aunts came back from work or by dinner time. They asked me where she was. I didn't know.

I went to my room. She had taken what few belongings she possessed. I suppose I wasn't expecting her to, but she didn't come home that night. Or the next. Had I said or done something? Was the fact that she had taken her things and not left a note reassuring? Did it mean that she had planned to leave and therefore hadn't been arrested, assaulted or kidnapped but left of her own free will. But she could have left a note.

I cycled the streets, went to the dissidents' cafe which was almost deserted and cycled to the railway station. It was a hopeless quest. Why? Why didn't she say? I went back home late and couldn't sleep. I was listening for the whistle, for the bell, for her return. I wanted her here.

She didn't come.

I wondered night and day as to where she'd gone. I went to the police and realized half way through talking to some idiot desk sergeant that it was foolish to pursue her; she had gone of her own free will.

I tried to distract myself by writing up the interviews I had done, featuring them as innocent and illustrative of a deep wound in the satisfactions of Western life. It's the material I had and I exploited it.

My aunt Shera only once said, 'I don't think that girl was good for you. Maybe for someone else.'

Amy said, 'You will find lots of girls.'

I tried to write but sat for hours facing the blank screen of the computer. I used to check my e-mail three or four times a day to see if there was anything from her. Then, in one of these idle, tormented moments I turned to America On Line and typed the name I knew she used as her identity which was DICRIMSONINDIA. And I filled in the password. I didn't know it but I tried SAPPHIRE and the e-mail address was active.

I shouldn't have snooped, but I told myself I was looking for clues as to her whereabouts. There were several messages from someone called JOEYLASSO. I opened one:

> Hey Hon,
>
> I read about your Ash-bum implosion and it's quite a story. Murder, huh? Is that the spirituality you're chasing?
>
> Di honey, Steve and Charity have got back here and are they one set of disillusioned dudes. They told me about the last days of your Pom-pay and getting arrested and your fraud-God hightailing outta town and getting clean away. Charity's gonna go to an IVF clinic she's found in NY and Steve says it has a ninety-eight per cent success rate. So honey, come back. I miss you like I miss Granny Shapiro's gefilte fish—and worse.
>
> Please, honey, give this rat and his rat race another chance, now that the holy cow marathon is over.
>
> Diana, I don't mean to be frivolous, but you know me and I'm no good with words and the bestest I can say is I love you and think and breathe you every moment of the day and night.

I know you're getting these because they don't come back on the wire. Please reply, honey. Tell me you're OK. Ma says she misses you too.

A kiss from her

And me.

X

X

J

There were several more in the same vein, begging her to go back, some of them talking about his work as a bookkeeper in a firm and how it was possible that Mr Rosenthal had hinted that they would offer him a partnership and then they would have a better income and then.. and then…how if the IVF treatment worked and he was so sure it would, and they could have a daughter (because he was sure his genes would produce a daughter) they would move to a better neighbourhood and a larger flat. There was one sad mail reporting on how Joey was mugged as he left the subway one night and how he had found a herbalist who promised to cure his psoriasis.

In another mail he said: 'Honey-bun, when you get back you are gonna get blown away with the new mattress that's orthopaedic and the kitchen table that's real oak which I put together myself…'

He wrote like a combination between a cowboy and a furniture salesman and perhaps he thought that was how lovers wrote to each other… No, not lovers, an abandoned husband to a wife.

So this was husband Joey. This was the flat, this the life she left behind. The one she would rather face the storm than return to? The one which compelled her into this mad, turbulent spiritual and sexual quest?

She couldn't have had any money when she got to Poona. All she had to offer the Guru was her charm, her intelligence, her body. And it was all he wanted from her because he had everything else.

THREE WEEKS PASSED. THERE WAS no word from Diamond in that time and then an e-mail:

> Dear F,
>
> I must have had you worried. Believe me it worried me every moment I have been away, but there was nothing else I could have done. I had to go. You have been very kind to me and I shall be eternally grateful to you though you and I know these short eternities do no one any good.
>
> I have to tell you—I am in the Himalayas with Rahul. He is starting a new ashram here and the past has been swept away. He has the destiny of a God, an avatar of the eternal spirit. He has been in touch with me ever since he left the ashram and changed his life. I couldn't tell you. He said he spent deep meditation on the sin of profligacy and betrayal. So many have betrayed him and he wrote to me saying he had looked for the one spark in the dark delusion of his past when, through making love he was looking for love. And he said he found me as a bright star in the spreading dark of his memory. Isn't that spectacular? He wanted me to forgive him if there was anything to forgive. He, of course, confessed that he had wanted other women and discarded me in the game of poker he has been playing with his life. I had to confess that I too had had other partners— Praful and you and I once betrayed him with Vincent, you remember Vincent, the sex-analyst? Shameless and shameful arsehole. I told

Rahul all this, even when I was with you and he said none of it mattered. And through the messages, even through the ether, I knew he had changed and I could feel the vibration which says 'sincerity'.

There is no shame in declaring that I love him. All declarations of love are declarations of closeness to the humble, isolated, pitiable human spirit and the connections to the dynamo of the ultimate energy of the Universe.

I always loved him. All those lies, accusations, events were Maya, illusion! He forgives me for having lied out of jealousy and the rage of being finished with, of being shuffled off like a dirty sock. I wrote those hateful pamphlets, or PS wrote them for me.

And then the kidnaps. Which again PS wanted me to do, to extract money from them and to discredit the ashram. And I did it to hurt him, to get back at him for rejecting me and taking on others. But it was illusion, maya. Still, I had those kids for three weeks and I loved them. Rahul now says I can be in charge of the Indian orphans he is determined to adopt. Guess what the first girl we have to name will be called?

F, I have always known, and I know you realized it, He and I were made for each other. The doctrine of love is the doctrine of possibilities—what the body can do, what the soul can do, what the heart can acknowledge. There is shame in none of it—none of it.

He hates me saying he has changed. He wants to think of himself as constant, such a sage! (Such a baby, really!) And in the last few weeks he has taught me so much. I have advanced a humble step towards enlightenment, by which I mean nothing arrogant, except my own peace.

F, I am writing this to you now, as he urged me to do,

not simply because you helped me when I mistakenly thought I needed something outside of the realization he was bringing to me. I am writing because I feel you need to pass through where you are and we want to help you.

I know you are going to return to the West, England, wherever. It is a false world. Its people are just people but the systems by which they live defeat the purpose of life. I don't want you to fall into that.

You remember when we went to see Vincent and he called you the man of facts, the man of evidence, the man who mistakes truth for the correspondence between language and material existence? Even then, as he said it, I knew he was right, though I loved you and hated him and couldn't say it.

You need to move beyond, my beloved, my friend. I have told Rahul all about you and he understands why I was attracted to you in this false passage of time through which we all have lived.

Trying to be eternally shining, and now knowing that I am,

Diamond

So that was it. The simplicity of the Western world, of life in New York, in London and where there was the order of routines understood and accepted. And then the complexity and chaos around the still centre of the spiritual quest. Yes, they had made a disciplined brave new world, as Praful put it, within the ashram, but the release of lusts and the permission to break all taboos was chaos, a chaos one could crave. It reflected the confusion and the world with flexible rules just outside the hedges and fences, the India in which one could buy most things and all abstracts—justice, fairness, truth, loyalty, love—could be bid for. It was the chaos of a bazaar auction. The contrast generated the electricity as when disparate metals at different temperatures touch and generate a current. That's what she must have felt. She couldn't go back to the simplicity. She had embraced the chaos and was in love with it, especially as it seemed to be its opposite, the paring away of the material concerns till there was only the spiritual void, the ego at peace with itself.

MY EDITOR E-MAILED ME FROM London to say he had managed to convince the fellow editors of bigger publications that I was the man to cover the entire story of the fallen prophet, the death of an illusion, the birth and death as I had written (quoting Praful, but he didn't know that) of the conceit of a brave new world. I was going to be paid well to cover the whole thing. Tony, the editor, fancied himself as a humorist and a supporter of multiculturalism: 'Massa day done, bwoy. Big Wonga on way' he wrote, mixing his argot.

I told my aunts I was staying. They said they were overjoyed. They asked about Di as politely as they could, knowing I must have heard from her because my behaviour had changed.

'She has gone with some friends to the hills,' I said.

'Good, good. Hope she stays away. We thought you were getting too sweet on her,' Shera said.

'And what was wrong with that?' I teased.

'Nothing wrong with that, but we told you, she should go somewhere else. These people don't understand men like you,' Amy said.

'Not right in the head, actually, if you ask me,' Shera said.

'You don't have to say that Shera,' Amy objected. 'These

are modern people and maybe we don't understand them, you know.'

'I think your understanding is respectable and good,' I said.

'Is she coming back?' Shera asked.

'No,' I said.

I wrote Di an e-mail:

Di,

Thanks for your communication and for your interaction with me. You have granted me the great gift of humility. As a student, second-rate scholar, struggling journalist and ambitious writer, I garnered the conceit that I understood or was beginning to understand how and why people behaved and believed. Truly. My short and happy encounter with you has taught me that I know nothing about some deep human founts of behaviour.

You know, I understand or think I understand why Shanti and the idiot Bhavnani did what they are accused of doing and how they proceeded. Believe me, I have known Praful Surti from my childhood and I understand his truths and untruths and his motivations and suffer with him in his defeats.

In a broader context, I even understand the man who has nothing to sell but his words, a snake of eloquence, a vulture of vocabulary, a jackal profiting from the dead or discredited corpses of abandoned belief. Yes, I think I understand them and finally I think I understand you. I think I now know, and you explained it, while not explaining it, what you are after. I hope you find it.

I think the Prophet of Love has a few more lessons to teach you and hope they won't result in the pain he inflicted on you. He should be grateful for the devotion you've shown even in abusing him and trying to break up his so successful game.

I think of you and the others who fall for him as a force field of justified dissatisfaction—and then the whole fabric of that world, of that quest with the costumes and pretend names and humbug, dissolves, like Shakespeare's Tempest, the players vanish. You are the substance of a dream. I don't expect a reply.

X

F D

I didn't get a reply, but an e-mail in the next week. It was not from her, but from Vincent who said he'd journeyed to the Himalayas and had joined as a 'love therapist' the Monastery of Love.

Shanti, Mr Bhavnani and Surti denounced each other in a network of interactive trials. Surti was convicted for three years for blackmail, Shanti convicted to hang for murder with her sentence commuted to life imprisonment on appeal and the hapless Bhavnani given nine years for conspiracy to murder.

From London I sent aunts Shera and Amy a copy of the articles I wrote.

'Our dear nephew, we are so proud of you' they wrote on a postcard. 'You have such a great command of the English language.'